OLD BONES

ALSO BY HELEN KITSON

The Last Words of Madeleine Anderson

OLD BONES

Helen Kitson

2021
Louise Walters Books

Produced and published in 2021
by Louise Walters Books

ISBN 9781916112339
eISBN 9781916112346

Typeset in PTSerif 11pt by Blot Publishing

Printed and bound by Clays Ltd, Elcograf S.p.A.

louisewaltersbooks.co.uk

info@louisewaltersbooks.co.uk

Louise Walters Books
PO Box 755
Banbury
OX16 6PJ

For Louise Wood,
best and only sister-in-law.

1

DIANA

Antonia switches off the radio. I hadn't wanted it on in the first place, it's the same every day: a depressing catalogue of national political squabbles and international disasters. Occasionally a major crime perks things up a bit, but these days even murder isn't headline news unless it has some peculiar feature. Serial killers always make the news, but most murders are sordid domestic affairs that don't fire the imagination.

'No new developments,' Antonia says. 'They can find out all sorts, these days, from a few old bones.'

I grunt, neatly beheading my boiled egg with a knife. The bones in question were discovered in a quarry near the woods just down the road from us. We all, I think, expected the let-down of being informed that the bones were those of a sheep or a cow. But no, it seems they are definitely human remains, although only a partial skeleton was recovered.

'To be expected,' Antonia commented. 'I daresay animals made off with some of them.' A fan of detective shows, she knows about these things.

She spreads butter thickly on her bread and adds a layer of homemade damson jam. 'I wonder if it's anyone

1

we know? I mean, it's not likely to be some ancient Saxon king, is it?'

'Good lord, who knows?'

Damson stones lined up on her plate. Tinker, tailor, soldier, sailor. Or does it only count if you use cherry stones?

'DNA,' she says, setting down her bread after taking a bite. Her teeth-marks in the butter. We should both be dead, all that cholesterol gluing up our insides.

'They'd need something to match it against, wouldn't they?' I have only the haziest notion of how DNA testing works. 'They'll try to find dental records, I expect.'

'We don't know if there's a skull.'

I stare gloomily at my trepanned egg, the shiny yolk oozing over the side of the egg cup.

Antonia is my sister. Five years ago she turned up on the doorstep with two suitcases, and burst into tears. She'd been a teacher of home economics at a not very prestigious school for girls on the east coast. The tale she told was of being bullied by other teachers, even some of the girls. Her nerves, she said, were shattered.

I don't remember inviting her to stay, let alone move in, but five years on she's still here. She never returned to teaching. I run a little gift shop in the village, and at first Antonia was happy to help out. Customers liked her. She would gladly listen to their tales of woe, never complaining even if they purchased only a novelty eraser from the end-of-line discount bin.

For many years the shop was my pride and joy. I took it over when Vera Dodson retired and I made a success of it, particularly when the new housing estates sprang up on the outskirts of the village, bringing in more people, many of them commuters with money to spare. The quaint village I remember from childhood now has the feel of a small town, the newcomers having brought with them more sophisticated tastes, to which the village has adapted accordingly.

The shop doesn't feel truly mine anymore. When my mother fell ill ten years ago I had no choice but to cut back my working hours, leaving most of the day-to-day running to my manager, Stella. Things have never been quite the same since. Whenever I turn up at the shop she gives me a sympathetic smile and makes it plain I am not needed. I think she misses Antonia more than she misses me, but neither of us is necessary.

'Be nice for you to spend more time with your sister,' she says. What can I do but agree? Stella is barely thirty and believes I should be winding down at my age. I'm sixty-three, and it's true that I muttered about the benefits of early retirement when Mother was ill, and took a great deal of time off after she died. Stella says she can't wait to retire, but I want to do so in my own time, on my own terms.

'I think you're mad to keep on working,' Stella says. 'No kids, no mortgage. I envy you, Diana, I really do.'

Maybe she does. She has a husband who does something vague in IT, and three boys. I have no one but my younger sister.

'They don't give much away, the police, do they?' Antonia persists.

Morbid, I call it, her desire to know all the details. She's the same with any newsworthy mystery of the dead body/potential murder variety. It's human nature, she says, this need to know, this fascination with mortality, since death is the one thing none of us can escape.

3

Well; she's done her fair share of escaping it. It was I, not she, who nursed our mother through her final illness, I who had to jump to attention every time Mother rang the little brass bell with a red ribbon tied around it (the ribbon for the benefit of her failing eyesight); I who was forced to withstand the tears, the tantrums, the dirty laundry. Antonia away, teaching, unable to return home until the funeral, staying long enough to sort through Mother's jewellery, divvying up the spoils. She's always had a fondness for shiny things and she does like to have *possessions*.

And the funeral; dear God, the funeral!

But I won't dwell – it's not healthy. Instead I say something bland about the police knowing their job and that they'd tell us if there was anything we ought to know.

But whose bones are they? What circumstances brought them there?

'Perhaps there'll be a memorial service,' Antonia says, poking damson stones with the blade of her knife. 'When they find out who it is.'

'Who it *was*, I think you mean.'

She tuts. 'Always so pedantic. I taught cookery and sewing, not English.'

Yes – and what a disappointment *that* had been to our father.

'Chances are they won't find out whose bones they are,' I say.

'*Were*. All the more reason to give them some sort of religious blessing.'

'Why?' I ask. 'What good would *that* do?'

'It's proper.' Her face red, eyes narrowed. 'It's the right thing to do.'

Little enough she's ever cared about religion, about

form. As a family we'd all trooped along to church every Sunday, largely as a means of adding a bit of colour to the grey blankness of a typical dreary British Sunday. I haven't set foot inside the church since Mother's funeral, though I've heard on the village grapevine that there's been something of a shake-up since Mr Latham moved to a parish in Lincolnshire and the new vicar took over. Smells and bells and blessings for animals, an unlikely mishmash of hellfire and flower power.

'If you say so.'

My turn to wash up this morning. Rotas for every domestic task. A place for everything and everything in its place.

I like the kitchen. It overlooks the long, narrow back garden, which was once planted with potatoes and other vegetables, and fruit, but now grows wild, only some hardy rhubarb and a few gooseberry bushes surviving from my green-fingered parents' time.

I root around in the kitchen cupboard, trying to find a cake tin of the right size for a new recipe. I want to practice making the cakes I've promised for the village fete.

Later, while the cake is in the oven, I sit in the living room half-watching some rubbish on television, a show in which people scour their houses for valuables to sell at auction. Idly I wonder how much the bits and pieces I've inherited might be worth. The TV antique hunter is a middle-aged woman whose husband needs the cash for a mobility scooter. In the spare bedroom she finds a doll with woolly yellow hair and a startled expression. Although in poor condition, it might be worth as much as three hundred pounds according to the show's expert.

I think of my favourite childhood doll, a simpering thing with bright blue eyes and cherry lips. It was one of the many toys I'd been encouraged to hand on to Antonia, who didn't take the same care. She liked to own things, but once she'd got them she either ignored them or treated them roughly. She'd dropped my doll and one of its hands had fallen off. Barely eleven years old, I couldn't contain my rage. I'd taken hold of Antonia by the neck and picked her up. If Mother hadn't found us, what might have happened?

Over the years I've done my best to make allowances for my sister. If she had only apologised about the doll and many other similar but more significant incidents I might have forgiven her. Most of the time I keep the lid on my still-simmering rage, but I can only continue to do that by treating Antonia as a halfwit, someone to be pitied.

'Let's look at the photos,' Antonia suggests.

She likes to see pictures of herself as a girl: such a sweet thing, such possibilities.

'I was so pretty.' She sighs as she turns the page of the photo album. Antonia still takes great care over her appearance: her nails are always manicured and she wears earrings every day. I can't see the point of dolling myself up for the benefit of no one more interesting than Antonia and the postman.

'I should have liked a husband,' she says. 'Wouldn't you?'

'I've never really thought about it.'

I've always assumed that Antonia is a virgin, but I don't suppose it's for sex that she likes the idea of having a husband. She's old-fashioned enough to believe that marriage conveys status upon a woman. Antonia was always the pretty one, the one who had her pick of the men. Luckily for me, perhaps, my tastes were quite different, but my romantic adventures were no more successful.

'Women aren't supposed to care about marriage anymore, are they?' she says, gazing at a faded photograph of the pair of us in flared jeans and cheesecloth shirts, daisy chains in our hair. 'I could have married, if I'd wanted to. I had offers,' she says.

'Offers! What are you, a heroine in a Victorian novel?'

'I'm just saying, that's all. There were men who wanted me, not like you.'

'Grow up, Antonia.'

'At least I left home – I got away.'

'I had my shop. I could have left home.'

'So why didn't you? Why, Diana? I've never understood.'

As she well knows, I lived in the flat above the shop for many years, until Father died. Mother said it was silly, that I should move back to keep her company and make a bit of money renting out the flat. I should have stood my ground, but a long-term relationship turned sour and, feeling emotionally crushed, I caved in and asked the estate agent to find a tenant for the flat.

'Mother needed me,' I say.

'Now *you* sound like a character from another era. Is it because we don't have children or grandchildren to keep us up with the times?'

We have smartphones and we watch Scandi noir TV dramas; but much passes us by. Our taste in clothes hasn't changed a great deal in thirty years and my record collection comprises seventies classics like Pink Floyd's *Dark Side of the Moon* and Neil Young's *After the Gold Rush*. Antonia favours singer-songwriters of the Joni Mitchell type.

'Mother always used to say that age is a state of mind,' I say.

'She lived in the past as much as anyone ever did. She never really got over Father's death, did she?'

'No, not really. That's what comes of relying too much on another person.'

'I rely on you,' Antonia says, brushing her fingers over an air pocket in the film that covers a studio photograph of her in her graduation gown. 'I should never have become a teacher. I don't have your strength of character. The girls knew I was afraid of them. I don't think they meant to be unkind – most of them, at any rate – but you despise weakness when you're young, don't you?'

'I don't know.'

'Yes, you do. Don't you remember that awful new girl who started at our school in the fifth form? You offered to take her under your wing until you discovered how dreadful she was. You were spiteful to her.'

'Was I?'

'Her name was Leah something-or-other. Dutch. Thick plaits of yellow hair. You pronounced her name as Liar.'

'Lord, the memory you have! I never think about those days.' Leah had a sweet, lilting voice and eyes like a china doll's. She sensed my adoration of her. Spite was the only means at my disposal of protecting myself from the rumours, the insinuations. I laughed when I made her cry, but I went home and sobbed myself to sleep.

'Do you want to come for a walk?' Antonia asks.

'If you like. Where do you want to go?'

'Just to the pond to feed the ducks.'

'Just to feed the ducks?'

'There might be more news.'

'Antonia—'

'Don't tell me you're not curious. I know you are.'

Since hearing of the recently discovered body, Antonia has veered between obsessively needing to know every latest detail of the police investigation and then sinking into mini-depressions brought on by the awfulness of people. I've told her there's no reason to assume the dead person was a murder victim, but she's probably right, it is the most likely explanation. Why would the police be making enquiries, as the phrase goes, if the death had been a natural one?

I have heeded the advice about not feeding bread to birds, so I fill a plastic tub with mixed seeds and add some peas I've defrosted in the microwave.

'A bit of stale bread won't hurt them,' Antonia says. 'It's what we used to give them when we were children.'

'It's very bad for them.'

'We never used to see dead ducks lying around, did we? I can't think it's as bad as all that. I'll take some, it's too stale for anything else.'

When we reach the pond, Antonia bends down to examine a bunch of flowers tied to one leg of a wooden bench. 'There's a card on it. In memory of – can't read the name, the rain's washed most of it off. How awful. I wonder what happened?'

'An accident, I expect.' I disapprove of the modern

9

habit of leaving flowers at the sites of accidents or crimes. It's maudlin to make shrines of these places.

Antonia tears up the bread and hurls lumps of it into the water.

'Those pieces are too big, Antonia.'

'Oh, so what?'

I glance at her. 'What's wrong?'

'People are awful.'

'There are plenty of good people in the world.'

It's like when you buy a new top; for weeks afterwards you see nothing but similar tops. It's just because you're so aware of it, not because there really are many more of them around. Car drivers say the same thing. There must be a name for the phenomenon. Somebody-or-other's Law.

I notice Naomi Wilkinson walking in our direction and raise my hand in greeting. A frown on her face, she glances around before coming over to us.

Naomi is the head librarian and the vicar's right-hand woman. She does the flowers at the church and edits the parish newsletter. She's the same age as Antonia but I don't know her well. We used to think her stuck-up, but it's possible she's merely shy. Her first marriage lasted for barely six months, and there was some bad business when her second husband upped sticks and left her in what I can only describe as mysterious circumstances.

'Good afternoon,' I say, rattling my tub of seeds and peas. 'We've come to feed the ducks.'

'So I see.'

'You've heard the news, I suppose? The body in the quarry?' Antonia says.

'Yes.' With that, she stalks away.

'What was all that about?' Antonia murmurs.

'I've no idea.' I think for a few moments, and recall the unexplained disappearance of Naomi's husband in the nineties. 'You don't think the body could be her husband? Why else would she be so upset?'

'Brian? He was a bit of a lout, wasn't he?'

'Brian, yes, that was his name. He liked a drink.'

'Such a quiet area, isn't it? Just goes to show, you never know what's going on behind closed doors.'

'What do you mean?'

'If it's him – Brian – well, I can sort of understand why someone might have wanted to do him in. He was a bad 'un.'

'How would you know? You've spent half your life in Suffolk.' I stuff the plastic tub into my shopper. I have little interest in Brian or whoever it is. 'We shouldn't make assumptions. It might not even be him.'

'I bet it is, though. Who else could it be? And he *did* disappear very suddenly, I remember you telling me.'

When we return home, we listen to every bulletin, but there is nothing new about the dead man.

'What did *you* think of Brian?' Antonia asks.

'Not much.' He'd been into my shop a few times for a last-minute greetings card. He had a leering way of speaking to women, addressing their bosom rather than their face.

I haven't the heart to cook, so instead I cobble together a ploughman's that we eat off trays balanced on our knees while we pretend to watch a game show.

'Turn it off, Di. It's getting on my nerves.'

I do so and stare at the wall, which is no more entertaining. I pick up an Agatha Christie novel when Antonia takes the trays to the kitchen, but find myself staring at the same page for half an hour.

'Good book, is it?' Antonia asks. 'I'll put the kettle on.'

Tea. For goodness' sake! I'm sure what we both need is a stiff cognac. But I nod anyway. Tea is all that's on offer.

Antonia goes to bed early. I stay downstairs and try to read, but I can feel myself nodding off. A drunken shout from someone outside startles me into wakefulness. I lay the book aside and turn off the lights before going upstairs, trying my best not to step on the stairs that creak, aware of what a light sleeper Antonia claims to be. It's her house as much as mine, but I miss the five years of peace I had after Mother died and before Antonia had her "breakdown". I resent her constant presence, her fussy ways, her whining voice. My hand spasms into a fist when I hear her softly snoring. I've had enough of being strong, of looking after people, of putting another person's needs before my own. What choice do I have, though? I'm all Antonia has.

2
NAOMI

By the time Naomi has finished preparing her lunch it's time for the national news and weather followed by the local headlines, to which she pays more attention. The presenter is a young woman with bright red hair and prominent teeth. She gives a cheery smile when she utters her 'Good afternoon', but it fades as she reads out the first item, about the human remains that have been discovered during excavation work in one of the abandoned quarries near Minster Hill. 'The police,' she says, 'are treating the death as suspicious until the results of a post-mortem are known.' Naomi listens, her body rigid, trying to take in what she's hearing, wondering what conclusion to draw from the presenter's bland comment that the police are following several lines of enquiry.

So it's true. She thought Antonia was merely being mischievous. Silly woman, always was.

In a daze, she switches off the television and sits at the kitchen table, her hands trembling. She stares out of the window and wonders when the police will call to tell her that the body has been identified as that of Brian Wilkinson, her husband. Will they ask her to identify him? No, of course not – remains, they said. What does that mean, though? A few scattered bones, or a whole skeleton?

She reaches into the cupboard for a bottle of whisky. Not much of a drinker at the best of times, she swallows half a glassful and tries not to gag. Wiping her mouth with the back of her hand, she stumbles back onto the chair and tries to think of what she will tell the police.

Her shoulders slump at the thought of all the gossip starting up again. There was enough at the time.

The women will be the worst – how they'll talk! In her experience, women are much stouter-hearted when it comes to horrible events. They pretend to be shocked, but most of them are as bad as Macbeth's witches, picking over the gruesome details as if they're dissecting toads. Men tend to keep their thoughts inside their heads rather than chewing it over with their pals. She's never been much of a mixer, has never felt comfortable passing the time of day with other women, let alone sharing intimate details of her personal life. For all she knows, gossiping might have a talismanic function, a way of warding off evils, or of nullifying their effects.

She puts on her reading glasses and picks up a women's magazine. She reads the third part of an ongoing serial but can't concentrate and keeps getting all the characters mixed up. Victorian novels are more to her taste, but she has a weakness for magazine stories, which make no demands upon her intellectual capacities.

She starts when someone knocks on the front door, certain her visitor is a policeman. Before answering, she removes her glasses and hides the magazine in a drawer. No need to panic. Why should it be the police, after all? They will have no record of Brian as a missing person. He walked out on her, didn't he? Good riddance to bad rubbish. No, of course she wasn't worried when he never came home. That

14

was the sort of man he was. The sort who'd say he was going to the pub for half an hour and roll home two days later. Restless, he was, always. Said he felt stifled in this one-horse town, everyone knowing everybody else's business. Talked himself up, he did, playing the big man. Made it plain he could do better than Naomi. No, she has no idea why he married her. Maybe he thought she had money? No, she wasn't surprised that he walked out on her. Saw it coming. Only a matter of time. Why on earth should she have tried to contact him? Why would I want a divorce? He was my second husband. Not going through that again. Better on my own. He's the sort who always lands on his feet. A charmer when he makes the effort. Probably found himself some blowsy barmaid. If he wants a divorce he knows where to find me. His responsibility, not mine.

Deep breaths, then. She has nothing to hide. She hasn't seen Brian since 1999. No one cared what became of him then, there's no reason to believe they'll care now.

She opens the front door, takes a step back. There's a man holding a box. He's got one of those screens you have to scribble on with a plastic stick. She takes the box, has to put it down so she can sign for it. It looks nothing like her signature, anyone could have written that, but it's good enough for the delivery man.

'Have a nice day,' he says.

'Yes; thank you.'

Picks up the box, takes it into the kitchen. It's the digital scales she ordered, of course it is. She probably has an unread text announcing its imminent arrival, but she rarely checks her phone for messages.

She sits with her hands cupping her face. Months can go by when she never gives Brian a thought. People must have wondered why she ever married him. Not like her first husband, different kettle of fish altogether. She met Nigel at university, was proud to bring him home to meet her parents, happy to move to Hampshire to be with him. Married six months. He said they married too young. A trial separation. His relief. Married again a year later to Melanie, had probably been sleeping with her all the time he was married to Naomi, or a good portion of it at any rate. He sends her a Christmas card every year. The first few years she ripped them up, put them straight in the bin. She doesn't get many cards now. Displays Nigel's. No one but her to see it.

She shouldn't have married Brian. Obvious now. Obvious from the beginning. The snide comments, the laughter. Your bit of rough, is he? Perhaps he was. Five years their marriage lasted, God knows how. She didn't tell anyone when he left. She knew what people thought. Run off to join the French Foreign Legion, some said, because it was more fun than being married to Naomi. Sourpuss. That's what they think of her. Not that the jokes started immediately. Some people felt sorry for her, but she can't take praise or sympathy with grace. Awkward, always was. No people skills. Too churchy.

She'll miss Mr Latham, he was a man you could talk to. This new one, likes to be addressed as Father Daniel. Says "father" sounds more friendly than "mister". Newfangled nonsense. Be one thing or the other, she thinks. No good comes from trying to be all things to all men. You knew where you were with Mr Latham. He wasn't the type to pry. Good job, too. He let her get on with what she's good at, arranging flowers, organising rotas, editing the parish newsletter. She hasn't warmed to Father

Daniel. Give it time, he says, I know you miss Mr Latham. Thinks she's stuck in her ways, too old to adapt or just bloody-minded. What does he know about her? Nothing, that's what. Sees her like everyone else does, humourless, bitter, the sort of woman who can't keep a husband.

She removes the packaging from her new scales. Battery included, saves her from having to find one the right size in her DIY drawer stuffed with cables, Allen keys, screwdrivers. She's a capable woman, can turn her hand to most things. Has to be, living alone. Always alone. Better that way.

A new day, another chance to make a fresh start, to tip the past into the bin. Her work clothes are laid out ready. Crisp white blouse, knee-length navy skirt, narrow black belt. A pair of those clever tights that pull your tummy in. Under the chair, her patent leather court shoes, easier to clean than matte leather and always smart, always right whatever the occasion. She hates leaving anything to chance, so there's always a spare pack of tights in her bag, a strip of paracetamol, an umbrella.

From the fridge she retrieves her lunch, made the night before. That, too, never varies. Pasta salad, falafel balls, a yoghurt for pudding. She saves on washing-up by having a cereal bar for breakfast with a cup of strong coffee. Brian always insisted on a fry-up to start the day. Muesli's for rabbits, he used to say. At least he cooked his own breakfast, said he learned to cook in the army. A meat and two veg man, sneered when she told him about the dinner parties she and Nigel used to host. Prawn cocktails, gammon with pineapple rings, Black Forest gateau. These days Nigel and Melanie doubtless offer their guests much more sophisticated fare, something rustled up with the aid of Jamie or Nigella or whichever celebrity chef is currently in vogue.

She walks to the library. In bad weather she wears a pair of flat shoes to work, slipping her court shoes on at the last moment. Many of the younger staff wear jeans and trainers. It's a library, they tell her, no one expects them to look smart. She feels more comfortable in her chosen uniform, it gets her into a professional frame of mind. She's been working at the library longer than anyone else and enjoys her position of seniority. She takes pride in knowing the tastes of regular users, keeping new books aside if she knows who would particularly enjoy it. Here is where she feels most at home, surrounded by books, by people who love books.

It's getting on for closing time when she sees Diana Littlehales walk through the door. Probably come to see if the book she's reserved is in yet. Naomi acknowledges her with a wave of her hand. They've known each other for most of their lives, but they don't really know each other in any meaningful sense. Naomi admires Diana's taste in novels, if not her taste in clothes. She's never seen her in anything other than trousers. Diana's silver hair is cropped, a severe style that suits her strong features. Naomi is aware that her own collar-length mousy hair could do with a trim.

'Are you in a tearing hurry for the book?' she asks Diana. 'Only your copy is coming from a larger branch. I'll check on the computer, but it might be a few more days yet.'

'No great hurry, no.'

'I should warn you,' Naomi says, 'the book deals with some strong themes, sex-wise.'

'I have read *Lady Chatterley's Lover*,' Diana says. 'I'm no stranger to strong themes, I do assure you.'

Naomi bites her lip. She knows that too many people assume anyone over sixty can't cope with anything more challenging than a soft-focus medical romance. 'Lesbians,' she says. 'There are lesbians in the novel. I'm afraid one or two people complained when they started to read it.'

Diana grins, assuring her she is equal to anything literary that Naomi might care to throw at her. The smile softens her expression and makes her look almost pretty. She's a difficult woman to read. Naomi suspects there's a great deal going on under the surface. 'Have you read it?' Diana adds.

'Not really my cup of tea,' Naomi says, 'though historical fiction is very much my thing.' Damn. Now Diana will think she's small-minded, even bigoted. How to make amends? 'You'll have to let me know if you enjoy it.'

'In spite of the lesbians?'

'I shouldn't be so quick to judge. I've heard that it's a bit *graphic*, that's all. There are some practices I really don't need to read about.' That sounds worse, doesn't it? "Practices" – what is she wittering on about? 'I like to think I'm reasonably broad-minded,' she finishes.

'I do know what you mean. Kathy Acker always managed to defeat me.'

'The poor man's Jean Genet,' Naomi says. That will help to redeem her in Diana's eyes, won't it?

'I like proper stories,' Diana says.

Not Genet, then. Radclyffe Hall, should she mention her? No, too old-fashioned. Who on earth these days would choose to read a novel where people are referred to as "inverts"? *Maurice*? No, better not lay it on any thicker. Digging herself into a hole. What is she trying to say, exactly? She doesn't have to prove anything to Diana. Villages, though. You think you know everyone. People will talk. How well does Diana remember Brian? And it's unlikely Antonia ever met him, so what is it to her? Best not make any mention of him. No one else has mentioned the news, the "human remains". Just down the road from Diana, though, that quarry. More peculiar to mention it or not to mention it? But why should she mention it? This is a library, not a newsroom.

'I'll have a look round while I'm here,' Diana says. 'A few cookery books, perhaps. I've offered to make some cakes for the summer fete. I'm still using my mother's *Be-Ro Home Recipes*.'

'People around here aren't very adventurous. A few Victoria sponges and butterfly cakes are all they'll be expecting.' Naomi checks her computer screen. 'The book should be here by the end of the week. I'll give you a call when it's arrived.'

Diana gives a perfunctory smile and wanders off towards the cookery section. Naomi sighs. She would like a friend, of course she would. Someone like Diana. A no-nonsense kind of woman who reads books, who isn't averse to difficult themes, but defeated by Kathy Acker.

She ought to have known her marriage to Brian would fail. He liked what he called men's books. Harold Robbins, James Patterson, John le Carré. The opposite of Nigel, who was a stylish man. Always nicely turned out, expensive tastes, knew when to use "who" or "whom", read Proust and Gide in the original French. Classy.

All wrong from the start, of course it was. Her wedding

20

ensemble a cream suit, pure silk, with a little pillbox hat. Staring mournfully at her reflection, at her mother who stood behind her, lips pursed. It wasn't too late to call the whole thing off. Her parents would have helped her face it out. But the honeymoon was booked, two weeks in Spain, and how she looked forward to sending Nigel a postcard with a Spanish stamp on it. *Dear Nigel & Melanie...* Nigel insistent on having a "civilised" divorce, no need for them not to stay friends, it was such a short marriage, after all, hardly worth talking about.

Naomi swallows her tears and switches off the computer. The young ones, they can't wait to escape, the air is sour with their resentful breath, life for them begins the moment they step outside, work brushed away like dandruff from a collar. She's glad they don't linger to watch her going through her evening routine, putting off the moment of going home. They all troop off together to the pub on Friday evening. She's invited, but she's never yet put in an appearance. She imagines them talking about her behind her back, passing judgement, longing for the day she's pensioned off. That's something Diana would understand. Diana's three years older than her, put her life on hold to look after that sick mother of hers, dead now, Naomi went to the funeral, made some fatuous comment to Diana about their mothers having been great friends. Well meant. Mr Latham in his element at a funeral, that lugubrious face of his, the narrow, bony hands of an ascetic.

She sets the burglar alarm and switches off the last of the lights. How long will it be before the post-mortem has been completed? How will they match up their findings with a real person? It's frightening how much they can find out these days, but there are limits, even now. It might still be all right. Brian's not my problem, she'll tell them, if they ask. He ceased to be my problem twenty years ago. I'm a respectable woman. A librarian. Top of my pay scale. But her position is a precarious one. It will only take a word, a disbelieving look, and the life she's made for herself will collapse like a house built too close to the edge of a cliff.

3

DIANA

'Where are you going?' Antonia calls down the stairs.

'To see the vicar about this wretched fete.'

'Wait a bit, can you, and I'll come with you.'

'What on earth for?'

No answer. I shrug and wait for her. Can't I go anywhere on my own? Me and my shadow.

When she comes down, she reeks of stale perfume and has smeared orange lipstick over her mouth. When she peers into her mirror I'm sure she sees a young woman (glossy hair, dimpled chin, cornflower blue eyes – I admit she was a fine looking girl, once). Even now, she regularly has her hair permed, and dyed auburn. My grey hair is cut short and I wash it in Fairy Liquid if I have no shampoo to hand.

'Is that Mother's old lipstick?'

'There was only a stub left. It was a bit hard, but it seemed a shame to waste it. Does it suit me?'

I haven't the heart to tell her the truth. 'You'll do,' I say. 'Though I can't imagine why you feel the need to tart yourself up just to visit the vicar.'

She's wearing a hairy tweed suit with high heels. 'Trousers?' she says, looking askance at my outfit: silky blouse, black slacks and flat suede shoes.

'Yes, trousers. The Anglican Church hasn't banned them yet, has it?'

She blushes and bites her lip.

'What *is* eating you, sister mine?' I ask.

'You'll make fun. Or you'll sneer.'

'Why will I? What have you done?'

'I've decided to start going to church,' she mumbles.

'You! God Almighty.'

'Diana, please.'

'What's brought this on?'

'I never took to Mr Latham, but this new man, he's—'

'Good looking, is he?'

'No! Well, yes, I suppose he is, but that's not what I was going to say. You've always assumed I'm not a believer, but you're wrong. I used to attend church every Sunday.'

'With the girls?'

'No. Morning assembly was enough for most of them. There were a few RCs, but they made their own arrangements.'

'So you've started bothering God, have you?'

'You see – I said you'd make fun.'

'I'm sorry, dear, it's just rather unexpected.'

'Anyway, this new man, Father Daniel—'

'Father! I shall continue to address him as Mr Fielding.'

'Shut up, Di. I wish you wouldn't keep interrupting. It's a very bad habit.'

I mumble my apologies and pipe down, but it seems Antonia is done with confession for the moment. Is this how she has chosen to come to terms with the hand she's been dealt? I've heard that Mr Fielding (Father Daniel indeed!) is keen on personal redemption, on what he calls "reconciliation", which I've since discovered is the re-branding of confession. I understand the need to make sense of life, particularly if you've reached our age and feel you don't have much to show for it, but I can't see what she can get from God (or "Father Daniel") that she couldn't get from joining the local over-fifties group or taking up watercolour painting.

'Diana,' she says as we stump along to the vicarage, 'I would like to invite him to tea. Father Daniel, I mean. Not today, but sometime.'

'You may invite whomever you please, though I don't see why we should extend our hospitality towards him. If we'd seen some benefit from the Harvest Festival, it would be a different matter. But not so much as a tin of mushroom soup has ever found its way to us.'

'Don't be ridiculous. Harvest bounty is distributed among the needy. You know that as well as I do. Why do you have to be so sneering about everything?'

'Just trying to lighten the mood.'

'Well, don't. It's not... seemly.'

I stick a toffee in my mouth and vow not to embarrass her in front of Mr Fielding. She's right, I do sneer, and it is a bad habit. No excuses. Chew the toffee. Keep my snarky thoughts to myself. Nevertheless, I can't rid myself of the suspicion that Antonia's interest in Mr Fielding is libidinous rather than religious. For her sake I hope she doesn't act the giddy goat in front of him; I know how silly she can get in the company of men, even holy ones.

A woman answers the door to us. I know she works as a cleaning lady, but for the life of me I can't remember her name. I repress a giggle when I imagine the look she'd give me if I addressed her as Mrs Mop. Not that I ever would. It's how my mother used to refer to our endless stream of cleaning ladies when I was young and we were comfortably off.

'Come in if you're coming, me ducks. Vicar won't be long.'

'Thanks, Mrs...'

'Anslow. You know me right enough, duck. Our Gillian's friend, weren't you? I'm her auntie.'

I feel the blood draining from my face. Yes, Gill did have an uncle, and I remember how Gill used to laugh about his wife. No side to her. Cheerfully referred to herself as "a common piece from Blaby".

'You ever hear from her?' she continues.

'The odd postcard.'

'Not seen her in years. She always remembers us, though. Expensive presents on our birthdays. A case of wine, last year. We don't really drink it, but it was high-class stuff, not a three quid from Aldi job.'

'Yes... she always was thoughtful.' Thoughtful my eye! She couldn't wait to get away from our "parochial, small-minded backwater". Her words, not mine.

Mrs Anslow shows us through to the living room and tells us to make ourselves at home. 'He's one of them trendy types,' she says. 'If you ask me, he'd do better in the city with some young folks around him. Still, mine not to reason why, and one's the same as another when it comes to cleaning up after them.'

Antonia and I gaze at each other, wondering where to sit. 'Less awkward to stand,' I say. 'We'll only have to stand up again when he finally decides to grace us with

26

his presence.' I pick up a little white china carriage clock from the mantelpiece. Pink lovebirds decorate the top. It looks like an iced cake. My empty stomach rumbles as I imagine biting into a pink sugary bird, letting it melt on my tongue.

'He's a busy man.'

'Which is why I phoned to make sure he was free for a quick chat. He could have answered my few questions over the phone, but no, he insisted I call round. Said he wanted to get to know people.'

'We might as well sit down,' Antonia says. 'We're making the place look untidy.'

The vicarage is ugly, the rooms too sparsely-furnished to be cosy, the carpet a cold shade of blue, and threadbare in patches. Two massive sofas are upholstered in leather-look plastic that offers no purchase and squeaks when one shifts position. The carriage clock is so at odds with the rest of the décor I can only assume it's an heirloom.

Mr Fielding hasn't been here long enough to impose his own taste on his home, other than to put up wind chimes in the hallway and replace a framed print of a fox hunting scene with a more tasteful reproduction of Martini's *Annunciation*. The white-painted walls are otherwise bare. There are no bookcases or personal items to speak of Mr Fielding's interests. The coffee table with its smoked-glass surface looks like a relic from the seventies. Mr Latham had no interest in home decorating.

Mr Fielding pops his head round the door, catching Antonia mid-yawn. She will be mortified. 'Sorry to keep you, ladies,' he says. 'I started writing my Sunday sermon and lost track of the time. I'll be with you in two shakes of a lamb's tail.'

He's handsome all right, with thick black wavy hair and what Mother would have described as "dancing" eyes. I'm not good at guessing people's ages, but he can't be more than thirty-five. Antonia's blushing, wouldn't you know it.

'He has a nice smile,' she says. 'He seems friendly, doesn't he?'

I glare at my watch. Good looks and nice smiles don't make up for being a poor timekeeper.

I can't help sighing. The new breed of clergy lacks gravitas. This young chap seems nice enough, but would I trust him with my deepest, darkest thoughts? Could I rely upon him in an emergency? I rather think not. *Two shakes of a lamb's tail*, for goodness' sake! What kind of expression is that for a man of the cloth to use? What possible experience of life can he have?

'He might at least provide magazines for people to read while they're waiting,' I say. If Antonia wasn't with me, I'd have gone home by now, but she wants to make a good impression, wants to get herself on Mr Fielding's radar.

It's impossible to get comfy on such slippery sofas. Antonia is gazing out of the window, a gormless smile on her face. I wave my hand to attract her attention. 'We can't stop here all day,' I say. 'Why don't we arrange to come back another time, when he's less distracted?'

'We can't just leave! How rude he would think us.'

'We wouldn't "just leave". I'd tell Mrs Mop. It's no skin off his nose.'

Eventually Mr Fielding returns, his face a high colour with a sheen of sweat, as if he's been running. 'My apologies, ladies – I've just asked Mrs Anslow to pop the kettle on.'

'Goodness, there's no need for that,' Antonia says with a giggle.

I roll my eyes. Antonia would have moaned all the way home if she hadn't been offered any refreshments.

Mr Fielding's eyes dart between the sofas, as if he can't decide which one to sit on. Instead of making that difficult choice, he drags a fold-out chair from in front of the writing bureau and perches on it, his legs crossed, back hunched, his features forming themselves into a suitable expression, suggesting polite but disinterested concern.

'This is my sister, Antonia,' I tell him.

He asks a few banal questions about us, Antonia making it clear she's a potential customer for whatever's on offer God-wise. He's delighted, naturally, and Antonia gives me a smug smile as if he'd begged her to join his congregation and can't believe his luck that she's said yes.

'It's the fete I really wanted to talk about,' I say. 'As you know, I'm in charge of the cake stall, and—'

'First let me say that I'm most grateful to you for offering your assistance. My previous parish was also a rural one, and there's nothing finer than seeing a whole community come together with a common purpose. You're setting a fine example.' He stops when Mrs Anslow enters the room bearing a tin tray decorated with a photograph of unnaturally healthy-looking red roses. She sets the tray on the coffee table with a small crash, and leaves without speaking.

Mr Fielding smiles warily. 'She's a treasure, she really is.'

'Now, about my cake stall.'

'Do help yourselves to some tea first.'

We'll be here all day at this rate. I pour out the tea and hand the first cup to the vicar, who accepts it with a polite nod.

'Please do tell me what I can do for you, exactly,' he says.

'I can't get any sense out of that woman who's supposed to be in overall charge of organising the fete. She hasn't told me how many cakes I'm to make, and she says I'm to decorate my stall, but she's very vague about theme.' It doesn't much matter; I can't say I have any great enthusiasm for the fete; but if I'm going to do a thing, I want to do it well.

'Mrs Wilkinson has taken over the organisational role,' he says. 'Her predecessor found it too overwhelming. You should liaise with her. Of course, she does have a demanding job, but I know she'll do her best to answer any questions you have.'

As head librarian, Naomi Wilkinson does, I suppose, hold a position of some significance, though the library is a small one and I can't imagine her duties are terribly onerous.

'Organising a fete sounds like tremendous fun,' Antonia says. 'And nothing to do with God at all.'

Mr Fielding winces, but – give him his due – his smile never falters.

'I mean,' Antonia amends, 'it's something to bring everyone together, isn't it? Whether they're believers or not.'

I finish my tea as quickly as possible, before he can start trying to convert me. I'm sure he wouldn't, but religious types always make me uncomfortable. I don't think I'm a bad person – no more than average, anyway – but my atheism will always be a barrier between me and this mild-mannered man who, no doubt, has the best interests of everyone at heart, regardless of their beliefs.

I stand. 'We mustn't take up any more of your time, Mr Fielding.'

'If you're quite sure. You're more than welcome to another cup of tea, if you'd like.'

'I haven't finished my first cup yet,' Antonia says, looking daggers at me.

It was a pointless visit. Why didn't he tell me to contact Naomi when I rang him up? I hope he's not going to be the flighty type. I can't imagine him thumping his fist on the lectern and damning sinners to the eternal fiery lake. Perhaps he's like a professional actor, only comes alive when he's playing to a full house.

Antonia and I take our leave of him. On the way home, she natters about the house ('Very much a man's house, don't you think? The décor could do with a woman's touch'), the refreshments ('Not even a biscuit! You'd think he could manage a few custard creams, wouldn't you?') and her own faux pas ('Honestly, I could kick myself! He won't hold it against me, will he?'). I nod or shake my head in the appropriate places, but she's the sort who can witter on for hours without realising that you've stopped listening to her.

Nights like this, depressing and lonely, always bring my memories into sharp relief. A streetlamp casts a jaundiced glow over the path, slick with rain. I remember walking along a road at night, a beautiful woman at my

31

side. She grabbed me by the lapels of my jacket and kissed me beneath a streetlamp. *There*. We'd laughed up at someone's bedroom window – a hastily-drawn curtain, the imagined pursed lips – but the bravado, my unspoken cry – 'I own the world!' – had disappeared by morning, with the leaking-in of the light.

Rain taps against the window like small stones. I drag the curtains shut and haul myself into bed. I lie with my eyes open, bedevilled by missed opportunities, chances not taken, the road less travelled.

A high-pitched noise rouses me. Cats fighting? It's barely one in the morning. I start when the noise comes again. 'Antonia?' I call, pulling myself up. 'Is that you?'

I hear Antonia sob. I'll have to see to her. I force myself out of bed and pull on my dressing gown. Slippers on my feet, I shuffle over to Antonia's door and knock. She doesn't respond, so I go in.

She lies awake, clutching her blankets. Her staring eyes remind me of the grandma in *Little Red Riding Hood* – what big eyes you have.

'Did I wake you?' Antonia whispers. 'I had a bad dream, that's all. But I'm fine now. You get on back to bed.'

With reluctance I turn to leave, while Antonia stares ahead as if she can see something terrible in front of her.

I hear nothing more from her until it's light outside, when she cries out. I dash into her room. 'Antonia? What is it?'

She sniffs and holds a tissue to her nose. 'I'm not feeling too clever, Di. Just a cold coming on, I expect.'

I pretend not to notice the tear sliding down her

cheek. I tuck her up with a freshly-filled hot water bottle and a Georgette Heyer. What else can I do to make her feel better? I go through a mental list of invalid staples: chocolates, flowers, grapes. (And why grapes? Why fruit? Do the ill crave fruit, and why should it have become such a cliché, the paper bag of grapes, damp and awkward in the visitor's hands?)

Best to ask first. 'Can I get you anything else? Tea, or a Lemsip? We've got fruit, I think...'

Antonia closes her eyes and shakes her head, frowning as if she has a bad headache. She has these little jags from time to time, some kind of hangover from the rough time she had with those over-privileged schoolgirls. I've told her it might help if she could talk about some of her experiences, but she won't. Speak to a doctor, then, I tell her, or pay a shrink, anything's better than suffering like this. She says it's post-traumatic stress disorder and she'll never get over it. My mind runs away with me, imagining all the cruel things they might have done to her, those callous girls and the teachers who didn't take her complaints seriously.

She refuses lunch, so I heat up a tin of soup and eat it in front of the telly with a chunk of French bread, sneering at the naivety of a young man who bought a house at an auction without viewing it or looking through the information pack. His face, when he sees the state of the derelict monstrosity he's bought, is a picture.

Burning a hole in my apron pocket is a postcard from Gill, which arrived yesterday. Normally I'm lucky if I get a couple of lines of scribble, but this one is almost the length of a letter. She popped it in an envelope, so at least I can be sure Antonia didn't read it.

Hope you're keeping well, Di. Currently in Crete, a painting holiday with my local art group. Fabulous scenery & company. You should travel more now you're not working such long hours at the shop. How's Antonia? I'm thinking of coming back to visit Morevale. It's been such years, hasn't it? It's something I've always meant to do, but you know how it is, and frankly I couldn't wait to get away. Still, we're none of us getting any younger, are we? I'd like to see you, Di. Would that be all right? I don't have your phone number, so could you send it to me? I know I've been appalling at staying in touch, but I never know what to put in a letter, and email is so impersonal, don't you think? Speak soon, I hope!

  Love,

    Gill

I've lost track of the number of times I've read this message, trying to read too much into it. I've responded in kind, chatty and bright, in a National Trust greetings card depicting a sunny day in Carding Mill Valley. It was one of the places we visited together, do you remember, Gill? That picnic we shared with dozens of skinny, greedy sheep. Not skinny, you said. Lean.

I turn off the telly and use the carpet sweeper to clear up the bread crumbs. I call up to Antonia, 'I'm just nipping out. Do you want anything?'

'Get me a nice magazine,' Antonia calls down.

'*Nice*,' I mouth. That's Antonia's trouble – she wants things to be *nice*, she can't stand confrontations, can't stand to acknowledge that sometimes we have to take the rough as well as the smooth.

34

I walk to my shop, which still bears the name given to it by Miss Dodson: Buttons & Bows.

'I like the window display,' I tell Stella.

'I can't take any credit for it. The new Saturday girl is studying graphic design at college. She's got a good eye.'

I wander around the shop hoping Stella doesn't think I'm checking up on her. I'm really only needed when she's ill or on holiday, and to check the accounts.

'The animal cards are selling well,' she says.

'Good.' They are the work of a local artist; we make a point of stocking products from local craftspeople, and customers seem to appreciate this. It's a lovely shop, but I can't help feeling wistful, remembering how it looked in Miss Dodson's day: shallow wooden drawers, each one meticulously labelled, for the knitting patterns; carousels holding embroidery silks in jewel-bright colours; sets of fancy buttons sewn onto card.

'Doing anything nice today?' Stella asks. 'You should get a car, there's lots of lovely places around here you and your sister could visit.'

'I never learned to drive.'

'Sorry; I keep forgetting. I suppose women didn't so much back then, did they?'

'I'm not that old,' I say. 'You're thinking of my mother's generation.'

She smiles blandly and eases a biscuit from the packet on her desk with a thumbnail.

I'm tempted to buy something nice for Gill, a welcome home present, and eye the display of handmade silver jewellery before realising it would be entirely inappropriate.

In the post office I read the cards in the window, as I always do. There are at least three women offering their wedding gowns for sale. "Never been worn". Never mind: I doubt any modern girl would do a Miss Havisham, sealing herself away with a wormy wedding cake covered in cobwebs. Instead, sensibly, she sells her wedding dress and moves on to the next chap. I wonder if anyone will feel put off buying a "tainted" wedding dress? Perhaps the acquisition of a bargain outweighs any superstitious thoughts.

I post my card to Gill, then look for a suitable magazine for Antonia. Something *nice*, filled with touching stories, gardening tips, adverts for Stannah stairlifts: nothing to frighten her, no sex, no swearing. I choose a magazine and glance through it as I wait in the queue to pay. What a cosy world it paints! I'm ridiculously irritated by the determination of the magazine not to acknowledge that terrible things happen, and at the same time I yearn for a world like that to be real and to be able to live in it. Does Antonia believe in this fiction of happy-ever-after love, knitting patterns and tray bakes?

After all this time, could she really learn to love again? Story corner – a charming story to read to your grandchildren. The Best of British home cooking special. Enjoy continuing chapters in our thrilling, heart-warming serial. The "Letter of the Week" comes from a lady in Devon who explains how she recently met up with a woman she hadn't seen since they worked together in a Carnaby Street boutique in the "Swinging Sixties": *It was as if we'd seen each other only yesterday! We had many laughs, and a great deal of chatting over old times, as you can imagine.*

If I could make a home for Antonia and myself in that inviting world where nothing ever happens to rock the boat, where the worst that can happen is a touch of greenfly on the roses, I would do so, without hesitation.

4

NAOMI

She has a reason to ring the doorbell. The book in her hand is the one Diana has ordered. *Tipping the Velvet*. A pair of pretty pink shoes, satin most likely, on the cover. Not velvet. The velvet in the title is something quite different.

She sees something in Diana, a sense of solidity, a person on whom you could rely. Puts up with that daft sister of hers, doesn't she? Naomi remembers Antonia from school. Prissy. Hair in neat plaits tied with red ribbons. In the same classes, both of them staying on for A levels, Antonia full of herself when she landed a place at Portsmouth Polytechnic, nose put out of joint when Naomi was accepted at Exeter University. Would never admit to jealousy, oh no, not that one! Clear as anything, though, and Diana had congratulated her, actually shook her hand.

She can't imagine those two getting along. Chalk and cheese, always were. Diana the reliable one, Antonia flaky, too high an opinion of herself. Still, she stuck it out, polytechnic, fair play to her, and held down a decent job. A teacher, that's something to be. Naomi wonders what went wrong, but will never ask. Not her place. Wonders, though.

'Naomi! I was just thinking about you. We really should get together, talk about the fete. I'm sure if we leave it up to those others nothing will ever get done.'

Naomi holds up the book. 'I'm afraid the library copy hasn't come in yet, and as I promised you it would be in by the end of the week I thought I'd lend you my own copy, if that's all right.'

'That's very kind of you, but really there's no hurry.'

'I insist.' *Please*. Please take it. I want to be useful and I so rarely am, these days.

'Are you sure? I'm a very quick reader so I won't keep it long. Nothing more annoying than lending someone a book and never getting it back, is there?'

'I wouldn't lend books to most people,' Naomi says. 'I know I can trust you.'

Diana gives her an odd look, as if Naomi has spoken out of turn. They barely know each other, after all. Three years was a big age gap when they were younger. Nothing now, of course. Sixty or sixty-three, what difference does it make?

She'll invite her in, won't she? To thank her for her thoughtfulness. Not that she wants any thanks. But a cup of tea never goes amiss, does it? The cup that cheers... Stop it, you old fool! Get a grip of yourself, woman. You run a house, you're at the top of your pay scale, you've no cause to feel inferior to anyone.

'I was just going to put the kettle on,' Diana says. 'Do you have time for a cuppa?'

'Only if it's no trouble.'

There's a lump in her throat when Diana brings the tea through to the living room. It's such a nice, comfortable house. Cosy. Homely. A plate of sandwiches on the table. She's interrupted Diana's lunch. A pretty plate, decorated with flowers. No man to muck up the place. Sometimes Naomi thinks she can still smell Brian on the pillow slips.

Not unpleasant. He wasn't a *dirty* man, after all, not like some she could mention. Uncouth, that's all. Said Nigel must have been a pansy when she told him that he always wore cologne. Jealous of Nigel, of course, annoyed because Naomi refused to hear a word said against him. 'If I didn't know better,' Brian used to say, 'I'd think you were still soft on him.' And she'd turn her head away so that he wouldn't see the sorrow in her eyes, the disappointment.

'Help yourself to cream and sugar,' Diana says.

'Where's Antonia?'

Diana tuts, raises her eyebrows. 'Church, would you believe. The eleven thirty service. She seems to have found God in her old age.'

'Hardly old,' Naomi says.

'You know what I mean. We're not *young*, are we? We can't even call ourselves middle-aged. There's no word for people like us.'

'We're in the autumn of our years.'

Diana shudders. 'I much preferred spring. The promise of youth.'

'Promises it didn't always keep.'

'Thank goodness for books.'

'Yes, thank goodness.'

There is something she wants to say, something she must tell someone. The moment isn't right, though. She's sure Diana wants to get rid of her, to finish her lunch before Antonia returns.

'It's wrong of me, probably,' Diana says, 'but I have this fixed idea that people who work in libraries can barely tear their eyes away from the page. Perhaps you don't have to love books to work with them, though I imagine it helps.'

'I love them,' Naomi says. 'Always have. The younger ones haven't the same fondness. Of course, I can see the attraction of Kindles and what have you, but a proper book, with foxed pages, that smell! There's nothing like it, in my opinion.'

Diana gazes at her. Realising, perhaps, that there's more to Naomi than meets the eye? Wondering what she earns? And her with no family, can't be badly off... The state of her clothes, though!

Naomi pulls at her cardigan, wishing she had the courage to be bolder in her fashion choices. The hem of her knee-length beige skirt is coming undone. Her yellow blouse has unfashionably large lapels and the colour's all wrong for her skin tone. Not that Diana's any kind of fashion plate. Antonia was always the one for clothes, a snappy dresser her mother would have said, probably did say, with a seasoning of scorn in her voice. Antonia always could wear anything well, but then, she always was one for the lads, wasn't she? Strange she never married. No, not strange, not strange at all. The things we keep to ourselves! Wonders if Diana knows. Must do, surely, a thing like that?

'Not at work today?' Diana says.

'No... Trying to cut down on my hours a bit. I'm not ready to retire just yet, but I've been there a long time. It'll come as a shock to the system when I don't have work to go to every day.'

'Yes, of course.'

She was keen on clothes when she was younger. She likes to keep up with current trends, even if she can't wear them herself. Some of the younger women often leave magazines lying around and she has a peep when she's eating her lunch in the staff room. She's not behind the times. She knows who Kim Kardashian is, even if she doesn't understand why she's famous. She grins, sometimes, when she thinks how much her mother would have disapproved of these young women flaunting their bodies, their lovers, their celebrity lifestyles.

They spend a couple of minutes having a rather stilted conversation about Naomi's work at the library and the new vicar, though there's precious little mileage in either of these topics.

She admits she's not too keen on Mr Fielding, though she's still happy to fulfil her obligations. The flowers, the rotas. There will be a second-hand book stall at the fete, she says. A good way to get rid of surplus stock from the library.

'You don't get involved with any of the church social groups, then?'

'To be honest, I'm not much of a mixer. Once I get home from work I just want to put my feet up.'

Diana nods but makes no comment. Probably doesn't want to sound like she's prying into Naomi's domestic arrangements. Knows, as she does, that you get far more out of people if you let them tell you their business in their own time, rather than trying to prise it out of them.

Naomi is ready to blurt everything out, but the moment is ruined by Antonia returning from church. She's flushed, her bucket hat askew over one eye. 'Oh, tea, how lovely! Is there some in the pot for me?'

Diana grunts. Naomi senses a tension that has crept into the air.

'To what do we owe the pleasure?' Antonia says.

'Naomi kindly brought a book round for me,' Diana

says, flourishing the book with its pretty cover, its peculiar title. Please don't let Antonia ask what it means!

'She reads far too many books as it is,' Antonia says, showing no interest in this one. 'The house is full of them. I can never like library books myself unless they're brand new. You never know what germs people have on their hands, do you?'

Diana glares at her.

'It's true,' Antonia says. 'Some of them have a most peculiar smell. You have to wonder what people's homes are like.'

These two probably spend half their lives bickering, but at least they have each other. Naomi is stuck with talking to herself or to ghosts.

Antonia peers into the teapot and frowns.

'Make some more if you're thirsty,' Diana says. 'I didn't know what time you'd be back.'

Antonia shrugs, looks as if she wants to say something, then thinks better of it.

'You can tell me all about the fine time you had at church later,' Diana says.

'You wouldn't be interested. I'll make a fresh pot, shall I?'

'As you wish.'

Naomi waits until she can hear Antonia clattering around in the kitchen then she uncovers her face, which is wet with tears.

'Good heavens!' Diana says. 'Did Antonia say something to upset you?'

Naomi shakes her head. If she tries to speak, she will sob, she'll feel such a fool.

'Naomi... we don't know each other well, and asking

42

if there's anything I can do sounds so trite, so patronising. Here.' She hands Naomi a box of tissues.

She must look a fright, a woman too old for these shows of emotion, with her unfashionable blouse, her hair in need of a cut, her pathetic attempts to show the world a brave, competent face—

'You have no idea,' she says thickly. 'No idea at all what I've been through.'

'No, I haven't. No one ever knows. We see people, more or less like ourselves, going about their daily business, and we assume their lives are more or less uneventful, more or less ordinary.'

'I need a drink.'

Diana opens a cupboard door, removes a bottle of sherry, and pours a good measure into Naomi's empty teacup.

Naomi takes a gulp before continuing. 'That body they found – the one in the quarry. It's Brian, I know it is. All these years I've lived with it, waiting for the body to be found, waiting for the knock on the door.'

Diana remains silent. Cat got your tongue, has it? Go on, ask me how I know. Go on, ask!

'I don't remember Brian well,' Diana says. Choosing her words carefully, tiptoeing over the minefield, Naomi can tell.

'He deserved it,' Naomi says with a watery smile. She swallows loudly. 'He—' She pushes her fingers through her mousy hair. 'I probably shouldn't have told you, but I had to tell someone, and I don't have... well, I live alone, as you know...'

'I'm sorry.'

'No need to be. I hated him. That's a terrible thing to say, isn't it? It's not something I say lightly.'

'Of course. Have they— How can you be sure it's him?'

'Who else could it be?'

'But he left you, didn't he? Walked out?'

Naomi hangs her head. Silly of her to hope that Diana would understand.

'I'm sorry, Naomi, I'm probably being thick, but... I don't quite know what to say.'

'No. Of course not. I've always known he's dead. He'll be just a lot of old bones now, won't he?' A sudden, nervous laugh escapes her lips, which she stops with a hand over her mouth. 'I'm sorry. In life he caused so much heartache. I thought we'd seen the back of him. Might have known he'd turn up again, the proverbial bad penny.'

'Did you... I mean... I'm not quite sure what you're trying to tell me, and I'm not being much use.'

Naomi takes another sip of sherry then puts the cup down, wrapping her hands around it. 'What should I do? I can't carry on living with this, knowing what I know.' She wipes her eyes. 'I suppose you're going to say I should tell the police.'

'Tell them what, though? That you suspect the husband who left you twenty years ago is the body in the quarry, but you can't tell them how you know?'

'Won't, not can't.'

'Did you kill him?'

Finally, the right question. 'Not as such,' Naomi says.

'What does that mean?'

'It's as much as I'm prepared to say. It's not fair to burden you with my...' My sins, she wants to say, but Diana would misunderstand.

'When he left, did you report him as a missing person?'

'No, he was never that.' Something has hardened inside her. The tears were a momentary weakness. No more of that, now. Some things are best kept bottled up. Another nip of the lovely warming sherry. 'Perhaps it's just that I prefer to think of him as dead than shacked up with another woman.' That's reasonable, isn't it? Not a logical thought, but it's credible, the sort of thing an abandoned wife might think.

'Why would you care, if you disliked him so much?'

'Guilt, I suppose. I wanted him to go. It was a terrible marriage. A mistake.'

'You could have got divorced.'

'Yes, we could, couldn't we? I don't know why it never occurred to either of us.' That's what she'll tell the police. She won't lie, that would go against her beliefs, but why bore them with irrelevant information? Brian left. I was glad. No, he was never violent, we simply had nothing in common. 'Besides... I knew he'd leave, sooner or later. He was as miserable as I was.'

The sherry really has done her the power of good. She's not used to it, that's probably why it's acted so quickly.

'I still don't understand why you think he must be dead.'

'Bodies don't turn up in quarries every day of the week, do they? It would be too much of a coincidence.'

'That sherry has certainly put the colour back in your cheeks. I take it you're feeling better?'

'I am, thank you. I rarely drink, seeing what it did to Brian, but it has its uses, in moderation.' How many times had she made excuses for Brian? Yes, he liked a drink, but he wasn't a bad drunk. The shame of it! Funny looks from her colleagues and even customers coming into the library. She knew what they were all thinking. Blaming her.

Diana rips another tissue from the box and hands it to Naomi.

'I feel so alone.'

Diana, frowning. Taken up too much of her time already. She's no help, no one is. 'You needn't be. People find you a bit stern. If you'd open up a bit more—'

She gives a hollow laugh. 'Open up!'

'Not about the past.'

'The past is where I live.'

'Stop martyring yourself, Naomi!'

Naomi bites her lip.

'Are you eating properly? I bet you're not.'

Pasta salad for lunch. A yoghurt. Sometimes an apple. Not like these lazy people who spend a fortune on pre-packed sandwiches. A proper cooked meal some evenings. Too much effort; but cheese and crackers can be quite filling.

'Here,' Diana says, thrusting the plate of sandwiches under her nose.

'Thanks.' She stares at it, but makes no move to take one. 'You're too kind to me.'

'Don't talk daft. Eat.'

Naomi takes a nibble from a sandwich, watching Diana put the sherry back in the cupboard. Probably thinks she's had enough. More than enough.

'I'm normally quite... quite sensible. It's just this body... A post-mortem, they said. It can't take that long, can it?'

'Depends how much body they've got to work with. Naomi, you've told me nothing of any substance, but... I wouldn't advise you to go to the police. It might look a bit... odd.'

She thinks *I'm* odd, that's what she means. I am behaving in a most peculiar fashion. It's the sherry, not used to it. Sherry on an empty stomach, what was I thinking?

'Naomi?'

'Sorry. Yes. I'm supposed to be a Christian, you see. It's my duty to love all my fellow creatures. I didn't love Brian.'

'Why did you marry him? We all wondered, at the time...'

'Of course you did. He asked me, that's why, and he couldn't have been more different from Nigel – my first husband, you never knew him. But you can't wipe out the past like that, can you? He sent a wedding present, Nigel did. From him and Melanie.' She looks at her hands, bitten fingernails, could do with a good clean. 'Stupid, stupid woman.' Old enough to know better. Brian with his vulgar charm, his roguish good looks, laughing with her when she told him that Nigel used to bore her to tears with his opera recordings and she hadn't had the heart to tell him how much she loathed them.

She stands up. 'I'm going now. There's no hurry about the book. You can always pop it into the library when you've finished it, someone will put it aside for me if I'm not there.'

'Naomi...'

'I'm right as rain now, really I am. Thank you so much for the sandwich.'

'Naomi, listen—'

'Maybe put a Post-it note on the front, so it doesn't get mixed up with library stock.'

Diana follows Naomi to the front door. Young people,

always hugging; not right for two sensible women of their age.

'Thanks again,' Naomi says, giving Diana a cheery wave when she reaches the front gate. Nice woman; thoughtful. It must come from having had to look after her mother for all those years. And now she's got Antonia, who's worse than a child.

She can sense Diana watching her through the living room window. She made a fool of herself, didn't she? Oh, the stupid things she said! But not too much, no; no cause for panic, we all say foolish things from time to time, it's perfectly natural.

Instead of going straight home, she takes a detour at the fork in the road, pauses near the cemetery, peers through the wrought-iron gates. Her parents' graves are marked with small white headstones, the writing in black. The white was a bad idea, it gets dirty quickly. Green glass chippings on the graves, a small metal pot filled with dead flowers. She ought to replace them, but she doesn't like going in there.

The older headstones lean at odd angles, they look as drunk as she feels. So many beloved wives and husbands, the inscriptions meaningless now that everyone who loved them is also long dead. They'll put Brian in there, she supposes. What's left of him. What will she put on the headstone? The vicar, he'll know.

She leans her forehead against the metalwork and groans. She'd looked forward to confiding in Diana, but it's no use. A mistake. Bile in her throat, that nasty sherry, a cheap brand. Pull yourself together, woman! No one must see you looking like this.

She takes a deep breath, consults her shopping list.

She'll make a proper nourishing meal tonight, pull out all the stops. There's no sense in meeting trouble half way, after all. A nice bit of fish, perhaps, with boiled new potatoes. She pats her hair. All better now, thank you. Right as rain.

5

DIANA

I have no idea what to make of Naomi's visit yesterday. I shouldn't have given her sherry. I sensed there was more she wanted to say, but I couldn't find the words that would have invited her to confide in me. Perhaps I should be glad. Did I really come out and ask if she'd murdered Brian? And her peculiar response: "Not as such". What on earth could that mean? It's tempting to believe that living alone has made her a bit strange, and her life certainly hasn't been comfortable. An early marriage that failed, then she waited fifteen years and the best she could do was Brian, of all people.

This morning I raced through the final few pages of Elizabeth Taylor's masterpiece, *Angel*, so that I can make a start on *Tipping the Velvet*. Rereading *Angel* has been a sobering experience. The story is, of course, hilarious; Angelica Deverell is pitiable for her self-delusion, egotism, and complete lack of a sense of humour. Now, though, it's the latter part of the story that gives me pause for thought. Angelica's trashy novels become unpopular and no longer sell. She and her put-upon companion, Nora, decline into old age and eccentricity.

These two characters remind me uncomfortably of my own situation. True, I have never been a novelist, nor am

I as self-deluded as Angel. But Antonia and I have become old before our time, a little eccentric, and probably pitied by younger people – and by those of our own age who have done something with their lives. Not that "doing something" always amounts to much. Look at Naomi, twice married but still as innocent as a schoolgirl in many ways.

I shouldn't be reading. I should be helping Antonia to prepare lunch for Patricia and Sheila, our cousins, the only relatives with whom we are still in contact. They persist in staying in touch with us and have a fondness for sending us notelets covered with their spidery handwriting, keeping us abreast of their news, such as it is. They're both in their seventies, sprightly though, a Med cruise every summer, bingo every week; but of course, as they like to remind us, they have children and grandchildren to keep them young and up to the mark.

They descend on us every year before they take their cruise. I can't begrudge the visits, trying as they are. Mother was fond of them. With their husbands, who were alive then, and their sons and daughters and grandchildren, they bulked out the otherwise thin crowd at Mother's funeral. The other mourners huddled around the grave were elderly and largely consisted of villagers who knew Mother before she took to her bed and turned her back on them all. Quite what was wrong with her all those years I can't rightly say: diabetic complications, she announced, after a particularly long visit from the doctor. I'd long suspected her of making rather too much of it. She lived, after all, to the age of ninety.

As the funeral got underway, there weren't the floods of tears I expected from Antonia, and I wondered if she was as fond of Mother as she always made out. Then again, she had her job, a life of her own, and her visits home were brief even during the long school summer holidays.

We left the church and trudged up the road to the cemetery, where we watched as Mother was buried in a mahogany coffin. 'Such a pretty colour,' Antonia whispered when she saw the box. 'Seems almost a shame to bury it. Someone's polished it up and it's just going to get all mucky in the ground.'

'You chose it.'

'I liked the colour in the catalogue. I suppose I didn't think about where it was going.'

Mother specified that she wanted to be buried without her wedding ring and I had it safe in my pocket in a black velvet pouch, feeling like a pickpocket who'd palmed it from one of the mourners. I considered throwing it into the grave, but decided against so melodramatic an action. Our cousins peered into the hole and the vicar looked a little worried, perhaps fearing the two women might topple in.

'They both look like the old Queen Mother,' Antonia whispered in my ear. They were dressed in pearly grey outfits with matching hats.

'Shh!'

All went according to plan until it was time for the coffin to be lowered into the grave. One of the webbing straps supporting the coffin slipped, and instead of a stately descent, the coffin clattered into its final resting place. Antonia screamed, Sheila buried her head in her husband's chest. Patricia's son tittered. The funeral directors couldn't have been more apologetic, but as Antonia said, it spoilt the whole day. A moving, dignified occasion turned into something from a sitcom.

I found myself having to deal with an hysterical Antonia while Sheila and Patricia acted as hosts for the "nibbles at our house" funeral tea. They kept the wine flowing, they made extra sandwiches, and expected no thanks. My gratitude for that one day means I am prepared to put up with the boastful notelets and their annual visit spent telling us about the cruise they took the year before and the one they are about to enjoy.

'Everything's ready,' Antonia announces. 'Help me bring it to the table, would you?'

Antonia puts on a good spread. She likes the fiddly work of stuffing vol-au-vents and cutting the crusts off cucumber sandwiches. She likes the excuse to get our best china out, and she arranges cakes artistically on their stands.

'I do hope they like it,' she says.

'You know they'd find fault even if you hired caterers from the Ritz.'

'Why do they have to be like that?'

She knows as well as I do. 'Never mind. *We* know it's an excellent spread.'

'Aren't you going to change into something smarter?'

I don't see the point of dressing up for relatives, but it matters to Antonia and so I dig out my black tailored trousers and a long-sleeve blouse with a paisley pattern, bought many years ago on holiday in Edinburgh, and ridiculously expensive.

From my bedroom window I watch and wait for the taxi to draw up. And there it is, bang on time. A lot of fuss with money and paper bags. They always bring presents and I always suspect they are unwanted Christmas gifts: bath bombs, hand lotion in tiny, fancy bottles, squares of fudge in cellophane packets. We eat the fudge and donate the "smellies" for prizes in the tombola at the village fete. At some point, I suppose, the chain of giving will end and someone will watch a bath bomb fizz disappointingly in their bath.

'Diana!' Antonia calls up. 'They're here!' A quiver of excitement in her voice. This is, after all, an Occasion.

I open the front door, but before I get a chance to say hello, Sheila produces a paper bag from within the folds of her jacket. 'I didn't know how you were fixed for food, dear,' she says, 'so I brought along a few sandwiches.'

Patricia nods. She has tightly-permed hair and looks like a blue-rinsed sheep.

'We took a taxi from the railway station,' Sheila says. 'You can't rely on the buses. The price of it! Quite exorbitant. You wonder how they get away with it, you really do.'

'I would have paid the fare,' I say. 'I wouldn't expect you—'

'You've let it go a bit, haven't you, dear?' Sheila says. 'You should get someone in to see to those window frames before they get much worse. It'll benefit you in the long run.'

The house is large by modern standards, but it's the only home I've ever known and I've never given a thought to what it might be worth. Painted white, it's known locally and unoriginally as the White House. The front garden has grown rather wild, but the hollyhocks and wild roses are what Antonia and I like to see, having no fondness for manicured gardens or smooth lawns.

'Still, it's not as though you've anyone to leave it to,' Sheila adds. She is very proud of the fact that she has known marriage and motherhood (but the husband is long dead and the son is never talked about since he "broke his mother's heart" when he left his wife for a "painted hussy" no better than she should be).

We usher the pair inside and settle them in the living room. Antonia went through a silly phase of referring to this room as the drawing room, insisting that "living room" is a common expression. Poor Antonia always had ideas above her station. She's forever buying home décor magazines and trying to replicate the "little touches" that apparently have the power to turn a pig sty into a chateau. Nothing ever quite works as well as the magazines promise. She bought throws for the sofa and armchairs, but they creased and were forever coming adrift.

She does us proud now, though, producing a pot of tea and a plate of French Fancies. She offers the plate first to the cousins. 'They're very moreish, don't you think?'

'We tend not to eat cakes,' Patricia says. 'Not bought ones, anyway. Though these look lovely, of course.'

'Oh, but the bought ones are always so much prettier,' I say quickly, seeing Antonia's mouth turning down. 'Besides, we don't want to spoil our appetites, do we? Antonia has made sandwiches, cheese scones, and vol-au-vents.'

'Did you use polyunsaturated spread? Butter's so unhealthy, my GP says I shouldn't eat it.'

'Only butter, I'm afraid. We don't like margarine.'

'So long as it's just a *scrape*,' Sheila says. 'I get bilious if I have too much fat.'

'Do help yourselves,' I say to the cousins, gesturing towards the table. They make a great production of picking over the food before Antonia returns from the kitchen with yet more sandwiches.

'I don't suppose you have any Arabica coffee?' Sheila asks. 'I'm trying to cut down my caffeine intake.'

She seems purposely to want things we can't provide; not anything exotic, but the fact that I can't supply her small needs seems to indicate some measure of failure on my part.

'Only ordinary. Or there's sherry?'

'Not with my stomach,' Sheila says.

'It was good of you to come,' I say to the cousins once they've eaten their fill, and even ask if they want to stay the night (at which suggestion the disappointed expression on Antonia's face is replaced by one of abject terror), but Patricia says they want to get back.

'You like your own bed at our age,' she adds.

'In any case we've ordered a taxi,' Sheila says.

'It's my youngest grandson's birthday tomorrow,' Patricia says. 'Did I tell you he's got a PhD now? The first doctor in the family.'

'I don't hold with this endless studying,' Sheila says. 'Life experience is what counts. You did all right for yourself without any degrees, didn't you?' she says to me.

'And so good to your mother,' Patricia adds. 'She was lucky she had you to look after her. Funny how neither of you ever married. What *was* the name of that boy...?'

'Philip,' I say. The chap Antonia wanted to marry, until his parents decided he was too young to get married and needed to concentrate on his brilliant career.

Patricia prods at a tooth. 'Philip, that's it. What happened with that, exactly?' She looks from me to Antonia and smiles. 'I'm too old to care about offending anyone, I'm afraid. Disappeared off the face of the earth, didn't he?'

Antonia puts her hand to her mouth and runs from the room.

I hurry after her. 'Come on, Antonia, take no notice of them. It's always better to brazen it out than show they've upset you.'

I take hold of her arm rather more roughly than I should, and march her back into the living room. Patricia sits on the sofa munching a French Fancy; Sheila is poking around the oak dresser, lifting up ornaments and examining them.

When the taxi draws up outside, the cousins scramble to their feet and make a great fuss about collecting their handbags and coats before tumbling outside and into the taxi. We stand by the garden gate and wave them off.

'What a pair of old trouts,' Antonia says when they've gone.

'They're like us, Antonia. You get like that, when you live with a female relation.'

'What a thing to say! What nonsense you talk sometimes.'

'It's true. We're just as awful as they are.'

'They didn't show much appreciation for the food. And they didn't make much of an effort at conversation. I expect they just like to keep an eye on the house. Perhaps they think we're going to leave it to their children in our wills.'

'Probably. They can assume what they like, for all the good it'll do them.' I link arms with her and lead her back inside.

'You don't really think we carry on like them, do you?'

'We've no grandchildren or fancy cruises to boast about, but we do get on each other's nerves, don't we?'

'But we're always there for each other, aren't we, Di?'

I'll be quite happy for Antonia to put me in a nursing home when the time comes. At least I'll have someone other than her to talk to. Even if I get stuck with a gaggle of senile old biddies, it will be better than having her look after me, buying my underwear and emptying the chamber pot.

I nibble on a leftover cucumber sandwich as I help Antonia clear the table.

'Make a pot of coffee, there's a dear,' I say.

'We only have Robusta,' she says, mimicking Sheila.

I smile, feeling at peace with my sister, but then she has to ruin it by telling me she overheard my conversation with Naomi the day before.

'You couldn't have overheard. You were in the kitchen, weren't you?'

She gives me a hangdog look.

'Oh, God – you were listening at the door, weren't you?'

'I'm sorry,' she says, shrugging. 'My curiosity got the better of me. Only... the things she said... what did you make of it all?'

'I don't know.' I had lain awake mulling over what Naomi told me, wondering if she'd actually told me anything at all. 'I gave her a tot of sherry, which was probably a mistake.'

'They say she drinks.'

'They?'

A quick shrug as she lowers the plunger of the cafetière. 'People.'

'Silly gossip.'

'Do you think she killed him?'

'Of course not! She's—' A librarian, I want to say. But why should a librarian be less likely than anyone else to murder someone?

'It's your duty to inform the police,' Antonia says.

'Inform them of what? A half-cut woman with a half-baked, rambling story about her missing husband.'

'That's enough, isn't it? She couldn't know he's dead unless she killed him herself. Stands to reason.'

'The mind plays all sorts of odd tricks. It's possible she's never come to terms with him leaving her.'

She hands me a mug of coffee. 'What are you going to do, then?'

'Nothing. It's none of my business.'

'You'll be an accessory after the fact. Diana, you might go to prison! How would I cope without you?'

'Is that all you can think about? Is that my only function in life, to look after you? You're not a child, for God's sake. Perhaps I *should* go to prison, it might force you to grow up.'

'Diana, how can you say such awful things?' She presses a hand against her mouth. Tears aren't far away.

'I'm not the one who goes around listening at doors. Oh, do stop crying. You know how you hate having red eyes.'

'I know. And it never even mattered what I looked like, except to me.' She scrubs at her eyes with a piece of kitchen towel torn roughly from the roll. 'It was wrong of Patricia to drag Philip's name into the conversation. She only did it out of spite, didn't she?'

'Yes; quite probably.'

'Put them off next year, can't you?'

'It's only for a couple of hours.'

59

'It's too much. All that preparation, and for what?'

'Antonia, about Naomi—'

'Just like you to change the subject.'

'I didn't – you did. Anyway, it doesn't matter. I have no intention of telling the police about a private conversation.'

'Don't blame me if—'

'I won't. This is my choice, nothing to do with anyone else.'

She pouts. I hope we can find a way to see out our days on friendly terms. Every New Year's Eve I resolve to be nicer, kinder, but I can barely get through January without scowling or snapping at her.

'You must see that I couldn't betray a confidence.'

'You don't owe Naomi anything. Things might have been easier for me at the school if other members of staff hadn't taken sides, covering up for other people.'

'It's not quite the same thing.'

'Isn't it? They made my life hell, Diana. You can't know what I went through.'

Naomi had used similar words. Of course I don't know what either of them has been through and I've never claimed otherwise. 'Talk to me about it, then. You never do.'

'I'd rather forget all about it,' she mumbles.

'You can't have it both ways.'

'You're hard, Diana, do you know that? You've no empathy. Remember how you carried on when I damaged your doll?' It's always the doll we talk about, as if it was the worst thing that ever happened and defined the rest of our lives. 'You've never forgiven me, have you? As if it mattered! And it certainly doesn't matter now.'

'I know it doesn't. What are you getting at?'

'You thought I over-reacted, but I was genuinely scared of what you might do to me.'

'Nonsense,' I mutter. 'Anyway, what does that have to do with my supposed lack of empathy?'

'It was an accident, the doll. I thought, once you'd simmered down, you would realise that, understand that these things happen. You've never quite believed it wasn't deliberate, have you? You're prepared to cover up for Naomi, but not to give me the benefit of the doubt.'

I must make allowances. Sheila and Patricia's visit has been too much for her. All those sandwiches, the baking, the lack of gratitude. I tell her I'll finish the clearing away. 'You go and put your feet up,' I say. 'You've tired yourself out.'

'But the mess—'

'Don't worry about it; I'll sort it.'

She doesn't take much persuading. She picks up her knitting and her magazine.

Later I'll take her a cup of tea. She regards cups of tea as small treats, a trait she's inherited from Mother. 'But if you do want to talk...' The words drift up the stairs, unheeded, spinning like dust in the air.

6

NAOMI

Naomi wakes early on Monday morning, even before the alarm clock can bully her with its shrill, incessant ringing. She's promised to go into work even though Monday is her day off. One of the assistants is on holiday, and one of their regular volunteers is at home with a sick child. Since Naomi has no other commitments she feels obliged to help.

She switches on the portable television and sits at the table to eat her cereal bar and drink her black coffee. Some famous chef or other flings chicken livers and herbs around a frying pan in a devil-may-care fashion.

Naomi pushes up the sleeves of her baggy brown cardigan. 'I can't watch this rubbish,' she mutters, pressing the off button with a bit too much force, causing a little ornament, a china salt shaker in the form of a Dalmatian, to tremble on the edge of the dresser. The Dalmatian is one of the many bits of nonsense Brian brought home for her. Never one for the grand romantic gesture – no box of chocolates, no dozen roses, no bottle of champagne – he tried to please her with the oddest assortment of trinkets. A pink teddy bear, once, and it was then she realised he brought her things he'd won at the fair or in a game of darts down the pub.

Naomi rinses out her mug, jumping at a knock on the front door. She opens it and finds a woman with brassy bleached hair and black roots. On her arm she carries a basket filled with tiny bunches of white heather, their stems tightly wrapped with tin foil.

The woman winks. 'Lucky heather and I'll tell yer fortune for yer.'

'Oh...' Naomi fiddles with her hair. 'No – thank you – I'm not—'

The woman leers at Naomi and pokes her head forward, as if to kiss her. 'Only fifty pee to you, lady.'

A kiss or a curse. Brian was always superstitious and a bit soft about Gypsies. One year for Christmas he'd given her a pair of rather vulgar gold hoop earrings of the type worn by Gypsy women in sentimental Victorian paintings. 'Maybe I should drape a scarf over my head and parade around with a basket of pegs,' Naomi said. 'Maybe you'd like me better that way.' That familiar come-here-girl twinkle in his eyes. 'Maybe I would,' he replied.

The Gypsy woman clutches Naomi's forearm. 'Your man's gone, hasn't he? Dunna you worry, though – he'll come back.'

'You haven't even looked at my palm.'

It's all nonsense, this fortune telling lark; it's all guesswork and slyness, there's no magic to it. And this woman, what are her credentials? Brian used to refer to some of his relatives as "Gypsies", but they weren't, they were itinerant showmen, travelling around the country in search of the next shooting gallery, the next screaming rollercoaster, the next customer to fleece.

'It's in your eyes, my lover.' Gently the woman rubs her thumb over Naomi's naked ring finger. 'You'll see him again, but you'll wish you hadn't. It's not going to end well.'

Naomi snatches her hand away. She digs around in her pocket for a pound coin, which she gives to the Gypsy hoping it will get rid of her.

'I can tell you more,' the woman says. 'Let me see your palm.' She tries to force Naomi to turn over her hand, but Naomi pushes the woman away and bangs shut the front door.

She hears the woman calling, asking her to open the door, she hasn't taken her sprig of lucky heather...

She tries to forget the incident, but it haunts her all day, like the faint but noxious smell of fried fish, clinging to her. However hard she rationalises the fortune teller's visit as a bit of nonsense, the woman's words bite into her.

The job keeps her sane, and it also gives her a place to go, away from the house she's learned to hate. Maybe they'll let her stay on past retirement age. What will she do with herself without a daily routine? Voluntary work is a possibility. Anything to get her out of the house for the bulk of the day.

At lunchtime she sits alone in the staff room, as she always does, gazing miserably at her pasta salad. Why shouldn't she splash out, spend frivolous money on fancy sandwiches? Everyone knows food tastes better if you haven't made it yourself. The habits of a lifetime, though, run deep.

One of the young admin assistants pokes her head round the door, backing away when she sees Naomi in there. 'Sorry – didn't think you were in today,' the girl says.

'I'll be out of here in a minute,' Naomi says. Do people find her company so burdensome? She tries to get on with people, she really does.

The young woman sidles in and sits on the chair furthest away from Naomi, who tries to remember her name and how long she has been working here. The young ones never stay long, it's hardly worthwhile getting to know them. Sloppy dressers, too, like this one: scruffy jeans, shapeless T-shirt, ugly thick-soled trainers.

'You OK, Naomi?' the girl asks.

'Sorry, miles away.'

'You look a bit flustered, that's all.'

'Do I? I'm quite all right, thank you.' Interfering hussy! She snaps the lid back on her tub of pasta salad, most of which remains untouched. It'll keep till tomorrow; she'll pep it up with a few fresh toms and a splash of salad dressing. Absurd to waste good money on pre-packaged muck, full of things with long names that belong in a chemistry lab. Look at that one over there with her pappy white bread sandwich oozing tuna and mayo. She's not even eating the lettuce, which she delicately teases from the sandwich and deposits in the packaging. The stink of it! There ought to be a rule against eating strongly-smelling food in here. It will seep into the main body of the library.

The girl catches her eye and blushes. 'Should have got the ham.'

'Yes, it might have been wiser.' She's not being fussy, it's simply common courtesy. She'll have a word with the office manager, see if she can't find a polite way of letting staff know they need to think of others when making their food choices.

The girl stuffs the uneaten portion of her sandwich back in the box. 'I'll save it for later,' she mumbles.

'I've got some clingfilm in my desk if you'd like some.' There's milk in the fridge; the smell of the tuna will taint it. The girl stares at her, uncomprehending. Gormless. People just don't *think*.

At four o'clock Naomi decides to return home. She calls in at the Spar then walks towards her cottage, the handles of the two plastic carrier bags cutting into her fingers like cheesewire. A migraine nags at her right temple. Sometimes she wishes she could lie down and sleep forever.

'He'll come back,' the Gypsy said. Naomi shakes her head, trying to dislodge the words. She's done her best to keep life normal, but it hasn't been easy. People were bemused when she came back to Shropshire after her divorce, but tongues wagged after Brian's desertion. Naomi wasn't just unfortunate, so the gossip went; bad luck followed her around like a needy child.

She should have tried harder to make her first marriage work. She blames Nigel for suggesting a trial separation. A couple of months, he said, which had turned into six, then eight, which was longer than they'd been married. She shouldn't have kept pestering him, asking him for a firm date, a decision one way or the other. 'We both need to grow, as people,' he said. 'Grow away from each other you mean,' she responded. She didn't want the divorce, but he was so reasonable about it, so concerned for her welfare, so adamant that the marriage was not worth saving.

She puts the bags down and stands for a few moments

outside the cottage. Without warning she vomits by the gate. She groans and wipes her mouth with a tissue, knowing that the migraine will begin to subside now. Forcing herself onwards, she picks up the bags and tramps into the cottage. Bags on the table. Glass of water to rinse out her mouth. Paracetamol. Coffee. She forces herself to unpack her shopping, averting her eyes from the pictures on the food packaging. She'll have something light for dinner. A bit of toast, that's always good for settling the stomach.

A wave of tiredness overcomes her. No point fighting it, she's still trembling from the unpleasantness of being sick. In her bedroom she closes the heavy curtains to shut out the world, which she both wants and fears. To break the silence, she switches on the radio. A bit of music floats in, something classical – Bach. Or is it Handel? Her parents had never been big ones for music. She tried to learn to appreciate classical music under Nigel's tutelage, but she hasn't the ear for it, just as some people have no palate for wine or quality whisky. Still, the music is soothing, it will keep her company while she dozes. Didn't she read somewhere that listening to Mozart while you sleep can make you cleverer? Or is that babies in the womb?

She won't stay in bed for long, an hour or so, that won't hurt. Best set the alarm clock anyway, just in case. That's one blessing, she's never had any difficulty getting to sleep. She'll feel better after a rest, she might even be able to face boiling an egg – no, best not to think about food yet, still a bit queasy. There's no hurry; her time is her own. No one to cook for, no one else's wants and feelings to consider. Many would envy her, she's sure; mothers with fractious and food-fussy young children, wives whose husbands come home late from work, irritable, demanding food on the table, right now. Everyone has their own burdens, their special cross to bear.

She's settling down for a relaxing evening of books and telly when she hears someone knocking on the back door. With some trepidation, in case the fortune teller has returned, she puts the chain on the door before opening it.

'Father Daniel!' Bloody man. She's tried, but she can't take to him. All this high church malarkey he wants to introduce, out of place in a village like this. If that's what he wants, he should become a proper Catholic or else find himself a more congenial church frequented by intellectuals who read Graham Greene and fret over *Guardian* editorials.

'I do apologise for bothering you at home. I tried the front door, but there was no reply.'

'The doorbell's broken,' she says. 'I keep forgetting to have it fixed.'

'Might I come in for a few moments?' He looks awkward in a casual jacket, though still wearing his dog collar. She wonders if vicars are allowed to take them off. The women ones must be, surely?

'Of course. Let me just take the chain off.' Despite her lack of fondness for this man and his absurd appellation, religion has always been a big part of her life. She views her church duties – the flowers, the parish newsletter, her occasional stints as a guide selling postcards of the church at fifty pence for one, or three for a pound – as doing God's work, albeit in a smaller way than Father Daniel's.

She ushers him into the house.

He has on what she calls his "serious face", the one he uses when he needs to sound sincere, or when there's trouble of some kind. 'I really just wanted to check that the preparations are all in hand for the fete,' he says.

'Of course.' How can he doubt it? She's nothing if not conscientious.

'And – you're getting on all right with everyone? Including Miss Littlehales?'

'Diana? She's a hard worker, and intelligent. Why do you mention her particularly?'

He gazes around the kitchen. 'Oh, no reason. Good, good.'

'Was there anything else?'

'Not really, I just... wanted to make sure everything was all right.'

'Why wouldn't it be?'

Father Daniel clears his throat. 'I do wish we could be friends, Mrs Wilkinson.'

'Friends?' She switches on the kettle, just for something to do with her hands.

'I realise I've not been in the parish very long, and I daresay it will take a while for people to warm to me, as it were, but I should welcome having you as an ally. Well, ally is the wrong word, perhaps. But I thought you could help me keep a finger on the pulse... as it were.'

What on earth does he mean? Does he want her to spy on people?

He touches her arm. 'I like to be... a hands-on kind of vicar. I don't like being too remote from people. I would like to think you could confide in me, if ever you needed a friendly ear.'

She takes one step back. 'Have people been saying things about me?'

'No, no, nothing like that!'

She doesn't believe him. Everyone knows how her first husband couldn't take being married to her for more than six months. How her second husband walked out on her. Everyone leaves Naomi. He must have heard it all. She wrenches open a dresser drawer and pulls out a small figurine. 'See this?' she says, holding up a china crino-lined lady.

Father Daniel nods.

'It's been in that drawer for years. My husband – my first husband – bought me this for my birthday. Every part of me tells me to throw it against the wall, smash it to pieces. And yet look at me, cradling it as carefully as if it were an heirloom.'

'Well, memories–'

'This is all I have to remind me that he once loved me.' She holds out the ornament like a trophy. 'He knew I wanted this particular figure – *lusted* after it – and it cost an arm and a leg. He thought it tasteless, a monstrosity. But he got it anyway because he knew it would please me more than anything else.' Afraid she might cry, she gently replaces the figure.

Father Daniel stares at a deep scratch on the table. It is obvious he doesn't want to be having this conversation.

'Six months our marriage lasted.'

'I'm sorry. That must have been difficult for you.'

The kettle switches itself off, but she makes no move to make tea. Instead she paces around the room, touching things: the dresser, the sink, the mirror on the wall.

70

She stands with her back to the vicar, her cardigan falling off one shoulder. 'He was a good man, despite what anyone else might tell you. I begged him not to end our marriage, there was no need for it. He wasn't like some I could mention, drinking their pay packets, messing around with other women. And I was a good wife to him – I was.'

'I'm sure you were,' he says, soothingly. 'I assure you, no one has said anything to me with respect to your personal circumstances.'

They have, of course they have. It's Brian they'll talk about, not Nigel. If they'd met Nigel, they'd have seen the difference, wondered at her making such an inexplicable second marriage.

She presses her fingers against her eyes, not wanting to see anything of the past. An appalling self-pity takes hold of her. All her life she's scrimped and saved. She can afford to buy nice things for herself, but persists in buying her clothes in the cheapest shops. They are always of poor quality, with seams that split and buttons that come off after one wash.

'I never wanted anything special,' she continues. 'I didn't want luxuries. Raising a family would have been enough for me. That's all I wanted. Just the normal things.'

Receiving no response, she moves towards the kettle. 'I'll make some tea. Would you like some?'

'Thank you.' He gestures to the embroidery hoop on the table. 'I see you're a seamstress,' he says.

'Not a particularly good one.' She prepares the tea, hoping he won't stay much longer. He can be of no help to her, and he's plainly uncomfortable in her home. She

71

doesn't have the gift of the gab like some people. He appreciates her, seems to trust her judgement, but she can tell he's not easy in her presence.

'Here you are, vicar. Nice and sweet.' A ridiculous thing to say. This tea is no nicer or sweeter than any other.

'I'm always available,' he says, patting her hand. No doubt he's being perfectly sincere, but the sort of availability he means isn't the open-ended variety. He will be available when it suits him, that's what he means. Besides, why should she care? If she were the type who wanted to confess all her sins, she'd have become a Catholic. Father Daniel will likely end up going over to Rome, but she's too set in her ways to jump ship now.

'I'm sorry I said those things, about my husband. I know it's the "in thing" these days to spill your troubles, like on those dreadful chat shows, but it doesn't come easily to me. I expect you can tell.'

'Many people find that talking helps, but I appreciate it's not for everyone.'

'It's certainly not for me. I'm quite happy to attend to such church duties as you see fit to allow me to do, but I'd ask you to forget any idea of us being friends or allies. I'm not a cold woman, but I'm old-fashioned enough to believe there should be some distance between men of the cloth and us mere mortals.'

'Thank you for being candid with me, Mrs Wilkinson. But I do want you to know there is more to me than sermons and fundraisers for the church spire. I think you're a troubled soul and I'd like to help, if I can.'

'Troubled? Aren't we all?'

'You live alone, you have no family. It's not a sin to get lonely from time to time, to need someone to talk to.'

72

'I'll bear that in mind, but I prefer to keep myself to myself.'

She hopes Father Daniel isn't going to make a habit of dropping in. It's what people do, but she was brought up to believe that you visited other people's houses only by invitation. Once he's finally gone, she sprays the room with air freshener, washes up the cups and saucers, and wipes the chair on which he sat with a J-Cloth soaked in disinfectant.

7

DIANA

'I couldn't half fancy a bowl of porridge,' Antonia says on Sunday morning. 'With salt and milk, like in the old days.'

'Old days? Don't talk daft – we never had salt on our porridge.' I might be a dreamer, but it's Antonia who tries to romanticise our childhood. She thinks they were the best times and she might be right, but I don't see the point of living in the past. Happy though some of those days were, they are gone and can't be recaptured.

Nevertheless, I make Antonia's porridge the way she claims to like it, in a puddle of milk and without the brown sugar that is the only thing that makes porridge edible.

Everything in the house speaks of Antonia's taste. The frills, flowery fabrics and fussy little details have even found their way into the kitchen. Finicky, useless things – the milk jug cover, for instance, a circle of fine linen weighted with coloured glass beads. Antonia's world, not mine.

Even the velour cushion covers in the living room have some fancy basketweave design. They are green to match the carpet and curtains, but no two shades are the same and each has a different pattern. Antonia buys our soft furnishings from a mail order catalogue. She turns down pages and circles all the items she likes; including rings, watches, children's toys. Whenever I come across one of these catalogues I feel a rush of pity.

Later in the morning Antonia attends church. She says she likes the ritual of churchgoing, the rousing hymns, and most of all she likes to watch the rest of the congregation.

'The Matthews girl looked particularly miserable today, I thought,' she says when she returns home, referring to a dumpy teenager who is the daughter of our hairdresser.

'You sound almost pleased.'

'Of course I'm not!' After a pause, she adds, 'You've been in rather a funny mood lately.'

'What do you mean?'

'That business with Naomi. And that postcard you keep reading.'

'It isn't dignified to argue on a Sunday, and after church, too.'

'I'm not arguing. It's from *her*, isn't it, the postcard?'

I put the kettle on while Antonia arranges a selection of biscuits on a plate: another ritual, another small treat.

'I don't mind talking about it, you know,' Antonia says. 'About what happened. About Gill.'

I grunt. She might be happy to drag up things that are better forgotten, but I have no intention of encouraging her. 'It was all such a long time ago. What does it matter now?'

'You've never forgiven me, have you? I only did what I thought was best.'

I throw a teaspoon across the table. It almost hits Antonia, but lands harmlessly on the floor.

'What was *that* for?' she says.

'Oh, you!' I say, stamping my foot like a toddler. 'You knew I loved her – why did you have to say anything?'

Antonia stares at me, mouth gaping with surprise. 'But, my dear—'

'Oh, you'll dress it up and justify yourself – I know you.'

Antonia bites her lip. 'You've always treated me like a child.'

'And do you wonder why? I can't talk to you, Antonia – I might forget myself.'

I leave Antonia to drink tea and eat biscuits by herself. Safe in my room, I take out my photos; private photos, never shared with Antonia. Dear Gillian, such a pretty girl. And she loved me, I know she did. Here's a picture of her with her arm protectively around my shoulder. She sent a copy of that picture to her married sister. In the covering letter she spoke about how dear a friend I was, how fond of me she was. She couldn't say more than that, of course. Times were different, people wouldn't have understood. But her affection for me is patently clear in the photograph. Only a fool could think we were anything but lovers.

Antonia knocks on my door. 'Would you like your cup of tea, dear?'

'No. Go away.'

'Just a sip...?'

'Please go away. You're ridiculous.'

Antonia and I prepare to go into town, as we usually do on Mondays, to pick up any shopping that can't be purchased locally. When we're ready to leave the house, Antonia fixes a floppy brown velvet hat to her hair with a couple of vicious-looking hatpins that once belonged to our grandmother. As a child she admired them, believing the decorations to be real sapphires rather than the coloured glass she now knows them to be. The pins, no longer perfectly straight, are rough with rust.

We take the bus into town. I have nothing in particular to buy, so I trail after Antonia, who enjoys window-shopping. 'Look at the price of those!' she says, pointing to dresses in a shop she would never patronise.

I wish she wouldn't stare at some of the more outré fashions worn by the young, but she can't seem to help herself. You'd think she'd never seen a girl with dyed hair before, and as I always say to her, plenty of women our age still dye their hair funky colours. Personally I enjoy seeing the parading peacocks, although fashion has become much duller since the days of punk rock. Even some of our friends briefly sported Mohican haircuts and bondage trousers.

So many things are light years beyond Antonia's comprehension. Hard as she struggles to come to terms with modern life, with reality, I know she would rather avoid confrontation with anything that makes her uncomfortable. At her age, she would say, she has a right not to be bothered by "unpleasantness". She was eighteen when "God Save the Queen" was released, but to hear her talk you'd think she was born when the Queen was Victoria and safety pins were for emergencies, not for making a political statement.

Antonia and I head for the café where every Monday we treat ourselves to a pot of tea or fancy coffee and a selection of cakes. This has become one of our little rituals, something to look forward to, and Antonia makes a great fuss about our weekly extravagance.

The café would not have been my first choice; it lacks atmosphere. The floor and wood-panelled walls are made of varnished pine. Although it calls itself the Swiss Café, it is decorated in shades of brown and goes in for the *Brambly Hedge* and gingham look. Antonia likes it because the tables are always clean. The walls are decorated with a variety of corn dollies – things I haven't seen elsewhere for years, although they used to be the absolute staples of the church bring-and-buy sale.

While Antonia queues, I amuse myself staring at a black-clad girl at the next table. Shiny black dress, black leather jacket, even black fingernails and lipstick. She tucks into a jacket spud filled with cheese and coleslaw, but her lipstick looks untouched.

'Yeah?' the girl says, scowling at me.

'Sorry, dear. Didn't mean to stare. I was just wondering how you manage to keep your lipstick on while you're eating.'

The girl raises a pencilled eyebrow. Her pursed, darkly-lipsticked mouth puts me in mind of a juicy blackberry. For a moment I think she's going to shout at me, but a sudden smile illuminates her face. 'You fix the first layer with face powder, blot it, then add another layer of lippy.'

'I see. Thank you. Excuse my curiosity. It's a long time since I wore make-up.'

'You should wear lipstick. A pearly pink, maybe. It'd suit you.'

Antonia returns with a tray loaded with plates and cutlery and over-full cups of coffee slopping their contents into the saucers. I get a tissue ready to place between my cup and saucer.

When Antonia sips her drink, her thickly-applied orange lipstick leaves a sticky mark on her mug. I itch to wipe it off. 'Who's your friend?' she whispers, indicating the girl in the leather jacket.

'Just a girl. We were discussing make-up.'

Antonia raises her eyebrows. 'Fancy.'

The girl gets up to leave. 'Bye, then,' she says to me.

'Goodbye.' When she's left, 'What a nice girl,' I say to Antonia. 'Just shows that you can't judge by appearances.'

Antonia has lost interest. 'Have you seen what they're asking for those?' she asks, pointing to the corn dollies pinned up on the walls. 'For a few stalks of corn and a manky bit of ribbon!'

'Shocking,' I say, tucking into my millionaire's shortbread.

Her gaze drifts to a young mother at the table behind ours, her two young children sticky with orange juice and strawberry jam. 'People these days think they've a God-given right to have children. In our day we accepted God's will and got on with our lives.'

I clench my teeth. 'No, we didn't. The first test tube baby was born in 1978.' Why does she persist in saying things she's said a million times before? I unfold my newspaper. The front page story is about a young woman who's been murdered: beaten up until she was unconscious and left in a car, which had then been set alight. I brush shortbread crumbs from the photograph of the murder victim.

Antonia glances at the news story. 'What an awful thing. It said on the news that a man walking his dog found the body. It nearly always is, isn't it? Makes me glad we don't have a dog.'

What I most dislike about the modern world is the way everything is treated as ephemeral. Nothing is made to last, and tragedies seem to disappear from public consciousness like Alka-Seltzer dissolving in water.

Take this poor girl, for instance, her awkward, gappy mouth on the front page of every tabloid. In a year's time, will anyone remember her name? It's true that people of a certain age remember the names of Maria Colwell and Ginette Tate; but there are so many more, so many short, forgotten lives. Many of them don't make the national press. Even on the local news, a murdered child isn't necessarily the lead item. I'm not sure why this suddenly bothers me so much. Perhaps because no one will remember me after I'm gone, either. Few of us leave much impression behind once our lives are over.

'Why do people like talking about murder so much?' Antonia asks, carefully cutting up her Bakewell slice.

'Do they?'

'Of course they do! A nice juicy murder. I suppose it beats talking about the weather.'

I can't help but recall the number of times I've wanted to bash Antonia over the head with a frozen leg of lamb, or slip a few drops of sparkling cyanide into her tea. What would I tell the police if ever I did such a mad deed? Money and lust are, I suppose, the most common motives for murder. I imagine trying to explain to the police how furious I still am with events that happened over forty years ago. I could hardly claim to have acted in the heat of the moment – four decades is an awfully long time to wait before taking one's revenge.

'Nice cakes, these,' Antonia says, catching hold of a plump cherry escaping from her Bakewell slice. She would be quite happy to stay in the little café all day, eating cake after cake – never a proper meal – and drinking foamy coffee.

I think of a restaurant I used to go to with Gillian. The tablecloths were real lace, no plastic or paper in sight. Bone china cups. Elegant, spotless cutlery, probably cleaned by hand, not in a dishwasher. Doilies, linen napkins, real carnations. Tears fill my eyes as I recall Gillian's effusive apologies when she tried to hold my hand and tipped the flower vase over instead. I had such fun saving up every detail of our meetings to describe to Antonia later, and she listened intently, her lips slightly parted, eyes shining as if – as if *what*, though? She seemed so pleased for me. Why had she chosen to ruin everything? *What harm did we ever do you?* – I said that to her, and Antonia had no answer, she just frowned, that slightly foolish, hurt look on her face, like a child who's been told off for something it can't remember doing.

'Was it a sex crime?' Antonia asks.

'What? What are you talking about?'

Antonia pokes the newspaper. 'That girl. The murder victim.'

'Oh, I don't know.' I fold the paper none too carefully and stuff it into my shopping bag, out of sight. 'What would you know about such things?'

'It's the way of the world, isn't it? It's all these short skirts that girls insist on wearing. Things were so much nicer in our day.'

'Don't talk rot. Things were never "nicer", as you put it. Was Mrs Crippen murdered because she wore a short skirt? Was Sharon Tate? Was whoever-it-is in the quarry?'

'Brian,' she whispers. 'We know it's Brian, don't we? Naomi told you.'

I roll my shoulders, but can't get rid of the band of tension around my head.

'Are you all right, dear?' Her eyes are filled with concern.

'Can we go, please?'

Antonia gobbles up the last of her Bakewell, and buttons her jacket. 'You should have said if you weren't feeling well. It's not as if we *have* to come here.'

Oh, but we do. I couldn't have faced Antonia's disappointed expression if I told her the weekly treat was cancelled.

8

ANTONIA

Antonia relaxes when she smells the steak and kidney pie cooking. *Lovely*. Diana has had a blitz on the fridge and pantry, chucking out all the ready meals and packets, having decided that from now on they're going to start eating proper home-cooked food. Antonia closes her eyes and pretends she's a child, Mother pottering around in the kitchen, clattering pans, her mission to nourish and please her little family. *It's only Diana*: Antonia has to remember this. It isn't safe to daydream about the past, it's too big a shock when reality bites.

Diana breezes into the room.

Antonia picks up the remote control and presses the BBC1 button. 'I used to like *Wogan*. Such a shame it isn't on anymore.'

'That show hasn't been on for *decades*, Antonia!'

'Damn soaps, that's all there is these days. They're very samey.'

'Very depressing,' Diana agrees. 'Pie won't be long.' She mutes the TV, but Antonia remains staring at meaningless moving pictures. The only sound in the room comes from the loud, monotonous ticking of the clock.

She picks up her knitting bag. She always has something on the go; always a project on the needles. Diana often asks who she's knitting for; there are no grandchildren and neither she nor Antonia wear woollen jumpers. Antonia wishes Diana would ask her to knit something for her, but she never suggests it. She knits two quick rows. That done, she stabs the knitting needles into a ball of yarn the size of a large grapefruit, and goes into the dining room.

Diana brings in the pie, puffing the steam away from her face, and returns to the kitchen to fetch dishes of Jersey Royals and runner beans.

'How delicious it all looks.'

Diana smiles, her book open on the table, which she reads throughout the meal, occasionally wiping from the pages a drop of melted butter or gravy.

After the meal and the washing-up are successfully negotiated, Antonia takes up her knitting again. Knit one, purl one, knit one, purl one. Antonia is glad she has something so rhythmically soothing to occupy her hands. Catholics have rosaries, she has her knitting. 'I could make you a scarf,' she says. 'Be nice for the winter.'

Diana grunts. 'If you like.'

Antonia holds up the knitting. 'Browns and oranges. You like those colours, don't you?'

The seconds tick on, loudly and laboriously. Diana flicks through a magazine and picks at the skin around her nails.

Antonia is sure her sister can't wait to spring up and announce that she's off to bed.

'How long?' Antonia asks.

'How long what?'

'Until you can go to bed. I can tell you're itching to go.'

Diana glances at the clock and sighs. 'These summer

evenings drag.'

'Oh, do say what you *mean*,' Antonia says. She's tried hard to keep a civil tongue, but it hurts her that Diana can't wait to get away from her.

'You take everything the wrong way, and when you feel got at – though goodness knows why you should – you start picking on me. It's very tiresome.'

Her fingers trembling, Antonia picks up the discarded magazine and stares at the cover. She's sure it's Diana who is quick to take offence, but if she tries to complain Diana will twist everything, as she always does. She thought things were going to be all right, but yet again Diana has managed to spoil the day.

So when Diana yawns, picks up her book and announces she's "bushed", Antonia waits ten minutes then makes her phone call. She'll withhold the number, she doesn't want police officers traipsing around the house.

'Police,' she says when she's asked which service she requires.

Her voice trembling, speaking softly so that Diana doesn't hear her, she says, 'I can't give my name, but I know the identity of that body found in the quarry near Minster Hill. His name is Brian Wilkinson.'

'I need to ask—'

'Just listen. Please. He was married to Naomi Wilkinson. She practically confessed to me that she murdered him.' She puts down the phone. She doesn't want to engage in further conversation. They'll make her say things she doesn't want to tell them. She thought of confiding in the vicar, but it's better this way. She hopes she didn't stay on the line long enough for them to trace the call, but there are no public phone boxes anymore. That must be why people use the burner phones she's seen in TV dramas.

Someone had to do something, didn't they? She doesn't care about Brian and she certainly doesn't care about Naomi, but she can't bear the thought of her sister going to prison. Antonia wouldn't know the first thing about running a house on her own. When she was teaching, she shared a house with another teacher, another old maid.

Besides, she thinks Naomi is quite capable of murder. Naomi has always hated her. The look of horror on her face when Antonia and Philip arrived together at Naomi's sixteenth birthday party. Poor Naomi, so desperate to have a boyfriend, so jealous of Antonia's beauty.

I didn't invite him, Naomi screamed; you had no right!

Antonia shrugged, triumphant, took Philip's hand and told Naomi she could stick her silly, childish party.

But Naomi married, and she never did. No children, though, that's one blessing.

Tears slide down Antonia's cheeks.

Knit one, purl one. The knitting is sloppy, with dropped stitches and variable tension.

9

NAOMI

'Mrs Wilkinson?' The taller of two men addresses her as they both brandish their identification.

'I am she.' Her voice is barely above a whisper.

'May we come in for a few moments? We did try the front door, but the bell doesn't seem to work.'

'You could have knocked. I would have heard you knock.'

Reluctantly she steps back for them to enter. The tall man introduces himself as Inspector Freeth, and his colleague as Sergeant Ward.

'Won't you sit down?'

'We'll stand, thank you. Hopefully we won't keep you more than a few minutes.' It seems the inspector is going to do all the talking. 'I expect you've heard about the body that's been found in an abandoned quarry near Minster Hill.'

Naomi worries at a loose thread on her cardigan. 'I saw it on the news.'

'For reasons we are not at liberty to divulge at this stage, we have received information suggesting that the body is that of your husband.'

'Brian? Are you sure?'

'Not at this stage. I understand you and he went your separate ways, but there was no formal separation or divorce.'

'That was years ago!'

He smiles as if pacifying an idiot child. 'Yes, we're aware of that. You didn't report him as a missing person, did you?'

Aware that her breath stinks of whisky, she retreats a few steps and sits at the table, as far as possible from the policemen. 'He wasn't missing. He walked out on me.'

'And he never contacted you again? You never tried to contact him?'

'Why would I? I was happy to see the back of him, if you want the honest truth.'

'The strange thing is, we can find no records to suggest he's alive and well. No evidence that he's working, or using a bank account, and no official death notification.'

'Well, as you doubtless know, he was my second husband. It wasn't a good marriage, but not a terrible one. Neither of us had any intention of remarrying, so I never had any reason to try to find him. He was always a bit of a drifter.' She has practised these lines many times over the years, in preparation for this moment.

'Surely there were other reasons you might have needed to contact each other? And you didn't move house, so it would have been easy for him to contact you, wouldn't it?'

Her hands are clammy. Why must they keep pestering her with questions? 'I can't answer for his reasons, can I? I didn't want anything more to do with him. I had a good job, the house is in my sole name.'

'I wonder, could you tell us the circumstances in which he left? Had you argued? Did he actually *say* he was leaving you?'

'I came home from work one day and he wasn't there. We'd had an argument that morning, but that wasn't anything out of the ordinary, and it was over something trivial. He didn't have a job, just odd cash in hand stuff here and there. Most of his clothes were gone.'

'So how did you know he'd left for good?'

'Because he'd threatened to do so many times before. He didn't like being tied to one place. As I've said, it wasn't a good marriage, and we had no children to keep us together.'

'And he left no note? Nothing to account for his actions?'

'That wouldn't have been his style. He never cared about other people's feelings. Everyone will tell you, he was a bad lot, always getting on the wrong side of people.' She swallows down rising nausea. Is she speaking too glibly, being too hard on Brian, giving them a reason to believe she might have wanted him dead?

'He had enemies?'

She pauses before speaking. How much should she tell them? No harm, surely, in telling them what is public knowledge. 'Put it this way, he had no friends. Not real friends. People he drank with, did favours for, probably not always strictly legal.'

'What did *you* think had happened to him?'

She clasps her hands, wishing they would stop trembling. 'Like I said, that he'd gone off to make a new life for himself. He had relatives who worked the fairgrounds, that kind of thing, I thought that might be what he'd done.'

The worst thing about the police is that you never know what they're thinking. If they have suspicions, they never let on, not until they have proof. And where will they find that, after all this time?

'What happens now?' she asks. 'I mean – if it's him – was he—?'

The inspector smiles. 'Our enquiries will continue. We'll let you know, of course, if we have anything significant to tell you.' He turns his mild gaze on his sergeant. 'I think that's all for now, don't you?'

Sergeant Ward nods. She's glad he didn't speak, suspecting he is the bad cop to Inspector Freeth's good cop. The sergeant has ginger hair and a mean, foxish sort of face, a permanent frown etched on his forehead. The terrier type, she thinks; the kind who never lets go once he's got his teeth stuck in.

They turn to leave. When they reach the door, the inspector twists his head. 'If you think of anything else about your husband that might be relevant to our investigation, you will let us know, won't you?'

'Of course.'

'Good day, Mrs Wilkinson.'

Once she hears their car drive off, she exhales loudly and pours herself another whisky. Her hands tremble. Diana is the only person who could have offered "information" to the police. Why would she have done such a thing? Giving her sherry, pretending to be concerned, but the moment Naomi left the house she must have been straight on the phone. Couldn't wait to share her juicy gossip. Telling herself she was acting like a responsible citizen.

Naomi curses herself for putting her trust in Diana.

You fool! She's tempted to go straight round to Diana's house, give her a piece of her mind; but if she does that she will likely blurt out things best left unsaid. She'll never speak to the damn woman ever again, that much is certain.

Anger gives way to a feeling of emptiness. In her head she repeats the word "betrayed", over and over, until it loses all meaning.

Naomi decides she needs something more substantial than a cereal bar for breakfast. She read somewhere that eggs are the most complete food, so she boils one and butters two slices of bread. Automatically she switches on the radio to listen to the early news, but her mind is fogged with the remnants of a dream in which the recently discovered body turned out not to be Brian's after all, but that of a tramp. The police came to tell her. Overcome with shock, she confessed to having murdered her husband, placing the palms of her hands together as if in prayer, ready for the handcuffs. They laughed at her; the notion of a murderous lady librarian too ridiculous to take seriously. The relief she felt on waking turned sour as soon as she realised it wasn't true.

Do dreams have any meaning, even if just as a way of tapping into the subconscious? Her mother always used to say that if your palm itched it meant you would soon be coming into money. Naomi often dreams of winning the lottery – who doesn't? – but she's never won so much as a church raffle, so how can she read any significance into one dream?

The police will, of course, return, and she must be careful what she says. She's been straight, up to a point, telling them that she and Brian didn't get on – anyone would tell them that, so there's no point lying about it.

It was only the booze; he was fine when he was sober. She shudders at the memory of the stink of his boozy breath in her face.

She sighs and drags herself back to the present, to the boiled egg she has allowed to go cold. She shakes her head. No point going over old ground, all those acres of memories, all the mistakes she's made. Did Brian marry her for her money? She doesn't have much, but the house is paid for and probably worth a bob or two. She tries to remember what they talked about before they married. They weren't often alone. Brian's idea of going out was a walk to the local pub. 'I'm a bit short at the moment,' he'd say. 'I'd like to get a round in, but...' And she'd slip him a couple of tenners, so that he could buy the drinks, so that his pride wouldn't be dented. Hail fellow well met as soon as he crossed the pub threshold, buying drinks for strangers with her money.

Egg disposed of in the bin, Naomi wanders into the living room and opens the curtains. She must find a routine to get through the days when she isn't working. As it is, she spends far too much time meandering around the house, brooding, moving ornaments a shade to the left or right, flicking a duster where it's not needed, and generally wasting precious time. It seems so wicked to pray for the days to pass when so many people have their lives cut short. She's fit and healthy and ought to be able to find suitable pursuits to occupy mind and body.

She has just settled herself in the kitchen with coffee and a cereal bar when there's a loud knock on the back door. Tutting at the interruption, she inserts the uneaten portion of her bar into its wrapper and slips it into her handbag.

When she opens the door, she is not surprised to see the two policemen there. Inspector Freeth and Sergeant Ward – she's always been good with names.

'Sorry to bother you again so soon, Mrs Wilkinson,' says the inspector. 'Might we come in for a few minutes?'

'Of course.'

The men look too big in her kitchen, too sure of themselves in their matching navy blue trench coats. The inspector smiles at her in what seems to her a pitying way. The sergeant is the cocky type, rocking back on his heels, hands stuffed in the pockets of his well-pressed trousers.

'Would you like a drink? Tea, coffee?'

'No, thank you,' the inspector says. 'We won't keep you long.'

She sits at the kitchen table. Whatever they're going to say, she wants to be seated when they break the news. She remembers her dream, remembers to keep a poker face even if they both lunge at her and clasp handcuffs around her wrists.

Inspector Freeth clears his throat. 'The post-mortem has now been completed. We'll need to check dental records before we can confirm the body is that of your husband, Brian Wilkinson. Can you tell us how old Mr Wilkinson was when you last saw him?'

Naomi clutches the cross hanging around her neck. 'He was forty-five. So you've not ruled out foul play?'

The inspector shrugs. 'A great deal of time has passed, and it may prove impossible to determine how he came to meet his death.'

'He? It's definitely a male, then?'

'It's a best guess. All we have are a skull and a few bones. Wild animals have no doubt made off with the rest.'

'But there's a skull – you said about the dental records—'

'The skull is in a damaged condition, although it does look as if it's the right age to have been that of Mr Wilkinson.'

She concentrates on maintaining her poker face. She mustn't show relief, or anything that might indicate she knows something about Brian's death.

'You said he left no note,' says Sergeant Ward. He has small, cold eyes and a mean little mouth. She took an instant dislike to him yesterday, and he's doing nothing to alter her opinion.

'No, no note. Like I said, it was quite in character for him to just up and leave. He'd no consideration for anyone.'

Sergeant Ward scrapes a chair back and sits, his knees almost touching hers. 'You seem rather anxious, Mrs Wilkinson.'

'I don't like it being dragged up again, that's all.'

Inspector Freeth paces the kitchen, peering into jars and even opening a drawer to peek inside.

'Are you looking for something, Inspector?' Naomi asks.

He regards her with a mild expression. 'No, no, not at all. I'm curious by nature, that's all. It helps, in this job.'

'I wonder if you could tell us what you remember of the day on which your husband disappeared,' Sergeant Ward says.

'It was such a long time ago. I can't remember that kind of detail after all this time. It was just a normal day, nothing particular happened.'

'So you *do* remember it?'

'No! All I'm trying to say is that if something significant happened on that day, I would remember it, wouldn't I? And I don't. When he wasn't home by nightfall, I just assumed he was – I don't know – fallen down drunk in a ditch or something. It wouldn't have been the first time.'

'And how long was it before you thought something might be wrong? Did you alert the police?'

'You know very well I didn't. As I keep saying, I had no reason to believe anything had *happened* to him. He was a grown man, wasn't he? It wasn't like a child going missing.'

Naomi takes a handkerchief from her pocket and blows her nose. She hadn't expected to be bombarded with so many questions, all of which seem designed to try and catch her out. 'What will happen now?' she asks.

'We have a few more enquiries to make,' the inspector says, gazing at a framed photograph of her, taken when she was nineteen or twenty.

'I don't like being badgered,' Naomi says. 'Haven't I been through enough? I just want to pretend Brian never existed.'

'I'm sorry if my questions upset you,' the sergeant says, not sounding sorry at all. 'You must realise, in a case of unexplained death, we have to investigate as thoroughly as we can.'

'Yes, yes, I know that, but I don't know why you're not talking to his drinking pals, or any of a number of the people who knew him.'

'And who, like you, disliked him?'

'I've been very frank with you. I could have pretended

95

we had a happy marriage, but I haven't. I've told you everything I can. I wasn't the only person who knew him well.'

'You probably knew him better than anyone. And disliked him more than anyone, by your own admission.'

'Do I look like a murderer? Brian was a big man – stocky.'

The sergeant smiles. 'It's amazing the strength people can find, when the need arises.'

Naomi stands abruptly, scraping back her chair. 'This is ridiculous! Trust Brian. Even in death he's causing trouble.'

'It's often the way,' the inspector says, his gaze roaming around the room. She feels he is looking for something in particular. 'We'll let ourselves out.'

Dumbly she watches the two policemen leave. She puts the chain on the door and leans against the dresser. She's read plenty of murder mysteries, in which everyone is given the same tongue-lashing, and everyone always has something to hide. They said themselves that the body is too incomplete to say for sure how he came to die. If she keeps her head, she'll be all right. But they know how nervy she is, how defensive. Doesn't she have the right to react in her own way? This is all Diana's fault, the interfering old baggage. She'll never speak to her again.

'Oh, blow this!' she says, snatching up her cup and pouring the coffee down the sink. She covers her face with her hands.

10
DIANA

I gave Gillian my mobile number rather than the land-line, for obvious reasons, but I held out little hope that she would call. After all, our communication in the previous forty-odd years amounted to no more than a few brief letters and postcards. She had moved around a lot – Bristol, York, Norwich and several other places – but never once had she suggested we meet up, and pride had prevented me from making any overtures.

I know very little about her life. She hadn't gone to university, instead working her way up from copy-typist to personal assistant in various organisations. She always had a cat or two, and whenever she wrote to me she stuck to conventional topics: places she'd visited, which plants were doing well in her garden, the pleasantness or otherwise of the weather. I followed suit, occasionally slipping in the titles of books I'd recently read and enjoyed, which she generally ignored.

Given all this, when my phone rings and I see the number with its unfamiliar dialling code I let it go to voicemail, assuming it's a nuisance call or a wrong number. Even when I see there's a message it never crosses my mind it might be Gill.

'Diana, hi, if you're there could you call back? I'll be around for another forty-five minutes or so. Bye!'

Her voice, after all these years. My heart thumping, I slip the phone in the back pocket of my jeans and walk into the garden. It isn't so much that I'm worried in case Antonia overhears, more a feeling of needing to be outside, with plenty of air to breathe, the breeze on my face, grass to walk through, as I compose myself to return Gill's call. I take deep breaths and lean against the apple tree, my back to the house in case Antonia happens to be peering out of a window.

'Gill?'

'Diana! I'm so glad I got the right number. I wasn't sure if you'd be at work.'

'I don't go in much these days. I have a very good manager, she's been with me for years, since before Mother died in fact.'

'When did she die? I'm sorry, I ought to remember, but the time does fly so.'

'Ten years ago.'

'I'm sorry. It's never easy to lose a parent,' she says with a not very convincing sad sigh. 'And Antonia is still living with you?'

'Yes. Five years now.'

'A pity she had to leave teaching. She was terribly bright. She always made me feel the most awful fool.'

And then, silence. Have we run out of things to say to each other so quickly? I must say something, but I can't bring myself to ask any of the questions that burn on my tongue.

'I did say I was popping down for a visit soon, didn't I?' Gill says.

'Yes.'

'I'll be down the week after next, and I'll be staying for three weeks or so. Really I just wanted to see if you'll be around at all, if you think it would be nice to catch up.'

'Yes, I'll be around, and of course I'd love to see you.'

'I won't make any firm arrangements, but I'll call you when I've arrived and settled in and we can fix something up. We might have a drive out to a nice country pub, something like that?'

'I don't drive, I'm afraid.'

'Oh, that's all right, I'm driving down, we can use my car.'

'That would be lovely,' I manage to say, already imagining myself seated next to Gill, pointing out landmarks as she drives us deeper into the countryside. She might ask me to fish a bag of sweets out of the glove compartment or find a carton of orange juice buried under a bundle of jackets and blankets on the back seat and I would feel useful. She would realise how comfortable we were together.

'Then I'll see you in around a fortnight's time,' she says. 'I'd love to stop for a chat, but I've got a dental appointment at eleven and I daren't risk being late. I forgot my last appointment and they charged me ten pounds for not turning up.'

'How dreadful,' I say, trying to read some intimacy, some affection, in her voice. But she could be speaking to anyone. Perhaps that's a good sign, that she can talk to me without any hesitancy, the years between today and the last time we spoke melting away like snow after a heavy fall of rain.

'See you soon, then, Diana. Bye!'

I will have to tell Antonia that Gill called, and I have no idea what her reaction will be. The phone lodged securely in my back pocket, I stride back to the house, bracing myself for tears, angry laughter, or the silent treatment. Possibly all three.

'Antonia, where are you? I've got something I need to tell you.'

'What is it, Di? There's no need to shout.' She's seated at the kitchen table, leafing through an Argos catalogue, turning down the pages showing things she'd like to buy.

I take a deep breath, which doesn't help at all. 'I've just been on the phone. Gill called.'

She turns down the corner of a page, pressing her thumbnail over the crease. 'Gillian Anslow?'

'Yes.'

'And what did *she* want?'

'She's coming up for a visit. Wanted to know if she could see me while she's here.'

'I hope you told her where to go.'

'Of course I didn't. Why would I?'

She glares at me. 'She led you a dance, and you were too blind to see it.'

'Rubbish,' I mutter. 'It was you that spoiled things, you know you did.'

She sniffs. 'If that's what you think, fine, you go on believing it. But don't blame me when she lets you down again.'

I grit my teeth. 'We're going to have a meal together, that's all. A pub lunch, all very casual.'

'For old times' sake?'

I shrug, unable to look Antonia in the eye.

11

ANTONIA

Antonia wakes early. Gillian bloody Anslow. Why does *she* have to turn up again, after all these years? She knows exactly what will happen. Diana will be smitten all over again, and Gill will let her down. But what if she doesn't? What if Gill is on her uppers? She knows Di is a soft touch. Antonia would like to think Diana will always choose her own sister over anybody, but she knows that isn't true. And Gill hates her, because Antonia knows the sort of person she is. It wouldn't take much for Antonia to find herself friendless and homeless. And if Diana finds out about the anonymous call she made to the police, she will despise her. Antonia doesn't even know if the house is in both their names. Surely Mother would have split it equally between them? But it was Diana who nursed her, Diana who sacrificed so much; Antonia who left, who made her visits home as brief as possible.

Diana never wanted her, she knows that; she never did. Antonia is still the troublesome kid sister, always in the way, resented. Diana puts up with her, but her face would show her relief if Antonia announced she was leaving. That's what she wants.

In a moment of pique, Antonia decides to show her

sister what life would be like without her. She decides to run away – oh, not far, only to Birmingham, an hour's journey by train from Shrewsbury, and not for long – but she will leave no note, no clue for Diana to follow. See how *she* likes being frightened. Antonia worries that Diana might phone the police, but pushes that thought to the back of her mind as she packs a small bag and leaves the house before Diana wakes.

Her step is light, a smile tugging at her lips, as she makes her way to the bus stop. All her life she has tried to placate Diana – Diana the perfectionist, Diana the leader. Antonia allowed herself to slip into the role allotted her – the slightly scatty younger sister, probably a screw or two loose. Most of the time she puts up with it, playing up to the role if it suits her to do so. But sometimes Diana goes too far. She must be taught a lesson.

When they were children, Antonia inherited one of Diana's cast-off dolls, a thing she never remembered Diana playing with or liking. Admittedly Antonia treated the doll a little roughly, but after all toys were *meant* to be played with. One day Diana marched into Antonia's room, lifted the lid of her toy box, and held up the doll by one leg. She howled with rage, her face tomato-red. Antonia had cut off most of the doll's hair and removed its dress. One porcelain hand was missing.

Antonia rushed to comfort her, but Diana pushed her against the window.

Diana didn't say anything. She didn't need to. Her rage was in her eyes and in the hand that held Antonia around the throat.

Antonia touches her neck. Even now she can't bear anything around her throat, not a necklace or a scarf. It brings back the choking sensation that scared her half to death all those years ago.

She catches a bus to Shrewsbury and checks her timetable. She can't help but feel a bit excited: she still associates train journeys with childhood outings to the seaside.

Her stomach rumbles, reminding her that she's eaten no breakfast. In the spirit of adventure, she decides to try a burger bar, one of those bright and shiny places she's never visited before, nor even considered visiting.

She dislikes the way her bottom slips about on the plastic seating. Why do young people like these places so much? The lighting is too bright, the décor cheap and nasty, the food unsatisfying. She burns her mouth on an apple roll and wishes she'd gone to Marks and Sparks instead.

Apart from her, all the customers are school-age children, some in their uniforms. Are they bunking off? She can remember the staff at Marks refusing to serve teenagers who should have been at school. No such tough love in the burger bar. The staff themselves look as though they should be in school. They also look bored to death.

Antonia takes her tray back to the girl at one of the tills.

'Trays over there,' the girl says, pointing to a series of racks next to a thing like a giant letterbox.

Antonia posts her leftovers and meal packaging and slides her tray between the wooden slats. She turns back to the girl on the till, who is picking varnish off her nails. 'Have you worked here long?' she asks, noting that the burgers come from the kitchen ready wrapped, so at least the girl's nail polish chippings won't find their way into the food.

The girl eyes her suspiciously.

'Is it nice, working here?' she asks.

'Crap,' the girl says.

'Why do you stay, then?'

'It's a job, innit?'

Times haven't changed much in some ways. For the well off – the middle-class, the happy few – it's possible to get an education, to "get on". For the rest, it's a case of leave school at sixteen, work in a burger bar till you fall pregnant, wind up in a council flat with some unsatisfactory boyfriend (undependable, replaceable), getting by (just about) by fair means or foul. Antonia has seen it in soap operas and believes in the reality of it.

'Do you want to order anything else?' the burger girl asks, jolting Antonia back to the present. 'We're supposed to kick people out if they stay too long without buying anything.'

'But I *did* buy something! I had one of those apple things. It nearly took the skin off the roof of my mouth, it was that hot.'

'But if the manager comes out, he'd see you hadn't got anything, wouldn't he?'

What a silly rule! Perhaps she's making it up, to get rid of her.

'I'll have a coffee, then,' she says. She's wasting her money; never mind. The girl makes no pretence of her annoyance at Antonia's continued presence. Antonia decides to leave her in peace and goes to sit at a window table where at least she has something to look at besides the bleak, brightly coloured plastic interior of the burger bar.

Self-service is an invention Antonia doesn't particularly care for. If you're going to fetch and carry all your own stuff, you might as well eat at home. In the old days waitresses went out of their way to be polite and cheerful to customers. That sullen piece by the till would have been out on her ear, quick as a wink.

It looks as though the girl has run out of nails to pick at. She moves on to her ears next, methodically twisting the plain gold sleepers, three in each lobe. For some reason, Antonia's eyes are drawn to her rather than to the windows. The only people around are people obviously on their way to work, most of them with their heads down, grim expressions on their faces.

The girl stands up and smooths down her nasty brown nylon overall. Shocked, Antonia notices that her belly bulges. It isn't flab; the girl has a tiny frame, rather skinny if anything. Antonia shakes her head and angrily stirs her coffee. *Stupid little girl!* Why do the young have such a taste for self-destruction? The girl cleans the counter with a grubby grey cloth.

It's too painful for Antonia to look at her. That swollen belly. *Poor little thing*, she thinks. *Both of them. Poor both of them.*

The coffee has the unfortunate effect of filling her bladder to an uncomfortable degree. The toilets are at least clean: she appreciates an hygienic loo. She has often thought, if she ever wrote a book (because she likes to believe there is a book in everyone), it would be a guide to the best loos in England. She told Philip about that and he rocked with laughter. Together they even did some preliminary research, giving marks for cleanliness, lack of odour, the smooth action of the soap dispenser.

In the old days... She really should stop harping on, she's getting as bad as Diana, but she *does* remember with fondness a time when every public loo had a paid attendant. Who'd do such a job now? Who'd want to risk the drunks, the young men spoiling for a fight?

She ambles across the road to the railway station, wondering if Diana has noticed her absence yet. According to her timetable, the next train to Birmingham is due in seven minutes. The platform is deserted but for a few staff in grey uniforms, milling about. Antonia sits on a wonky bench and studies the advertising posters. Oddly, one of them is an advert for God. There's some biblical text in large, shouty letters and something about church being "for YOUR sake and for GOD'S sake". The other poster advertises the latest blockbuster film, and the final hanging space is reserved for a Network Rail poster exhorting passengers not to feed the pigeons: "If you want to feed birds, buy a budgie" is the message. Well, they *do* make a lot of mess, pigeons. Splats of white decorate the edge of the platform and the canopy overhead.

A man blows his whistle and the scratchy PA system announces that the Birmingham train is approaching the station.

Trains have certainly improved in the years since she first went on one. She wouldn't like to be stuck in a compartment either on her own or with some stranger; the open plan system is much better. It being a Wednesday morning, and after the rush hour, she has a double seat to herself. Stupid not to have bought a magazine to read. A nap would be nice, but she's terrified of falling asleep and missing her stop. She doesn't want to end up in Penzance. That isn't part of the plan.

Once she's in Birmingham, she has to find something to do to kill the time before she can return home. She needs to be away for most of the day, so that Diana will really start to worry.

The main shopping street is busy, filled with people pushing and laughing. Unused to the bustle of a big city, she feels almost as if she's travelled into the future. In her village, life has stood still for the last fifty years or more. The number of black faces startles her, as does the noise – so many noises – music blaring from shops, gangs of young people speaking in loud voices, the words incomprehensible to her. With relief she turns off the main street and walks up the hill to the art gallery.

The inside of the building is cold and quiet as the inside of her church. She expects to be asked to pay to go in, but the man on the door says it's free. 'Do you want to check my bag?' she asks. 'I'd rather not part with it, and you can see it's not big enough to hide a stolen painting in.'

'It's fine, you can take it with you,' the man says.

Two flights of cool, marble steps. At the top, she's greeted by the sight of an Egyptian mummy – *is* it a mummy? Is that the right word? Just a sculpture, perhaps...

She finds herself in a room full of Pre-Raphaelite paintings. Antonia thinks how much her mother would have liked the pale-faced young women and their rich, beautifully-rendered dress fabrics. You can almost feel the textures of the silks, the velvets, and the wavy red hair. Mother would have liked the prettily religious and the chastely romantic subject matter. Antonia finds it cloying and suffocating. The models look miserable and under-occupied.

When her feet begin to ache, she seeks out the café. She glances around and notices other women who are perhaps her age or older, yet they seem so much younger. Their clothes are more modern and their faces have a lightness she can't quite place. These women might have their troubles, but they are not trapped in the past like her and Diana.

Taking a bite of her flapjack, she wonders what Diana's reaction will be on finding her absent. Will there be tears? Remorse? A promise to herself to treat Antonia better in the future?

She's getting a headache from the constant echoey sounds of cutlery scraping against plates. Perhaps Diana will phone the police. For all she knows, Antonia might already be officially a missing person. But that seems unlikely. She's heard the police don't start to look until forty-eight hours have passed, unless it's a child or there are suspicious circumstances. Antonia isn't senile and has every right to go where she pleases without accounting for her movements.

Will Diana even bother with the police? For all Antonia knows, her sister is relieved at her absence and is using it as an excuse to phone Gill for a cosy chat, Diana making it clear how tiresome she finds Antonia, Gill happy to vindicate Diana's traitorous thoughts, saying how they'll see each other again soon, it'll be just like the old days. That would be like Diana, to take advantage of a situation for her own ends.

She checks her watch, visits the gift shop where she buys a few postcards, then returns downstairs. She stumbles as she reaches the door, the attendant giving her a hand, holding the heavy door open for her. 'There you go, safe and sound,' he says.

So much of the language we use, she thinks, is a string of meaningless words and formulaic phrases. Politeness matters, though; she's the first to say that.

'Have a nice day, now.'

'Yes, thank you, I will.'

Bemused by the unfamiliar city, she takes refuge in yet another burger bar. Staring at her plastic cup filled with scalding hot coffee, she almost cries from loneliness and fatigue. So much for her big adventure. She's not old, but she's set in her ways, too used to the quiet rhythm of her own small life to cope with this.

She wants to go home.

12

DIANA

The minutes tick by. I try to concentrate on the *Radio Times* crossword, but my heart isn't in it; once I realise I've made a mistake that throws out the whole thing, I scribble through it so roughly the paper rips.

Antonia isn't the type to go out without saying anything or, at the very least, leaving a note. In fact she rarely leaves the house at all, other than to go to church. Various scenarios play out in my head, ending with an intruder clapping a hand over Antonia's mouth and dragging her from the house. But who would want to kidnap a sixty-year-old woman? Or perhaps she banged her head and is wandering around the village in a state of happy amnesia. The only other possibility I can think of is that Antonia has taken leave of her senses and run away.

I leap on the phone when it rings. 'Yes?' I snap, expecting to hear a contrite Antonia, or possibly a police officer; no, the police would visit me in person, they wouldn't ring.

'It's Naomi,' the voice says. 'May I come and see you?'

I smile in spite of myself; Naomi isn't the sort to waste her breath on social niceties. She gets straight to the point. I admire that. 'It's not hugely convenient,' I say. 'My sister seems to have— Well, she's gone missing, not to put too fine a point on it.'

'I could come and sit with you. Or help you look for her. I wouldn't mind.'

I tap my chin with my crossword pen as I consider. 'All right, then. Yes, in fact, I should like to see you.'

Antonia would have prepared tea and biscuits for a visitor. I have no patience with such flim-flam. If Naomi wants anything to eat or drink she only has to ask. I keep watch through the living room window and wave when I spot Naomi, whose shaggy hair makes her look older than her years. Such a shame her hair is prone to frizz: a sharp, short cut might do wonders for her, if she had straight hair.

I meet her at the front door.

'Did you do it?' she demands, before I can even say hello.

'Do what?'

'Did you tell the police I killed Brian?'

'What on earth are you talking about?'

'Someone did. Someone has been poking their nose in where it's not wanted.'

'Come in and tell me all about it,' I say.

'I'm sorry – I thought – I mean, who else...?'

'I popped into the library this morning. They said you weren't working today.'

Naomi shrugs. 'I rang in sick.'

'Naughty girl,' I say, ushering her in. I'm shocked by her accusation. 'It's not that long since women weren't allowed to take a job, or were at least criticised heavily if they did so.'

'Of course. But things change, don't they? I can't spend the rest of my life being constantly grateful to the Suffragettes.'

111

I blush and let the subject drop. Mother was very anti-Suffragette, to an almost shameful degree. She considered them abnormal: ugly women who couldn't get husbands. She didn't seem to mind who we married, as long as at least one of us got married. She moved with surprising ease from discussing wedding gowns with Antonia to considering reception venues with me, however much I tried to tell her that the occasional date I had with a man meant nothing. Antonia had at least teetered on the brink of marriage before the horse-drawn glass coach turned back into a pumpkin and four quarrelsome mice. Mother sympathised at first, but after a while she got fed up with Antonia's tears and tantrums. Mother had a short memory and very little in the way of empathy.

'Even if I'd had my suspicions, I would never have phoned the police,' I tell Naomi. 'I'm old-fashioned, perhaps, or snobbish, but either way I don't approve of people who tell tales.'

She appears mollified with my explanation, but I know the doubts will remain.

'I'm sorry,' she says. 'There's me tearing strips off you when you must be out of your mind with worry about Antonia.'

Antonia... She never liked Naomi. Could she...?

'Where's she likely to have gone?' Naomi continues. 'Does she have any friends or relatives she might have visited?'

I wonder if Naomi went through all this when her husband disappeared.

'We have cousins, but Antonia doesn't like them, and they'll be swanning around the Med by now. There's no one else.'

I wondered if she might have contacted one of the teachers with whom she used to work, but she will have her address book with her. She never speaks about anyone in particular, though she must have made friends among the other members of staff. I try to remember who sends her Christmas cards. We never muster more than a dozen or so between us. Perhaps I haven't paid enough attention to her, too willing to accept her disinclination to talk whenever I've gently tried to prod her about what went on at the school.

Naomi sits on the sofa, elbows resting on her knees. 'You'll just have to wait for her to come back, if you can't think where she might have gone.'

Her tone of voice makes me blink. She seems entirely unconcerned about Antonia. 'Yes, but—'

'When children run away, it's usually because they want to have an adventure, or because they want to make their parents miss them. You know, to spite them, if they've had an argument or something. I rather suspect Antonia is behaving in a similar manner.'

'I suppose you could be right.' I sit in the chair nearest the fireplace and absent-mindedly jab at the empty grate with the poker.

'*Have* you argued?'

I speak slowly. 'We had a difference of opinion.'

'What about?' She casts her gaze around the room, before fixing it on the fruit bowl. 'D'you mind if I nick an apple?'

'Help yourself.' I push the bowl towards her. 'The row... it's childish of me, I suppose, to be so angry with her – still – after all these years. It's really myself I'm angry with.'

Naomi crunches into the apple, hunched forwards, her blouse gaping open where she's lost a button.

'Gillian Anslow rang me. She's coming down soon and I've agreed to meet her. Antonia thinks it's a terrible idea.'

Naomi nods, her mouth full of apple.

'I'm sure that's what set her off. She didn't say much, but Antonia hates change, and she always disliked Gill. And, of course, she thinks the world revolves around her. She was the same when we were children.' I twirl the poker in my hand, wondering why I ever picked it up. 'This isn't really helping us to find her, is it?'

'I'm surprised you *want* to find her.'

I let the poker fall from my hand and clatter onto the polished tiles around the grate. 'She's still my sister. She has no one else. Neither do I, for that matter.'

'It would have been better if she married. I always think some people aren't cut out for marriage, but Antonia...'

'Yes, indeed. She would have thrown herself heart and soul into keeping house for Philip. Do you remember him?'

'Vaguely,' says Naomi. 'Quite a nice-looking boy, I seem to recall.'

I fetch the relevant photograph album to show her. 'That's him – that's Philip. Do you really think he was handsome?'

'Yes, very. As far as you can tell from an old photo.'

'Quite. I wonder what happened to him.'

'Of course—'

We both start at the phone's ring. I stare at it and finally rouse myself to answer. 'Yes?'

The line goes dead.

'No one there,' I say with a scowl. 'I'll bet you anything that was Antonia. Now – what were you about to say?'

'Oh, nothing really. It's just... Fear often makes people say hurtful things.' She stands and pulls her blouse straight. 'You need to keep yourself busy. Shall we make something for when Antonia returns?'

I frown and shake my head, unsure what Naomi means.

'Scones or something.'

'But—'

'Come on – it'll keep your hands occupied and might help take your mind off her.'

Is this really the same woman who got in such a state, half-cut on my sherry, about the body in the quarry? In a daze, I follow her into the kitchen and together we make a batch of scones filled with chopped-up glacé cherries.

When we've finished, she washes up and I dry.

'Is Gill going to be staying in the area for long?' Naomi asks as I make a pot of tea.

'She didn't say exactly how long she's here for.'

'Has she changed much, do you think?'

'I don't know. It's hard to tell from one phone call. At least we're both sensible adults now. Young people talk an awful lot of tosh. It's only as we get older that we learn it's often better to curb our tongues.'

'You were great friends. I'm surprised you didn't keep in touch.'

I bring the pot over to the table and sit down opposite Naomi. 'Friendship, perhaps, is another thing the young take for granted.' I have the distinct feeling that Naomi is fishing. If so, she won't get much out of me. There are some things I have no intention of sharing.

A smile spreads across Naomi's face. 'I did know, you know – how you felt about Gill.'

I remove the quilted cosy and stir the tea. 'As you said, we were great friends.'

'Come now, Diana, don't insult my intelligence.'

I give her a sharp stare. Does she really know, or is she referring to something quite different?

She holds up her hands. 'Very well – you don't want to talk about it. Fair enough.'

I pour out the tea with a trembling hand. 'It was all years ago. Water under the bridge.'

'All right, let's change the subject.'

'The body in the quarry–'

Her face reddens; she dips her head. 'I hope you can forgive my bizarre outburst. I don't know what I was thinking.'

'Do you really think it's Brian?' No point in pussyfooting around. I'll never confide in her about Gill if she won't play a straight bat with me.

'The police can't say for certain that it's him, but it's a man of roughly the right age.' She looks me in the eye. 'They don't think they'll be able to say for certain how whoever it is came to meet his death. Not enough evidence. Too many bones missing.'

'That's good, then – isn't it?'

'Diana, some of the things I said... I wasn't thinking clearly. Brian *left* me. Walked out. My first husband divorced me, the second left. I felt responsible, I suppose – that my behaviour had somehow driven them away.'

'That's not the same as believing you're responsible for Brian's death.'

There's clearly more to Brian's disappearance than

116

him simply walking out on her. But she can't backtrack now. He might yet be positively identified as Brian, and Naomi's slipperiness will then look very peculiar indeed.

Her face is suddenly haggard, her shoulders visibly slump. 'Oh, God,' she says. 'I'll never be rid of him, will I?'

You chose him, I think. Any fool could see it was an unwise marriage.

'Do you remember him?' she says softly.

'Not well. We didn't exactly mix in the same social circles.'

She manages a half-smile. 'My mother called him my bit of rough, the gamekeeper to my Lady Chatterley. It was never quite like that. It's the one action in my life I truly can't explain. I earned a decent salary, I wasn't desperate for children. But I never stopped missing Nigel, that's the thing. I suppose I thought if I remarried it would break the spell he had over me.'

'But why Brian, of all people?'

'Perhaps because he was everything Nigel wasn't. I don't know, I really can't explain it. Everyone knew I was making a big mistake. Even the wedding reception was a shambles. Brian got drunk and almost got into a fight with a man who accused him of trying to get off with his girlfriend who was one of the waitresses. Drink, high spirits... I always found myself making excuses for him.'

'I'm sorry.'

She takes a deep, ragged breath. 'Why did you go to the library this morning? Did you want to see me especially?'

'I was simply going to ask you for some recommendations.'

'Fiction?'

'Yes. I want to broaden my literary horizons.'

Does Naomi still suspect me of telling the police about our conversation? I wonder about Antonia, but if I say this to Naomi won't it prove I'm the kind of person who snitches on people? Besides, I can't quite bring myself to believe Antonia capable of anything so underhand.

'I doubt there's anything I could suggest that would be new to you,' Naomi says.

She doesn't believe me. She thinks I went to the library to break down, to confess that I'd told the police they should speak to her. 'Naomi—'

'I seem to be reading a great deal of crime fiction at present,' she says. 'Unreliable narrators. Piecing together the clues to work out who's lying and who's telling the truth.' She pauses. 'It's never that straightforward, is it? Is that what makes us human, do you think? The ability to blend truth with lies until we believe the lies and doubt the truth?'

'I dislike unreliable narrators,' I snap, aware that I sound defensive. Aware that Naomi has picked up on this. 'I'm not good at following the clues,' I add. 'I tend to believe what people tell me.' Not true, surely? Life would be impossible if one never doubted what anyone says.

'Perhaps you should be more sceptical,' Naomi says. 'I know that I never tell the whole truth – if, indeed, there is such a thing. What do you think?'

'I've told you, I said nothing to the police, but I understand why you don't believe me.'

'They wouldn't tell me who tipped them off, of course, even if I asked.'

'No, I don't suppose they would.'

'I wonder what made Antonia run off like that?'

'I told you, it was my phone call from Gill.'

'Yes, you did say.'

And that's all I will say. It upsets me to think Naomi knows, as she must do, that I'm holding something back, but what else can I do? I can't throw Antonia under the bus, can I? I would never forgive myself. Nevertheless, I quail under Naomi's steady gaze, the scorn I read in her eyes. Damned if I do, damned if I don't.

13

ANTONIA

Antonia feels in her handbag for her front door key. Perhaps Diana won't even believe that she's been as far as Birmingham. Well, she can produce train tickets and burger bar receipts to prove where she's been. Not that it matters. What matters is that Diana should see she can't have everything her own way. That *is* what she wants to prove, isn't it? She's so relieved to see her own home again that she feels a bit silly about her very insignificant adventure.

The door opens. Diana stands there, arms crossed.

'Did you look for me at all?' Antonia asks.

'Come in.'

Antonia is about to give tongue to her feelings when she sees Naomi sitting on the sofa with a photograph album on her lap, a cherry scone in her hand.

Naomi looks up and smiles. 'We made the scones for you,' she says. 'Diana said cherry ones are your favourite.'

'Yes, they are indeed, but...'

'Where were you?' Diana's voice is as cold as a March wind.

Antonia lifts up her chin. 'I went to Birmingham.'

'Why on earth...?'

'I fancied a change of scene. They have some lovely pictures in the art gallery there.' She takes the postcards from her handbag and passes them to Diana.

'Souvenirs? You've... brought back souvenirs?' Diana slaps the cards onto the table.

'Yes, why not?'

Diana rubs her head and stands by the fireplace, one elbow supported on the mantelpiece. 'Antonia... did it not occur to you that I might be worried where you'd got to?'

'Of course it did. That was the whole purpose of going.' Antonia smiles, glad that Diana has grasped the point.

'Why, though? Why would you want to put me through that?' She glances at Naomi, who seems absorbed in looking through the photos.

'You upset me,' Antonia says simply. 'I was worried in case you wanted me to leave and have the house to yourself again.'

'Why on earth would I want that?'

Antonia can't say, not in front of Naomi. 'Mother would have wanted us to stay together. She would want to know that you're looking after me.' This, at least, is true. Many was the time Mother – seemingly so feeble in most ways, near the end – clutched her daughters' hands and refused to release them until Diana swore she would always look after her sister. 'She's the youngest,' Mother wheezed. 'She's not as strong as you are.' And Antonia heard Diana promise, in the way that one does promise things to someone who is dying, not wanting to think about the future.

'I would never ask you to leave,' Diana says, her voice colourless, the smile on her face small and contained. 'This is your home.'

'I'm so glad,' Antonia says. 'I think I might help myself to one of those scones.' She heads for the kitchen, handbag swinging on her arm.

121

14

DIANA

I shake my head. 'I'm afraid she's never grown up. Running off on a whim like that, coming back as if she's been no further than the corner shop... and because I'm tired and fed up I'll say no more about it. What fools we are!'

Naomi lets the photograph album slip off her lap and onto the sofa. 'I'll be going, then, now that she's back.'

'Yes... yes. Naomi—' She looks up sharply. 'Thank you for staying with me. I should have worried myself daft if you hadn't been here.'

'Oh, it was nothing. I'll let myself out.'

I pick up the iron poker. It's slim, but heavy. I'm sure I remember a case where a murder victim was bashed over the head with a poker; maybe an intruder, clonked on the head by an outraged householder. No matter. All houses are stiff with dangerous weapons, but not everyone notices they are there.

Munching on a scone, Antonia returns from the kitchen. She looks awfully pleased with herself.

'I hope you're satisfied,' I say. 'I nearly rang the police, you know.'

Antonia finishes the scone and flicks the crumbs from her skirt. 'Why didn't you, then?'

'Naomi said they wouldn't be interested. They take

the view that adults are entitled to go off and do whatever they want, regardless of the inconvenience they cause to other people.'

'What are you doing with that poker?'

I start and glance down. I hadn't realised I was still holding it, and I fling it with a crack onto the red quarry tiles in front of the fireplace.

'Very clean streets they have in Birmingham.'

'Is that so?'

'Far too crowded, though.'

'Good heavens, Antonia, what were you playing at! Couldn't you have found an easier way of making your point?'

'You would never have listened.' She rummages in her handbag and pulls out a packet of mints. 'Want one?'

I shake my head.

She pops out a mint and sucks on it for several moments, rattling it around her teeth.

I'm aware of the clatter of bottles announcing the milkman's arrival, and I'm still awake several hours later when I hear the postman stuff something through the letterbox. Why do milkmen always deliver so early – is it really necessary? I can't imagine anyone sitting at the kitchen table at five in the morning, impatiently waiting for the milk to come. I could, of course, shop for plastic bottles of milk in the Spar, but I like to support our local dairy, which has been delivering to our house since the seventies.

I sit on the side of the bed and look at my feet: long, bony, gnarled as a weather-beaten oak. As for my ugly toes, could anything be more unappealing?

Who will see my bare feet, though? As yet unknown and disinterested members of the medical profession, possibly. And then... and then – coroner, undertaker...

I've no idea why I'm so nervous about the fete. What could possibly go wrong, and why would anyone blame me if it did?

A part of me fears that Antonia will do something to scupper the day. She will plead illness or distress of some nebulous kind and force me to stay with her all day. Throughout life I've played second fiddle to Antonia. I became used to being ignored while people petted and admired my doll-like sister. At times I even preferred it that way. Being the centre of attention can, I imagine, eventually become burdensome.

Seven thirty seems a decent time to be up and about, so I wash and dress and make my way downstairs. The kitchen table is lined with cakes, each set on a paper plate and covered with clingfilm. I need to phone the vicar so that he can come and collect them, since neither I nor Naomi owns a car.

Antonia shuffles into the kitchen an hour or so later, her flannelette nightdress covered by a silky kimono she picked up at a rummage sale.

I bustle around preparing bowls of cereal for the both of us, my eyes studiously avoiding the display of cakes.

Antonia, though, fixes her gaze on them. 'They turned out well,' she says, sounding as if she wishes they hadn't. 'Still, the proof is in the eating.'

'Hurry up and finish your breakfast. I don't want you still in your nightie when the vicar comes round.'

'Fat lot *he'd* care.'

'Nevertheless.'

She takes her time over her cereal, heaving a big sigh when she finally stands up to take her bowl over to the sink.

I glare at Antonia's departing back, then make my phone call. Mr Fielding answers on the second ring. 'I'll be round in half an hour,' he says.

'Everything set?'

'Oh, yes. Naomi's already in situ and organising everyone.'

It looks like it's going to be a fine day, but I stuff a mac into my bag, just in case. The fete is being held outdoors, of course, but Mr Fielding seems to think we can move the stalls inside the church hall if, as he puts it, the heavens open.

The doorbell rings bang on time. I invite Mr Fielding in and together we put the cakes into his car.

'You look very nice,' he says.

'Do I? Thank you.' I'm only wearing an old faded print frock with comfy sandals. Still, it's always nice to receive a compliment.

I sit in the passenger seat of Mr Fielding's small car, my handbag on my lap. He drives with confidence, the radio tuned to a classical station playing softly in the background.

When we arrive at the church hall we remove the cakes from the car and carry them over to the stall set up on the adjacent playing field, nodding in greeting to the other stallholders: clothes, toys, white elephant. There is also a plant stall, Naomi's bookstall, and a tombola. Top prize in the raffle is a weekend break at a health spa. I decide to buy a few tickets in the hope of winning it for Antonia.

'Lovely day for it,' Mr Fielding calls out, striding towards Naomi. 'Diana's done us proud. What a variety of cakes!'

'I hope you'll be buying one or two yourself,' I say.

'Most certainly.' He wanders away to offer hearty greetings and words of praise to the other stallholders. In addition, there will be face painting and a bouncy castle for the children. Cups of tea and glasses of lemonade will be on sale at thirty pence each. Naomi and I have decorated the grounds with bunting and balloons, but there is a rather poignant air about all these festivities. When all's said and done, it's only a village fete: very British, very jolly, ever so slightly pathetic.

There's a lot of hanging around with nothing much to do until noon when the fete opens. I rearrange the display of cakes and accept a cup of tea from Naomi.

'Shall we?' she says, pointing to a couple of deckchairs.

We sit down and sip our tea.

'Will Antonia be coming?' she asks.

'She said she would, but you never know with her. She does like a bargain, though, and I'm sure she'd enjoy seeing the children playing.'

Naomi smiles thinly. 'I don't have much time for children myself. They say it's different with your own, of course, but I've never met a child for whom I felt anything approaching affection.'

'I suppose – in your line of work—'

'Naturally I do my bit, encouraging a love of books in them, but I'm more than happy to leave the storytelling sessions and so forth to the younger members of staff.' She sets her cup down on the grass. 'I was rather a serious child myself, very bookish. No one needed to encourage *me* to read.'

'Can I have a look through the books on your stall before the paying punters descend?'

She grimaces. 'A lot of old rubbish. Danielle Steel, James Patterson, that sort of thing. Books for people who don't really like reading. I donated a number of books from the library, but I doubt you'll find anything there worth a second glance.'

I have a look and see that Naomi is right, although I notice she's donated a copy of a novel by a local writer. 'I'll have this one, if you don't mind.'

Naomi waves away my proffered fifty pence piece. 'It's not as good as it's cracked up to be,' she says.

'Have you met her? The author, I mean.'

'Gabrielle Price? She used to host regular workshop sessions at the library. Too grand for that, I suppose, now that her second novel is doing so well.'

'It won a prize, didn't it?'

Naomi sniffs. 'I daresay. Too pretentious for my tastes.'

We sit in silence for a while, enjoying the sun on our faces, but eventually it's time to take our positions and wait for people to drift in. The vicar is charging fifty pence as the entrance fee, half price for children over the age of five. Some people will cavil even at that, although the money collected is to be donated to the church funds.

After a while I check my watch and see that it's nearly half past one. Antonia still hasn't turned up. I'm about to give her a call when I notice a woman in a striking turquoise silk blouse at the entrance.

I have to grip the table to stop myself from collapsing. I sit down heavily and run my hand over my mouth.

127

'Are you all right?' Naomi calls over. 'Heat getting to you?'

'I'm fine. Thanks.'

I stare at the woman again. Can it really be Gillian, after all these years?

I'm vaguely aware of a girl holding out money to me, for one of the cakes. 'That one,' she says, pointing at the Dundee and waving the coins in front of my face. 'It's for my mum.'

'What?' I snap. My hands tremble and my chest is tight.

The girl clicks her tongue and I grab the money, not even checking to ensure it's correct, and she shakes her head as she stalks off with her cake.

Gillian gazes around, the suggestion of a smile on her lips. After all these years, the mere sight of her causes my heart to pound. My guts twist at the memory of my last sight of her: her backwards glance, long fair hair blown into her face by the wind; her tentative wave; and me, rooted to the spot, wanting to cry out and beg her to stay, knowing it would be useless.

I smooth down the front of my dress and wonder if she will recognise me. Despite her white hair and thicker waist, age has been kind to her. What will she think of me? She's a good few years younger than I, of course. The last time I saw her I was twenty-two and she eighteen, which makes her nearly sixty now. Sixty! I swallow the lump in my throat.

Should I call out to her? And how do I greet her? Will I be able to speak at all? My urge is to run away. I can't stand to see the disappointment in her eyes when she sees the woman I am now.

The immediate problem is solved when I catch her eye and she strolls towards me.

'Diana! How lovely to see you.' She speaks casually, as if the past never happened. As if I'm an acquaintance, someone she once knew but who means little to her.

I nod. Much as I want to say something, I seem unable to open my mouth. I can't think of anything except the moment when she told me she and her parents were leaving Morevale for good; the light touch of her hand on my arm that made me shiver.

She shades her eyes from the glare of the sun. 'You've picked a good day for it.'

I blurt out, 'Is it really you?'

Goodness knows I've dreamt of her often enough, but always as she was back then, a slender girl in faded jeans and a white sleeveless blouse, her silver hairclip glinting in the sun, the smell of the rosewater she always doused herself in. When she wasn't with me, I'd spend ages just inhaling her scent on my clothes.

'I decided to come a little earlier than I'd intended. I saw the fete advertised on flyers as I was driving in.' She stares at the cakes on my stall. 'I wondered if I might see you here.'

'Here I am.' I laugh, but when she glances up again I fall silent, struck dumb by the sight of her face. Close up I can see the lines around her eyes and mouth, but age has not diminished her loveliness. Her hair, pure white, is beautifully styled in a sleek jaw-length bob. She has deep-set brown eyes, a hint of blue shadow on the lids. Her blouse, open at the neck, reveals a quirky necklace of blue and green glass beads. No wedding ring, I notice.

'We must catch up properly very soon,' she says, lightly.

'Yes, we must.' I can't help feeling bitter. She speaks of us catching up as if we last met a few weeks ago. But we have forty years of catching up to do – a lifetime. Does the past mean so little to her?

'Perhaps, after the fete, we could go for a coffee?'

I nod, not wanting to seem too eager.

'I think I'll have a look at the books.' She begins to walk away, then stops. 'Your sister...'

'She probably won't come. Too many school fetes when she was teaching, I think.'

Nodding thoughtfully, she wanders towards the book stall. In the old days we used to recite poetry to each other. Shelley was her favourite, after she'd worked through a weakness for Christina Rossetti's love affair with God and death.

In a daze I manage to get through the final hour or so of the fete, checking my watch every few minutes. I had offered to help clear up afterwards, but Naomi seems un-perturbed when I ask to be excused. 'An old friend turned up,' I tell her, unable to utter Gill's name, though I'm sure Naomi must have seen her.

'Then of course you must go and enjoy your reunion. Don't worry, I have plenty of volunteers on tidy-up duty.'

Gillian comes over to us. 'I managed to find a book,' she says, waving a battered hardback copy of Virginia Woolf's *Mrs Dalloway*. 'Not a first edition, of course, but it is Hogarth Press.'

'Very nice,' Naomi says. 'Are you a fan?'

'A half-hearted one.'

'This is Naomi, our head librarian. I'm not sure if you two remember each other.'

'Of course,' Gill says as the two women shake hands. 'Some people you never forget, do you?'

Naomi is then collared by Mr Fielding. 'Apologies. Very nice to meet you again,' she says as she leaves us, throwing me a quick frown.

'Shall we go?' Gillian asks.

'I'm afraid the café isn't very... that is, it's pretty basic.'

'No matter.'

Gillian's smile never wavers as she takes a seat and peruses the dog-eared menu. I try to think of an opening gambit.

'I suppose I should give you a potted history,' Gillian says.

'You've never given much away whenever you've written to me.'

'I've been a poor correspondent, haven't I? So many omissions, so many things I never knew how to say. It never seemed the right time, so I kept things light; superficial, even. My cats, my plants, the weather...' She takes a deep breath. 'Forty years is an awfully long time to compress into a couple of sentences, but I'll do my best.'

'When you left...'

Gillian shrugs. 'I had little choice in the matter. My parents... they felt it would be better for me, for us, to start again somewhere else.'

My mouth is dry, so I swallow and force my voice to sound natural. 'In Wales.'

'Yes. Very pretty, green valleys and all that.' She laughs. 'Very dull, to tell the truth.'

I fetch our coffees. Gillian stirs two lumps of sugar into hers.

131

'When I was twenty-five, I got married – not quite to the first man I met, but near enough.' She continues to stir her coffee. 'He was a good man.'

'No children, though.'

She shakes her head. 'I threw myself into work. I still work part-time, as a bookkeeper.'

'You always were good with figures.'

'Better with poetry, though,' she says. The comment takes my breath away. Is she making reference to us? We used to lie on my bed, our heads touching, fingers entwined, binding our love with beautiful words. 'You still have the shop, of course,' she says, breaking the moment.

'Yes; it's served me well, that shop, although I haven't been very hands-on since Mother died. Sometimes I think about packing it in altogether, but I might as well keep it going for the time being.'

'But you're all right, aren't you? I mean, living with Antonia…'

I grip the saucer. I don't want to talk about Antonia, who ruined everything, or so I tell myself. 'We rub along, I suppose,' I say. 'What made you come back now, after all this time?'

'A whim, I suppose. I wanted to make sure I saw the place at least once more.'

'Once more? You're not dying, are you?'

'Good gracious, no!' she says with a laugh. 'I'm sorry, my phrasing was a little awkward. It's simply that I had an invitation from friends to visit them for a while, and thought it would be a good opportunity to see the old place again. I have more time now that I've cut down my work hours.'

There are so many things I want to say, to ask her, but I don't know where to start.

'I do take note of all the book recommendations you give me,' she says. 'I've read and enjoyed many of them.'

'I'm glad.'

'Whenever I see a Thomas Hardy adaptation on the television, I always think of you. Do you still read him?'

'Yes.' Why do I suddenly feel as though she's patronising me? Her comment was harmless enough, yet I sense some pity in it. Why should I feel that way when books have, indeed, been such a saving grace? I have an urge to make some blatant reference to the past, to what we shared, but I don't want to scare her off. 'Your husband...'

'He died, some years ago.'

'I'm sorry. I noticed you aren't wearing a ring, and you're still using your maiden name.'

She gazes at me, steeliness in her eyes. 'Don't read too much into that. A dog bit my hand and my fingers swelled up after the tetanus injection. The ring had to be cut off. As for my name, I chose not to take my husband's surname simply because I think Anslow is more attractive than Bottomley.'

'I see.' I can't help wondering why she's really come back. Her coolness suggests that a desire to see me isn't top of her list of reasons. Perhaps it genuinely is a sentimental journey to see her childhood home again after a long absence. 'I didn't mean—'

'Water under the bridge.'

'And you can't step in the same river twice, if we're going to start swapping aphorisms,' I mumble.

This conversation has not gone as I expected. What *did* I expect? For her to say that her life has been a mistake, that she should have stayed here, with me; that her marriage was second best? But she says none of that. I

133

must not cry – I was just a phase, a first, immature love. I'm the one at fault for hanging onto a memory, making too much of our relationship.

'Just so.' She glances at her watch and drinks the rest of her coffee. She tears a piece of paper from her address book and writes down a phone number. Without telling me exactly where she's staying, she passes the paper to me. 'I really must go now,' she says. 'How much do I owe you for the coffee?'

'My treat.'

'Thank you, then.'

'Would you like to see my shop? We stock lots of handmade items. Local artists and craftspeople.'

Another glance at her watch. 'Another time, perhaps. I would like to see it before I go.'

A lump in my throat, I watch her leave, feeling almost as bereft as I did when she came to tell me she wouldn't be able to see me anymore. She couldn't wait to get away from me then, either.

134

15

NAOMI

Alone in her kitchen, Naomi retches, then clamps a hand over her mouth. Tears spill down her cheeks.

'Pull yourself together,' she mutters. She takes a deep breath and turns on the hot tap to fill the washing-up bowl. Focused on the work, she scrubs her mug and plate, placing them carefully on the draining board.

Once she's finished she leans against the wall, a film of sweat on her face, breathing deeply. Her guilt seems almost a physical thing, a tight constriction around her fast-beating heart.

Will she never be able to bury the past? Seeing Gillian Anslow again, after all these years, made her feel as if she were sixteen again. That terrible party! Naomi remembers getting horribly drunk. Her party, her house, so why was she the one hanging around in the kitchen with no one to talk to? Gillian had found her throwing up in the garden, had cradled her head, held her hair back so that she wouldn't get vomit in it. Later, weeping on Gill's chest while Gill gently stroked her hair. For a few weeks, they were inseparable.

And then, finally, Gill's admission that she had been seeing Philip on the sly and that she was waiting for the best moment to tell Antonia about Philip's betrayal.

'But why would you do that?' Naomi said.

'I think it's about time Antonia was brought down a peg or two. She thinks she's so perfect, so irresistible to boys. Why are you cross? You can't stand her any more than I can.'

'That's not the point. You're being cruel. She's done nothing to you, has she?'

Gill shrugged. 'It was so easy, though. Philip's an absolute pushover. In a way, I'm doing her a favour, so she can see exactly what he's like.'

Gill couldn't understand why Naomi was so furious with her. They argued, but that didn't stop Gill from sending an anonymous note to Antonia, telling her to be in a certain place at a certain time, when she would learn something to her advantage. Philip with his hands all over Gill, of course. 'Wouldn't you give anything to see the look on her face?' Gill said.

Naomi shook her head and wished she had the courage to tell Philip what Gill was up to. She told herself he wouldn't have believed her, so there was no point.

Upstairs, she selects a necklace from her jewellery box. A delicate silver chain with a tear-shaped amber pendant. Philip brought it back from Cromer, where he had been holidaying with his family, and gave it to Gill. 'It's hideous,' Gill had said to Naomi, wrinkling her nose. 'D'you want it?' Naomi has worn it once or twice and recalls Antonia admiring it.

It's time, she thinks, to make amends where she can. She walks round to Diana's house and asks if she can speak to Antonia. Diana ushers her into the living room, where Antonia sits looking through a fashion magazine.

'I'll leave you to it, then,' Diana says.

136

'What is it you want?' Antonia says, not glancing up from her magazine.

'We're both getting on. I'm tired of thinking about the past. Do you think about Philip very much?'

'Of course I do. Sometimes I torture myself thinking of how things might have turned out, but I do try not to. That sort of thinking sends you loopy eventually. What's done is done. I should have got over him instead of carrying him around in my heart, knowing he was never any good.' She looks up. 'He wasn't, was he? I thought he could change. I begged—'

'Please, Antonia, don't distress yourself.'

'Oh, you. As if you could ever understand.'

'There's something I'd like to give you.' Naomi takes the box containing the necklace from her pocket and shows it to Antonia. 'D'you remember this? I wore it a couple of times and you admired it.'

Antonia touches her throat. 'Yes, I remember.'

'I'd like you to have it.' Without waiting for Antonia to respond, Naomi fixes it around Antonia's neck and guides her towards the mirror over the mantelpiece. 'It suits you. I know Philip behaved like an idiot, but I'm sure he loved you.' She wants to believe this; she wants Antonia to have this, at least.

'I'm too old for exotic jewellery.' Antonia touches the amber pendant and makes as if to remove it. She wears earrings every day, and they're no fancier than the necklace.

'Please keep it. It should be worn.'

'Why don't you wear it, then?'

Naomi shrugs. The gift will be spoilt if Antonia knows where the necklace came from. 'I never really liked it, to tell the truth.'

137

Antonia winces and Naomi believes she understands what she's thinking. Sometimes it *is* too late. Too late for her to find a lover. Too late to bear a child.

'I'm sure you can find your own way out.'

'Of course,' Naomi murmurs.

16
ANTONIA

Seated in front of her dressing table to brush her hair before she turns in for the night, Antonia stares at her reflection in the mirror. A woman of sixty wearing a beautiful necklace intended for a teenager – it's almost obscene. She winces at the spurt of anger that overwhelms her when she thinks of the rage she has bottled up all these years. She remembers Diana's fury over her damaged doll; Diana's hands around her throat, the spiteful fingers digging into her flesh. That was what she wanted to do to Gill when she saw her with Philip. Gill, of course, who'd sent her that ridiculous "anonymous" letter. It wasn't enough for her to seduce Philip, she had to gloat about it, too.

Is the evil already there in some people, or does something happen to flick the switch, to bring out the evil that lies dormant in everyone? She wishes she knew. It seems to matter.

Diana, she knows, believes most people are decent and that everyone is capable of spitefulness, but that fundamentally people want to be kind and good; and most of the time, indeed, they are.

Her hand closes around the tear-shaped pendant. In one quick movement she yanks it from around her neck, breaking the chain. An accident, she will tell Naomi. And Naomi will understand, but she will say nothing – no tears, no recriminations, just an acceptance of what they both know to be true: that you can't change the past or mend wounds that have festered. Naomi thinks she's an idiot, but Antonia knows perfectly well how Naomi came by the necklace; knows Philip gave it to Gill, who never truly cared for him; knows Gill gave it to Naomi, it meant so little to her.

She creeps onto the landing and peers over the banister. She can hear Diana messing about in the kitchen. Back in her own room, she shuts the door and turns the lock.

Then she opens her special cupboard, smiling to see her girls, arranged in neat rows. Always ready with a smile for her, never a cross word or a tantrum.

She selects one from the middle row and gently lifts it out. She sits on the bed stroking Suky's soft golden hair.

'Such a pretty girl,' she coos. 'I know it's dark in the cupboard, but Auntie Diana wouldn't understand. She's never liked children. She doesn't know what it is to be a mother.'

She takes the brush from the dressing table and removes the tangles from Suky's hair.

If Diana saw them, how shocked she'd be to see how well Antonia looks after the girls. She would never treat them roughly. Diana can keep her silly books, she'd rather have her girls any day of the week.

'She wouldn't understand, would she?' she repeats to Suky, who gives Antonia her best smile. 'Course she wouldn't, and that's why you have to stay in the cupboard. If I had *my* way, you'd be sitting where everyone could admire you.'

At the last count she had forty-eight dolls, all girls.

Most of them she bought mail order. Diana never noticed – Antonia is always taking delivery of goods ordered from home furnishing catalogues.

One doll is not in the cupboard but under the bed in a dust-covered box – the doll that used to be Diana's, the one she made such a fuss about. That doll has no name and is not loved.

After putting Suky back, Antonia retrieves the box. She blows off the dust, removes the lid and glares at the doll. 'I'd like to wipe the smile off your face,' she mutters. She grabs the pendant and drops it into the box before replacing the lid and pushing it back under the bed. 'Little bitch,' she murmurs, enjoying a frisson of naughtiness in uttering the taboo word.

She walks across to the window and looks out onto the back garden, gently bathed in moonlight. For a moment she thinks she sees herself as she was when she was sixteen. A pretty girl, not a care in the world. Is that true, though? And is it wrong to pretend the past was a place where the sun always shone and she never had a moment's unhappiness?

Narrowing her eyes, she can almost see herself and Philip; he's pushing her on a swing made from rope and wood suspended from the apple tree. She remembers kicking her legs in the air and tipping back her head, pretending to be the woman in a Fragonard print she'd seen on someone's bedroom wall. So much of life is about pretending to be something other than what one is: prettier, cleverer, less ordinary.

Philip is locked in her heart like a fly in amber, perfectly preserved, but people are not flies and Philip is not still eighteen. Strange, but she rarely wonders what he's doing now. Did he marry, is he a father? He might even be dead. Ultimately, it doesn't matter. Even if he's alive, unattached, if she met him now it would do neither of them any good. He wouldn't be *her* Philip, and she'd despise him for that. *Her* Philip is dead.

She sits down heavily on the bed. Her room is much the same as it was when she was given it, at the age of thirteen, when her parents decided she and Diana needed the privacy of separate rooms. The room never altered in all the time she lived away, was always waiting for her to return. On the bed is the same silky counterpane, the colour of old gold, that she chose when she was a teenager. The same curtains, patterned with a design of stylised roses, threadbare now.

The bed is lumpy, the room an awkward L-shape, but it's hers. Her spinster's single bed, a framed photograph of her parents taken shortly after they got engaged, her mother awkwardly drawing attention to the solitaire diamond on her finger. The same ring Antonia would have worn if she'd married Philip.

No ring, no Philip. Throwing herself instead into her schoolwork, determined to make something of herself; but even then it was always in the back of her mind that if she did well, found herself a good job, Philip would realise the mistake he'd made and come back for her. That was enough to spur her on even when she suspected teaching was a mistake, that she hadn't the necessary strength of character to take charge of large groups of children. She thought she would be safe in an all-girls school. No one prepared her for how *feral* girls could be once they were with their own kind, away from the civilising influence of home and parents.

Bullying was not taken particularly seriously when Antonia began teaching. She knew who the bullies were, and which girls they would choose as their victims, and did her best to deal with both until she realised that she, too, had been marked as a victim. She was called in to the see the headmistress on more than one occasion, accused of having lost control of her class.

'They pick on me,' she said, shrinking beneath the headmistress's barely tolerant expression.

'You are the adult, Miss Littlehales. It's your responsibility to make them respect you even if they don't like you.'

She wanted to be liked above all else, her craving for affection turning her into a figure of fun. She was the soft teacher in whose classes girls knew they could misbehave with impunity. They knew she would never complain about the obscene drawings of her on the whiteboard. She suspected they knew, too, that one day her pent-up frustration, the constant little humiliations, would cause her to lose control in the most spectacular fashion.

The final train journey home was the bleakest of her life. She didn't write to tell Diana she was coming home. Sick leave, she claimed; rest and recuperation. The weeks turning into months, a new rhythm established, the school further and further away.

She is safe here, in this room, with her dolls and her faded photographs and the memories that shimmer in the air like damselflies.

17

NAOMI

The police again. Why can't they leave her alone? But they'll have news. The dental records they were talking about. They must be sure now. They've come to break it to her before she hears it on the television.

'Why don't you sit yourself down, Mrs Wilkinson?'

She feels a whimper bubbling up. Clamps her hand over her mouth, doesn't want them to hear her distress as well as see it.

She gazes at them, unable to read anything in their expressions or their body language. Do they have special training, she wonders, in how to hold yourself when breaking tragic news?

Get on with it, then! But she doesn't say that. It would be rude. They already think she's a bit odd. She can tell from the little glances they pass between themselves.

The officer in charge clears his throat. (What's his name again? Already she's forgotten it and she used to be so good with names.) 'We've now conducted all our preliminary enquiries to the extent possible given the nature of the remains and their location. Checks against dental records have confirmed that the body is not that of your husband, Brian Wilkinson.'

144

He waits for her reaction. But what *is* her reaction? She can't think. Her mind is completely numb. Not. He said "not", didn't he? Did she mishear?

'Mrs Wilkinson, are you all right? Is there someone we can call to sit with you for a while?'

She shakes her head. No one can help her.

'We are continuing with enquiries into the present whereabouts of Mr Wilkinson, but given the length of time that has passed and his itinerant lifestyle, I'm sure you can appreciate what a difficult task that is.'

The officers glance at each other, both shrugging. They think she's mad, don't they? Unhinged. Off her rocker. Incredible, they'll think, that someone so obviously not all there can hold down a responsible job. But what would *they* know about her responsibilities? They probably think she spends all day stamping books and making sure the teenagers using the computers aren't trying to access porn.

'We may never know where your husband is,' the officer says, more gently. Is he going to offer her sympathy? He hardly seems to know if the news he's broken is good or bad.

'Nothing to do with me?' she says. 'This body – this man—'

'We're still checking through the missing persons lists.'

'But you had a tip-off. You said. That it was Brian.'

'It's possible it was someone intent on making mischief. It does happen, I'm afraid.'

'Who would do such a thing?' She clutches her cardigan to her chest. 'People are dreadful. Why can't they leave other people alone?'

145

'I'm sorry. You understand we did have to follow it up—'

'Yes, yes; I'm not blaming you.'

Most people know that Brian deserted her twenty years ago, but which of her neighbours – those people to whom she says hello in Spar and the ones who browse the library shelves – suspect that Brian is dead? Why would they care? Do they all believe she killed him?

Someone with whom he made a date and never turned up? No, his women were fly-by-nights, they would have shrugged and found another man if he hadn't shown up. He never was the reliable type.

Someone who dislikes her, then, and wants her harried and upset. She can't believe anyone hates her that much.

Once the police have left her in peace, she walks round to Diana's house. She wants her to know that the body isn't Brian.

'Poor man, whoever he was,' Diana says once Naomi is composed enough to explain everything. Diana listens, she nods in the right places, but she keeps glancing at her mobile. Is she even taking in what Naomi is saying?

'Diana, this will sound ridiculous, but I think I can speak to you in confidence.'

'Of course.'

'There have been a number of difficulties in my past. I'm sure it's not the case, but I always feel as if people take a no smoke without fire kind of attitude.' She smiles apologetically. 'I'm sorry; I'm not explaining this very well.'

'You still think I made the call to the police, don't you?'

Naomi tugs at the hem of her navy blue skirt. 'I'm sorry... I know I should be relieved to know the body isn't Brian's, but in some ways that makes it worse. I thought – hoped – that part of my life was over. It's the thought of the talk there'll be that makes me feel ill. And people will talk, won't they?'

'Not if I have anything to do with it,' Diana says. 'No one has said anything, have they?'

'But the person who made the call – they'll tell other people, won't they?'

'It wasn't me.'

'*Someone* made that call,' Naomi persists. 'Why would they do that? Who would have suspected such a thing? I haven't spoken about Brian in years except to you.'

Diana bites her lip. 'I expect it'll be on the news soon, anyway.'

'Not until they've identified the body. They're not going to put it on the news, are they, that it's not Brian?' She mimics a news presenter: '"Oh, and by the way, it's not Brian Wilkinson, in case you were wondering". Until they know who that poor man was...'

'Try not to worry. I'm sure it'll soon blow over. If anyone drops hints to me, I shall put them straight. Don't worry, Naomi.' She pats Naomi's hand, but her eyes are on her mobile, on the notification that a message is waiting for her.

18

ANTONIA

In the living room, Antonia pushes the net curtain aside to stare out into the street. A man is about to mow his lawn, but there are no other signs of life.

Diana is out again. She always is, these days.

Neighbourhood Watch is a joke. The round orange plaques affixed to lamp posts are as toothless as those "Beware of the Dog" signs showing pictures of Rottweilers. She has to laugh when she sees the owner walking their dog and it turns out to be a scruffy West Highland terrier or a dopey old Labrador.

She sighs and lets the curtain fall back into place. For half an hour or so she watches telly, but there's nothing much on; there never is. A programme about a woman who met up with someone she hadn't seen for twenty-five years and promptly married him reminds her of Philip. Diana never could understand why Philip suddenly wasn't around anymore. Antonia remembers her sister's exact words – 'He's got bored with you, then, has he?'

Philip's parents made their dislike of her plain from the start. Flighty, they called her, just because she liked jewellery and make-up and having a good time. She tries to tell herself it's just as well she found out how faithless Philip was before she committed herself to him, but that doesn't make it hurt any less. 'Serves you right,' Gill said when she confronted her. 'You took him to Naomi's party even though he wasn't invited. You were showing off, because Naomi is plain and has to pretend she isn't interested in boys. You never think of anyone but yourself, do you?'

It was all so long ago, of no importance anymore, but now Gill is back and Diana is smitten all over again, and it's Antonia who'll bear the brunt when Gill goes away having given her this brief glimpse of what they might have had together. It's unkind, that's what it is. Gill doesn't give a damn about Diana's feelings, she never did.

For a moment when she heard about the discovery of the dead body she thought it might be Philip. Somehow it would be easier to bear the idea of him having been murdered than to think of him living without her, never missing her, never wondering what might have been. It was a wicked thought, with no basis in reality. She saw the removal van, Philip's family in their Morris Marina, bags and boxes wedged around Philip and his sister on the back seat.

Their similar experiences should have created a bond between her and Diana, rather than pulling them further apart. They've both been let down by someone, both of them pushed aside and abandoned. Of course Diana blamed her for Gill leaving, but it just proved that Gill was a weak person, unable to stand up to her parents any more than Philip had to his. Whereas Diana has spent the last forty years sulking, Antonia has buried her hurt. She doesn't wear her heart on her sleeve the way Diana does, but that doesn't mean her pain isn't as great.

Antonia picks up an old framed photo from the mantelpiece. In the image, she and her sister stand in front of

149

Diana's gift shop and smile for the photographer. They rubbed along together pretty well when they were both working. They saw each other at Easter and Christmas and every bank holiday, and they'd both had plenty to talk about, their lives were full. By the time Mother's condition deteriorated to the point where she needed full-time care, Diana had lost interest in the shop and Antonia knew her days at the school were numbered. She would have welcomed being able to confide in Diana about her problems, but her home had become as lowering as the school. If Diana sensed anything was wrong in her sister's life, she never said. Her life revolved around the needs of a crotchety old woman; she had no sympathy to spare.

And in her last few years Mother could be difficult, there was no doubt about that. Antonia felt like screaming every time Mother knocked on the ceiling with her stick, aware that Diana resented her presence, for Antonia was only an occasional visitor, and it was Diana who had to cope with the everyday grind of seeing to Mother's more intimate needs and dealing with her constant demands.

When she hears Diana's key in the lock she switches off the telly. It's five o'clock, and normally they'd be having dinner now.

Diana enters the room with a smile that vanishes as soon as Antonia catches her eye.

'You're late,' Antonia snaps. 'Where did you go?'

'We had lunch in town, then we came back and went to the children's playground, but it was rather noisy.'

Antonia wrinkles her nose. 'Nasty place.'

'How do you know? What call would you have to visit a children's playground?'

'You see such terrible things in the paper – they're always finding hypodermic needles and condoms in there. Even an abandoned baby once, I seem to remember.'

'I've decided to give up reading newspapers, they're too depressing.'

'Anyway, what were *you* doing in a children's playground?'

'It was just somewhere to go and sit. Besides, the weather was lovely and Gillian is fond of children. You're very inquisitive today.'

'Nosy, you mean. Why shouldn't I ask? It's natural, isn't it? You've been out such an age, I wondered where you'd got to.'

'I didn't think you'd care.'

'You never *do*.' Antonia turns her back on Diana and slumps into an armchair with a trusty magazine. She opens it at random and pretends to be gripped by its anodyne contents.

'It was Gillian's idea to go to the playground, if you must know our full itinerary. She enjoys visiting all the places she remembers from her childhood. So many memories, for both of us.'

Antonia fiddles with the corner of a page, tearing off minuscule fragments of paper. 'Did you talk about me? Did you talk about how awful I am?'

'Of course not. You hardly entered our conversation. Gill quite rightly says the past is over and done with, not worth talking about.'

Antonia glares at her sister. 'Is that what you really think?'

Diana presses her lips into a thin line. 'You might have put the oven on,' she says eventually.

151

'It's all ready to go in.' She's laid out two frozen shepherd's pies in foil trays on a baking sheet. Each pie has a topping of piped mashed potato that, she knows, will have the flavour and texture of soap flakes.

'If you'd waited, I could have cooked something.'

'But you just said I should have put the oven on. I wish you'd make up your mind.' Antonia flings down the magazine and stalks into the kitchen. She switches on the oven and tips frozen veg into a saucepan.

Diana lays the table, then settles down to read. If she's not out with Gillian, she's got her head stuck in a book.

Forty minutes later Antonia carries the food into the dining room on a tray. 'Come and eat, before it gets cold.'

Hot, cold, what difference does it make? Antonia sits and presses her fork into the stiff, dry potato rosettes.

Diana tucks into her food, apparently oblivious to its unpleasantness. 'I saw Vera Dodson's niece while I was out – Vera, you remember her?'

'Of course.' Miss Dodson used to own the gift shop, though in her day it was a shop selling wool, knitting patterns and accessories. Antonia believes she sold the shop to Diana for a paltry sum. Working in the wool shop had been Diana's first job after she left school and Miss Dodson wanted to help her, having no children of her own.

'Vera's in a nursing home now, poor thing,' Diana says. 'I really ought to visit her.'

But you won't, thinks Antonia, not while there's Gillian to fawn over. 'Yes, you should,' she says. 'She was very good to you.'

Diana nods, but her unfocused gaze suggests her mind is elsewhere.

Antonia clears away the plates and boils the kettle.

She makes the tea and brings the tray into the dining room, setting it on the table before sitting down.

'Has Gillian changed much?' she asks.

'It would be strange if she hadn't. She wasn't much more than a girl when I last saw her.'

'And you really haven't discussed me at all?'

'Why would we? We've far more interesting things to talk about.' Diana knocks the table as she pushes herself back in her chair.

'Don't be unpleasant.'

'For goodness' sake, Antonia! Sometimes you talk like a child.'

Tears smart in Antonia's eyes. 'I don't know what you mean.'

'You know full well.'

There is a long pause. They stare at each other, resentment burning between them. Who will break the silence and finally speak the things that need to be said? Antonia grips the corner of the table. 'Won't you ever forgive me?'

Diana's left eye twitches, and for a moment Antonia fears her sister is going to lose her temper; but the moment passes and Diana smiles tightly. 'Don't expect too much, Antonia. Sometimes I think you ruined my life.'

'How can you *say* that!' She slaps the table, rattling the cups and the little metal teapot. Pushing back the chair, she stands and stomps into the living room. She takes out her frustration on one of their velour-covered cushions, flinging it across the room. It bounces off the telly. She feels like smashing all the best china – cup by cup, dish by dish – but the act of throwing the cushion has made her tremble. The last thing she wants is for Diana to think she is losing her grip.

Diana comes in, and bends to retrieve the cushion, her knees cracking as she stands up. 'We're both too old for this.'

Is this an olive branch? All Antonia wants is for her sister to be kind to her; to treat her as a friend, confide in her, instead of behaving as if she'd rather she wasn't around. 'Then why can't you at least try to get along with me? We've no one else. Can't you at least try?' She picks up the photograph of herself and Diana. In the picture their arms are loosely linked, their heads almost touching. They were happy days, weren't they?

Diana shuts her eyes and massages her forehead. 'Don't upset yourself. Everything will be fine as long as we stay off the subject of Gill.'

'But how can we – now that she's back?'

'She'll be gone soon enough and then life can get back to normal.'

What does "normal" mean, though? Diana never gives any thought to what *she* wants. There's church, of course, and the Monday morning trips into town, but it's ages since she did more than exchange pleasantries with anyone. She was always the outgoing one, in the old days; but after the business with Philip she faded, something was lost that she has never been able to recover. Antonia gently replaces the photograph on the mantelpiece. 'You think I'm useless, don't you?' she says.

'I've never said anything of the sort.'

'No, but you think it. You've never taken me very seriously. The silly younger sister, that's how you think of me.'

Diana sighs. 'You're being very tiresome. Are you having one of your depressions?'

Antonia raises her eyebrows and opens her mouth to

protest, but immediately she frowns and admits, 'Perhaps I am.'

'You should see the doctor, then. I'm sure he'd give you some pills.'

Antonia sits down with a bump. 'Pills!'

'Isn't that what you want? I don't know what else I can do for you. Why don't you try to involve yourself more with the church? You know how much you enjoy the Sunday service.'

'There's no need to be so patronising.'

'Pull yourself together, then. There are plenty of things you can do, if you could be bothered.' Diana stomps out of the room.

Antonia clutches a cushion to her breast and forces herself not to cry. Her sister might be right, but it's easier for her. Diana's the strong one. Diana has no idea how much she has suffered, nor will she ever find out; not, Antonia thinks, if she has anything to do with it.

19

DIANA

I ring Gillian and we arrange to meet at seven thirty. I'm tempted to spend hours fiddling with my hair and outfit, but I'll feel self-conscious if I make too much of an effort. Anyway, I try to tell myself, Gillian is just an old friend I'm catching up with, there's nothing more to it than that.

Antonia sits with her hands folded in her lap, her fingers making tiny but continual nervous movements. 'You're seeing Gillian, then.'

'I made no secret of it. She'll be gone soon enough.'

'So you keep saying. I don't think you truly believe it, though, do you?'

'I know you dislike her, but I can't help that.'

'You just can't take to some people, can you?'

'You've always made *that* perfectly clear,' I snap. By now I should have decided that it's better to let bygones be bygones. After all, we've all done things we later regret. Nevertheless, some memories are harder to bear than others, and Antonia doesn't help matters with her barbed comments.

'You'll be late getting in, I assume.'

'I suppose I will.' My heart softens as I notice the tears in her eyes. 'Please don't wait up, dear. There's really no need.'

Her response is to open a *People's Friend* magazine at random and fix it with a fierce stare.

'Be like that, then,' I mumble. I check my watch as I shut the door behind me. Although I'm the sort of person who always arrives early for appointments, it wouldn't do for Gillian to find me waiting impatiently for her like a spotty boy on his first date. I take my time walking to the Indian restaurant outside of which we've agreed to meet, but I needn't have worried because Gillian is already there.

'D'you fancy going for a drink first?' she asks me.

I frown. 'A drink? But there aren't any cafés open at this time of night.'

She laughs. 'I meant an alcoholic drink. There are at least three pubs in the village to my certain knowledge.'

'Only two now. The Golden Lion closed down years ago. It's a charity shop these days.'

'Is it really? Good lord. The hours you must have spent in there.'

'I know.'

It was a biker pub in our day. Young men in leather jackets with denim cut-offs, girls in long skirts of Indian cotton, and cheesecloth blouses. The same songs on the jukebox, over and over: "White Room", "Stairway to Heaven", "Layla". I never saw Gill in there. She was four years younger than me, not allowed into pubs, and the landlord was a friend of her dad's so he knew how old she was.

I didn't get to know her properly until she was seventeen. I was twenty-one by then. I'd had the occasional boyfriend and a few drunken fumbles at parties, but I was, as they say in Victorian novels, "heart-whole". I'd known lust, but never love.

I knew Antonia disliked Gill, because of the falling out over Philip. When I asked Gill about it, she laughed and said they'd had a stupid misunderstanding and Philip wasn't good enough for either of them. I let it drop, I didn't want to make an issue of it, but in hindsight I should have dug deeper. Antonia's resentment of Gill never abated and she couldn't wait for the chance to pay her back.

'Shall we try the New Inn?' I suggest. 'I'm not much of a pub goer, but I think it's quite a nice one. Not, you know, full of drunken louts.'

The pub has changed surprisingly little. It's what my mother would have called a spit and sawdust pub – cosy and friendly, but hardly luxurious. The seats are old church pews and wooden stools, the carpet a grimy red-dish-purple. The horse brasses nailed to the walls seem to be the genuine article rather than replicas made for modern pubs wanting the olde-worlde look.

We buy our drinks and sit at a corner table.

'I wonder if we should have invited Antonia to join us?' she says.

I grimace. 'I don't think that would be a good idea. To be frank, it's nice to have an evening away from her.'

A wry grin crosses her face as she drapes her cardigan around her shoulders. 'And yet you still live with her.'

'The house belongs to both of us. Neither of us would like to see it sold, so we're stuck with each other.'

'Like a bad marriage.'

'Perhaps. Gillian, I—'

'Gill. I prefer to be called Gill.'

'Right. I was just going to say, about the past—'

She shakes her head. 'I prefer to live in the present.

The past is full of things I'd rather forget, if I'm honest.'

My mouth is dry, and I struggle to keep my voice from shaking. 'I see.' I've reached a point in my life where I want to stop regretting all the things I've never done, and stop fretting over the past. But it's proving difficult.

'I don't mean that in a nasty way,' she continues. 'There are good memories as well, of course, but it all seems so long ago, doesn't it?'

Not to me, I think, but I simply smile and take a sip of my gin and tonic.

Gill – not Gillian, I must remember that – rummages in her handbag and withdraws a photograph. 'This was my husband.'

I hold the picture by one corner and scrutinise it. It shows a stocky man in shorts and T-shirt, long socks and walking boots. He's balding but has a bushy beard and stands with hands on hips, one foot on a rock in what strikes me as a rather proprietorial pose. I'm surprised at how masculine he looks. Gill was always such a strong character. If I imagined a husband for her at all, it was a small nondescript man, happy to be bossed around by his wife.

She takes the photograph from me. 'We were very happy,' she says, looking me straight in the eye.

'Of course,' I murmur. I can't help feeling she's protesting too much, determined for me to accept that her marriage was what counted, not anything that went before it.

'I'm surprised you never married.'

I can barely disguise my shock, but try to keep my words light. '*Are* you? It was Antonia who attracted all the boys.'

'And yet she never married, either.'

'After that business with Philip I think she gave up on the idea of men.'

'That's a pity.'

'He broke her heart.' I expect Gill to say something glib about hearts being muscles and not prone to breakage, but instead she nods thoughtfully. I continue, 'Antonia always wanted children. She cried, you know, when we saw a story on the news about a woman who gave birth in her sixties. I half-expected her to ask if I'd pay for her to have IVF treatment.'

Gill laughs, but stops when she realises I'm not joking. 'Surely she would never—?'

'I don't suppose it seriously crossed her mind, but it bothered me, how much it affected her.'

'Poor Antonia. She was such a spirited girl. I can't believe she's changed so much.' After a pause, she adds, 'Have *you* changed? Do you think you're essentially the same person now that you were at, say, twenty-two?'

The age I was when we last met, as she must know very well. What does she want me to say? I can hardly make specific reference to our relationship. Why couldn't she mention some other, random age instead of one that's so significant?

I pause to consider my answer. 'I'm more aware now that we don't have all the time in the world. That life can slip away without us really noticing.' I look Gill in the eye, but her only response is a neutral smile, and I realise that I want to ruffle her, perhaps even worry her. 'We all delude ourselves to some extent,' I add. 'And I think most of us don't realise things about ourselves that are blindingly obvious to other people.'

'That's an interesting observation,' she says, dipping her head.

I am painfully aware of my feelings and my faults. I'm under no illusion that she will at some point declare her love for me and everything will be roses. What I want is for her simply to acknowledge that our relationship happened, and that she really did care about me. Otherwise, I will have spent the past forty years pining for someone who never loved me, and I don't think I could bear that.

Gill finishes her drink. I offer to buy another round, but she shakes her head. 'Let's go and eat.'

'Is your mother still alive?' I ask once we're seated in the Indian restaurant with a pile of poppadoms and a selection of chutney dips.

'Just about. She's eighty and a bit forgetful. Almost blind, too. She lives in a nursing home.'

'Oh.' The idea of putting Mother into a home was something I never considered. Is Gill more sensible in reneging responsibility for her mother, or simply heartless, as Antonia always said she was? 'I saw your aunt a while back – she's the vicar's cleaner.'

She frowns. 'My aunt? I don't have – oh, you must mean Auntie Rosemary, the one who married Uncle Pete.'

'Haven't you been to see her?'

'Not yet. I know I should, but... she's a bit full-on, if you know what I mean. That "salt of the earth" act.' She shudders.

'You're not staying with her, then?'

'Good lord, no.'

Where, then? Where are you staying, Gill? But I can't ask without sounding as if I'm prying.

She steers the conversation towards books and films but then, when I think she's going to ask for the bill and suggest we leave, she tells me that she has something she wants to tell me. Her expression is solemn.

My guess is that she's going to announce that she'll soon be returning home and therefore there won't be many more of these meetings. I always knew I wouldn't have much time with her, but I'd hoped she might be persuaded to stay for just a little longer.

'I'm afraid I shall be leaving Morevale very shortly.' She glances at me and I shiver. There's nothing in her eyes – no warmth, no understanding. Taking a deep breath, I stuff my clenched hands into my pockets and brace myself for what she will say next.

'It's likely I shan't have the opportunity to visit again, at least not for a very long time. I'm getting married, you see. He – my fiancé – lives in Devon. I'm sorry if it's a shock.'

I can think of nothing to say. I should leave now, go home and weep. It seems Antonia was right about Gill. Heartless, Antonia called her; heartless and manipulative.

'Are you all right?' she says.

'Surprised, that's all,' I say, my voice tight. 'You might have said something earlier.'

'I know. I haven't been entirely honest with you.' No apology, no sweetening of the pill.

'So who is he, this fiancé of yours?' I have no fear, now, of saying the wrong thing, and I wish I hadn't pussy-footed around her. She's not the only one who hasn't been entirely honest.

Gill blushes and glances down. 'We've been friends for a while, actually, through my late husband.'

I smile sourly.

'His name's Ian. He owned his own coach business until he retired – Welsh scenic tours, that kind of thing...'

She tails off, and for the first time since she returned I feel I have the upper hand in the conversation. I tell myself that I've hardened my heart against her. Whether or not that's true, it gives me courage to stand my ground.

'How nice for you both,' I say.

Gill frowns. 'You could sound like you mean it.'

I pour myself a glass of water, take a few sips then put the glass down with a trembling hand. 'I wish you'd told me sooner, that's all.'

'I'm sorry. I hoped you'd be pleased for me. I intended it as a surprise.'

How like a child she is, expecting everyone to be as pleased about her news as she is. 'Of course I am.'

'And it's not as if... well, you always knew I was only visiting.'

'Yes; but why now, Gill? After all these years?'

'Ian thought it would be a good idea. Laying the ghosts of the past sort of thing, before we start our new life together.'

I raise my eyebrows, but she seems entirely serious. I think I see how it is. Perhaps she really did want to see Morevale one last time, but it's clear that, if she had any interest in seeing me at all, this desire was occasioned by nothing more than curiosity. I imagine the purpose of school reunions is much the same. People attend not because they want to see their old friends, but to see how they've turned out, hoping they'll be less successful, less rich, less attractive than them. Then they go home and bitch about what a shower they were.

'We *were* friends once,' Gill says softly, 'but we were different people then.'

'*Were* we?' She might pity me, consider my life to have been a failure, but she hasn't changed any more than I have.

'I would like to think we still are friends,' Gill says. 'Once we're settled, I'll send you my address. We'll keep in touch.' She touches my arm lightly.

She'll send me Christmas cards, perhaps with those awful round-robins, but after a year or two they'll stop, and that will be the end of it.

'I wish you'd never come back,' I say, staring at my glass because I can't look her in the eye.

'I'm sorry you feel like that.'

Even now, she could make it all right with just a few words – *Did I hurt you so much?* And then I would say, *Yes, you did, you broke my heart*. And then she would apologise. She could even tell me she regrets what happened between us, that she really did love her husband, and it wouldn't matter. Why can't we be honest with each other, just this once?

I reach out and touch the cuff of her blouse. 'Gill—'

'Yes?'

Someone at another table knocks over a glass of wine, startling me, and the moment is gone, or else I come to my senses.

'Nothing; it was nothing.' I take a deep breath. 'So whereabouts in Devon will you be living?' And I sit there with a tight smile on my face while she raves about Dartmoor, cream teas, and Agatha Christie.

'Well, goodbye, then,' she says when her taxi comes, holding out her hand. I suppose it was too much to hope that she would kiss me goodbye. Nowadays everyone seems to have picked up the continental habit of kissing cheeks, but for us it would be awkward.

As I walk home I mull over the things I could have said. I've spent the bulk of my life bottling up my feelings. I am realistic enough not to harbour any hope of rekindling our relationship. I need to put the past to rest.

I have had other lovers since Gill, relationships that lasted longer, partners who cared about my feelings as she never did. I haven't always behaved well, or with consideration for other people. Too discreet, perhaps: from choice rather than necessity; reluctant to allow all the different parts of my life to merge. Easier when I had my own flat, of course, but even then I rarely allowed anyone to stay the night. My girlfriends thought I was fearful of what the neighbours might say, and to an extent that was true, even in the more liberal nineties. Besides, it's unfair to blame the times, which are never cut from a single piece of cloth.

I maintain that some people are simply better suited to living alone. In any case I've never been an activist and I dislike making grand gestures. If I'd fallen in love, I daresay it would have been different, I would have made a stand. Perhaps I've missed out, but so have many people, whatever their sexuality. Despite our differences, it seems Antonia and I have ended up travelling down the same road. Sometimes I wonder if we'd have done better living in a city, but you can be lonely anywhere, can't you?

When I get home, I find all the lights are out and Antonia has gone to bed. I'm glad for that, but I wish I had someone to talk to. Perhaps that's why people remain in bad marriages. However much someone gets on your nerves, it's still someone, another presence in the house. Sleep is the only way to shake off this melancholy, and I go up to bed without having a milky drink, without even reading for a while as I normally would. But sleep won't come, and I find myself digging out my *Oxford Book of English Verse*, tormenting myself with reading the poems that were Gill's favourites, looking for hidden messages I know I'll never find.

20

NAOMI

In the old days, Naomi would have had a fit if it had been suggested she eat anywhere but at the table. These days she often makes do with a tray in front of the telly. No point setting a table for one person. Nearly everyone she knows has a friend or partner to rely on. Claire at the library has been love's young dream since she got married, and even Diana and Antonia Littlehales have the support of each other.

Who does *she* have? She has tried to make friends, she really has. People tell her she's stand-offish, but she's simply shy. The only person who's ever invited her to tea is the vicar. They get on well enough, but she still can't make him out, can't take to him, certainly can't trust him. His sermons are interesting from a literary point of view, streams of consciousness that seem to owe more to Virginia Woolf than to God. He talks about "feelings" a lot, about "doing good", about "taking responsibility", but it's all rather airy-fairy. She wants someone to tell her exactly what to do, what to feel, how to exorcise her demons.

Still, he's a pleasant man to work for, she has to give him that. Not fussy in his ways like Mr Latham was. But Mr Latham was a man she could talk to. He understood temptation, sins of the flesh, shadows on the soul. When Brian left her, he let her sob, gave her whisky. She tried to tell him her sins, but he didn't want to hear them. 'Let it go,' he said to her, ever so gently. For a while she did, she thought she had left everything that hurt her in the past, but as soon as she heard about the body in the quarry everything came tumbling back. It was like the bursting of a dam she thought she'd built well, but it turns out the twigs and leaves were not strong enough. The grief, the pain, the twigs and dirt.

People have always whispered about her, she knows they have. Her odd life. Going away to university, getting married, coming back six months later with a degree but no husband. Then Brian. Christ, why did she ever—

She's not one for blaspheming, but Brian always brought out the worst in her. Compared him with Nigel. Wrong of her, but she couldn't help it. Nigel was so stylish, so cultured. They set up home in a one-bedroom flat, they bought furniture from second-hand shops, a squashy sofa upholstered in a wine-coloured velvety material. He'd come home with knick-knacks he'd found in junk shops, bought them cheap, got a bargain. Venetian glasses. Willow pattern plates. Everything a bit shabby in an expensive-looking way. Turkish rugs, lots of Indian brass.

And Nigel himself, he would have looked good in anything, Levis or a bespoke suit. A man at ease in his own body. Sometimes she thinks she married him because he always had to be near something he could read. The back of the cornflakes box would do if there was nothing else. He brought home as many books as he could carry, old orange Penguins, improving books of the kind that used to be handed out as school prizes for good attendance, some of them with the presentation plates still stuck inside. Sometimes a silverfish would fall out of one of those old foxed books. The flat always smelled of patchouli oil – graveyard dirt some people called it, because of its heady, earthy smell. In the evenings Nigel used to sit in a wickerwork chair that creaked with every small movement. There was always something classical playing in the background. They talked about getting a cat.

She knows if it hadn't been Melanie it would have been some other woman. There were tears, at first, but she had her pride. Poured out her feelings only in her diary. Saved up to buy her house, keeping herself short so that she could get it that bit quicker, gritting her teeth in the meantime living back with her parents. Though they never interfered, that was something; never made her feel ashamed of being divorced.

Most of the time she feels numb when she looks back on her life. Which mistakes were avoidable, she wonders? All of them, perhaps, but hindsight is a wonderful thing. Brian was the worst mistake; would the vicar understand if she told him she regrets her second marriage with every fibre of her being? He'd tell her she has to own it, her responsibility, but where does that get her?

She checks her watch. At one o'clock she's due at the vicarage with her amendments to the parish newsletter now that she's proofread it, which gives her half an hour to eat her lunch. Not being particularly hungry, she makes do with a couple of slices of buttered toast, washes the plate in cold water, then gazes around the kitchen. From the dresser she picks up a bottle of Blue Grass, the same stuff she's been using for years. A cousin buys it for her every Christmas. It's the same perfume her mother used to wear. Brian once came home with a bottle of Chanel No 5 for her, but she could tell from the label it was cheap knock-off muck he'd bought from a market stall.

She squirts herself with the Blue Grass, then decides she's overdone it and uses soapy water to wash most of it off, in case the vicar thinks she's wearing it for his benefit. Even as a young woman she was never a flirt, but as she gets older she wishes she hadn't been in such a hurry to get married. Her parents assumed she was pregnant, that they "had" to get married, but Nigel made it clear he wasn't interested in having children, and Naomi felt the same. He's my Mr Right, she told her parents. We want the same things, we have the same thoughts. How she cringed when she realised how many of Nigel's thoughts had been about Melanie.

They spent so much time together when they were at uni that she didn't really bother to make any other friends. Their friends were Nigel's friends. They'd drop in, loll on a beanbag, smoke a joint. They'd talk to Nigel about Nietzsche and Solzhenitsyn and apartheid and she always tried to join in, but if she retreated to the kitchen a great deal it wasn't because she felt that was her place, but to hide her tears. She was out of her depth, and she didn't like the way Nigel looked at Melanie. Jealousy, he told her, is destructive, it's a cancer of the soul. So she tried to make friends with Melanie, asked her over when Nigel was at work, gave her cups of tea and jam doughnuts, tried to have "girly" chats with her, but they never took to each other, although Nigel was pleased she made the effort.

There was a time when she had hopes of making friends with her deputy at the library, Lynne, a woman in her fifties who has always lived with her mother, and a regular member of Mr Latham's congregation. When Naomi was made head librarian following the early retirement of Viv Evans, she'd been relieved. Lynne seemed the sort of person she could get on with. Mrs Evans, whose deputy Naomi had been, never was. Naomi remembers the look on Lynne's face when a young woman came to church, bold as brass, with her two illegitimate children, rumoured to have been fathered by different men. Lynne caught Naomi staring at her, and a look of understanding passed between them. *In my day,* she imagined saying to Lynne, *she'd have hung her head in shame.* But the moment passed and they never got to know each other outside of work.

And it had been a terrible thing to think. When the young mother came into the library with her children, Naomi made a beeline for her, offering her advice on the nicest picture books. 'It's OK, thanks,' the woman said. 'I like to let them browse and choose their own books.' Naomi later found out the woman had started teacher training and worked at the local primary school helping a child with special needs.

'I'm too quick to judge,' she told Mr Latham, and he understood, he sympathised.

She has even tried to bury the hatchet with Antonia Littlehales, who has started coming to church recently, although Naomi believes it's only because the new vicar is what she calls "dishy". Maybe she should try harder. It's daft to let stupid things they did as teenagers get in the way, though she does wonder if it was Antonia who made that anonymous call to the police. She was always spiteful. It would be just like her. Diana wouldn't have meant to let anything slip, but Antonia isn't stupid, she would have latched onto any small hint. Naomi supposes she ought to tell Antonia that what Gill did was nothing to do with her, it was a cruel thing to do even if it was just as well Antonia found out what Philip was like, as she surely would have done anyway, sooner or later.

'Ours to have compassion, not to reason why,' the vicar says whenever she tries to talk to him about morality. He's full of things like that. Meaningless rubbish. If you turn the other cheek, she tells him, someone will only go and slap it. Still, she makes herself useful, and he appreciates her help: the flowers, the rotas, the newsletter. She's even credited on the back page. Editorial Assistant, Mrs Naomi Wilkinson. It's not much of a literary claim, but she's proud when she reads the printed newsletter, nowadays folded in half and stapled, so it's like a small magazine.

People tell her that eventual retirement comes more easily to people who've eased down during the last few years, but that's all very well for those with families and hobbies. Her house feels too empty, and she finds it hard to fill the days when she's not working. Voluntary work, perhaps, if she can find something congenial. Anything would be better than spending too long with her own thoughts.

She arrives at the vicarage on time. Mrs Anslow takes her to the office and taps on the door. 'Mrs Wilkinson to see you, Father,' she says, lifting her eyebrows as she always does, letting Naomi know that she too thinks this "Father" business an affectation.

'Come in, Naomi.'

Recently he's got into the habit of addressing her by

her first name. She'd rather he called her Mrs Wilkinson, but these days everyone seems to think they have the right to be on first name terms.

'Here you are, then,' she says, handing him the copy of the parish newsletter marked up with her amendments.

He glances up. 'You haven't seemed yourself lately. Is something troubling you?'

She hesitates. Although she vowed not to confide in him again, who else is there? 'It's that body they found,' she blurts out. 'I thought it was Brian – my husband. The police have told me it's not him, and now I don't know what to think.'

He twirls his fountain pen between thumb and forefinger. 'It's understandable that you should be upset. Whoever the poor man turns out to be, he was someone's son.'

'It's just… If I'm honest, I wanted it to be Brian.'

Mr Fielding puts his pen down. Now she has his full attention. 'Presumably you loved him when you married him?'

She snorts. 'Love! He was one of those men who could charm the birds off the trees, when it suited him. Once we were married, he showed his true colours.'

'In what way?'

'Getting drunk, going with other women.' She swallows. 'I'm sorry, I shouldn't have said anything. But people in the village, those who remember him, they know what he was like. It'll all start up again, the twitching curtains, the whispering behind hands.'

Mr Fielding leans back in his chair, a frown on his face. 'Why should it? In any case, *you've* done nothing wrong.'

She tells him about the anonymous phone call. 'You

know how rumours get around. People said some terrible things. Not to my face, of course, but I knew. I heard.'

'What sort of things?'

She shakes her head. 'I'd rather not say. It was all lies, of course. People like to think the worst of others – don't argue, it's true.'

He smiles. 'I wasn't going to argue. I'm aware of the weaknesses in human nature.'

'People said I drove Brian away with my behaviour. They said I was a cold, uncaring woman.'

'I'm not sure people will remember – or care. It was all so long ago.'

'Maybe. It was a dreadful time. Just dreadful. I've never really got over it, that's the truth.'

'I wonder if you might benefit from speaking to a professional.'

'You mean a psychiatrist, don't you? A mind doctor.'

'A counsellor. I think it would do you good to talk through your feelings with someone who understands how to channel them into something you can cope with.'

'You think I'm mad?'

'I think you might be suffering from stress. Not that I'm an expert on these matters.'

'I'm not sure I hold with spilling my secrets in front of strangers.'

'It's sometimes the best way. I think it can be more difficult to speak about such things with friends – easier to speak to someone impartial, who won't judge.'

'Maybe you're right.'

The idea of therapy revolts her. Americans go to therapists all the time, for years sometimes, so it can't do much good. If you've got a bad tooth, you visit the dentist once, he deals with it, and that's that. People who depend on regular therapy are simply too weak to cope with their lives. Her parents believed in keeping things to themselves. Speaking to a vicar is acceptable, but that's different. Trendy therapists, spouting their nonsense about Freud and Jung and the kind of relationship you had with your dad, that's not her style.

She returns her thoughts to the present. 'I hope you don't mind me saying, but I'd prefer to be called Mrs Wilkinson. I know it's old-fashioned of me, but—'

The vicar blushes. 'Of course; whatever you prefer. I do wish you'd told me earlier.'

Now she feels awkward, as if she's made a terrible faux pas. 'It's not really important...'

'If it's important to you, it would be churlish of me not to respect your wishes.'

She feels chastened, as if she's the one in the wrong.

Gossip is something she despises, but you can't have a proper talk with Mr Fielding – he's too careful in what he says, so determined to sound unbiased, with no opinion of his own. His words are sensible enough, but platitudes are no use at all. At least she knows anything she tells him will go no further.

'Leave this with me,' he says, tapping the newsletter with his fountain pen. 'And thank you, for all that you do.'

Is that it? she wants to say. And yes, it is. He's already writing again in the notebook on his desk.

Naomi is reluctant to go home. She stops to shake a stone out of her shoe before opening the front door. The small piece of gravel has made a hole in her tights. Glancing up, she sees the downstairs curtain twitch in the house opposite. Nosy old baggage, that Mrs Fisk, always with her face pressed against the glass. Sees only what she wants to see, though.

She slams the front door behind her and enters the living room. Brown carpet, curtains and cushion covers. Neat as a pin, clean as a whistle. Why do people say that? What can be so especially clean about a whistle? All these browns, though; very depressing. Perhaps she should invest in some colourful cushions like those jewel-bright ones in the flat she shared with Nigel. He had such good taste.

The rest of the day she passes with housework and reading, counting the hours until she can reasonably go to bed, but when she gets there she can't sleep. In her mind she keeps seeing Brian, lurching around the kitchen, knocking cups and plates onto the floor; sees herself cowering in a corner, screaming...

Towards morning she gives up her half-hearted attempts to sleep. She sits at the kitchen table, leafing through photographs of herself as a child. Snapshots taken by loving parents. Gap-toothed smile, hair bleached by the sun, her favourite yellow cotton sundress, her skinny legs crossed. What harm could possibly befall that ordinary, happy child? She pushes the photos away, maddened by the images of innocent contentment that seem to mock her. Somewhere it had all gone wrong. Dark grey clouds settled over the sun. Her smile has faded, her mind carrying its secrets like remembered bruises.

21

DIANA

I pop out in the morning to get a bit of shopping in and check on Stella. Not that she needs to be checked on, but I do feel guilty for my lack of involvement in the running of the shop. I'm sure Stella prefers it this way, but it is my ultimate responsibility. It would be good for me and for my relationship with Antonia if I spent a day or two each week at work. Once Gill has gone away I'll broach the subject with Stella, making it clear I've no intention of cutting her hours or her pay.

'Can't stop,' I tell Stella, 'just thought I'd better show my face once in a while.'

'You worry too much,' she says. 'Although, as you're here, what do you think of these?'

She flicks through her mobile and enlarges a picture of a felted badger, exquisitely made, wearing a top hat and sporting a monocle. 'My sister makes them. Foxes, otters, mice – all sorts. She asked if she could pop a few in the shop, see if we get any traction.'

'I don't see why not. Show me some more.'

The animals are beautifully observed, all with some quirky detail, without being at all sentimental. 'I love them,' I say, and Stella beams. We have similar tastes. Would she find it so terrible if I spent more time here? It *is* my shop, I tell myself again, but I know I need Stella far more than she needs me.

Yesterday, in a moment of madness, I phoned Gill and invited her to lunch. 'You'll have to take us as you find us, I'm afraid,' I said on the telephone. I don't know why I said that. It's not as if Gill is likely to be used to anything grand or expect us to ply her with champagne and caviar. Neither of us mentioned Antonia, and I have no idea how the pair of them will get along. There's no need for them to meet at all – it's not as if they were ever friends – but Antonia keeps asking why I'm keeping the two of them apart, so we might as well get it over with.

Once I've bought the food, I visit Challoner's, a general store that sells everything from tea towels to toy train sets. I'm looking for some smart place mats for the table to replace the old raffia things we've made do with for years. Having picked out the ones I want, I decide to splash out on a new tablecloth. It's a beautiful cream damask, far too fancy for everyday use, but I can't resist.

I take my purchases to the counter. The older Mr Challoner serves me. A paunchy man in his fifties with a comb-over, he beams at me and asks if I'm throwing a dinner party.

'Good gracious, no. I can't think of anything more dreadful.'

Unfazed, he nods and continues to beam. 'It was good to see your sister in here the other day.'

'Antonia? When was *she* in here? She never does the shopping.'

'It was nice, all the same. Did the little girl like her doll?'

'What doll? Antonia never bought a doll!'

Mr Challoner scratches his head. 'I thought it was a bit strange.'

'Are you sure? I'm sorry, that's a silly thing to say...'

'A doll, it was,' Mr Challoner says, sliding my purchases into a carrier bag. 'Couldn't have been more pleased – that line's been hard to shift.'

'What sort of doll was it?'

'One of them collectors' dolls.' He lifts up his chin and points towards the "Toys and Games" aisle. 'Dressed in tartan, it was, with one of them tam-o'-shanters on its head.'

'Would you show me, please?'

'Right you are.' He evinces no surprise. A shopkeeper of the old school, he's a great believer in the customer being right, and always tries to accommodate every request, however bizarre.

He lifts down a doll in a cardboard and cellophane box. It has a hefty price tag. It's meant to look like a small girl rather than a baby, and to be admired and displayed rather than played with.

'It's nicely made, if you like that type of thing,' Mr Challoner says. 'Hand-made, according to the label.'

I nod. 'Thanks for showing me. Antonia must have bought it for Patricia's grandchild.' Patricia's grandchildren are adults, and Mr Challoner has no idea who Patricia is, but he smiles and puts the doll back on the shelf.

'Don't forget your shopping,' he calls as I hurry towards the door.

I walk home in a daze, wondering why Antonia should buy such a thing and where she's hidden it. I decide not to mention it; not today. It's not worth the risk of putting her in a bad mood before Gill arrives.

I've decided to make a gooseberry pie for pud. As soon as I get home I dash into the garden to pick the fruit from our rather leggy bushes. The sun beats down on my bare head as my mind flits between worrying about Antonia's doll and fretting that she will ruin the lunch with some ill-considered reference to the past.

My hands falter as I try to pluck off another gooseberry, and the fruit falls to the ground. 'Clumsy article,' I mutter, then look up to see Antonia gazing at me through the kitchen window. My back aches, and I've collected barely enough to make a small pie, even if I combine the goosegogs with some tinned fruit.

I want to shout at Antonia and tell her to mind her own business, but I shut my mouth with the words unspoken. I mop my brow and lean against the fence for a moment, feeling the weight of years and memories pressing on my backbone.

The gooseberry pie idea abandoned, I change into a pale pink blouse and black trousers then go downstairs to put on an apron and lay the table. Everything looks so perfect – the cream tablecloth, matching napkins, the new place mats – that I get a lump in my throat, remembering other, more innocent times when Gill used to come to tea. Sometimes we'd all been there – my mother and father, Antonia, Gill and me – all of us talking over one another. One of the worst things about getting older is all the extra space, reminding me of the people who are no longer here.

Antonia placidly knits as I place food on the table: a bowl of salad, a plate of cooked meats, some Scotch eggs, and a veal-and-ham pie.

'You've put spring onions in the salad, haven't you?' Antonia says.

'Yes. I like them.'

'I shall have to poke mine out. They repeat on me dreadfully.'

I roll my eyes, but refuse to let anything put me off my stroke. 'Do as you please.' *Just be nice to Gill.* Of course I can't say this, but it keeps going round and round in my head. The table looks lovely and the sun streams through the diamond-pane windows. Only Antonia can spoil what should otherwise be a pleasant lunch.

When the doorbell rings I whip off my apron and stuff it behind a cushion. 'Get the drinks ready, would you?' I call to Antonia over my shoulder.

'What drinks?'

'Oh, I don't know – a jug of water, lemonade...'

Antonia sniffs. 'Pity we're all out of champagne.'

I hurry to the door and let Gill in. She is wearing smart jeans with a short-sleeved beige jumper.

'You always wear such wonderful necklaces,' I say, admiring her long strand of oblong glass beads that remind me of Fox's Glacier Fruits.

She fingers the beads. 'Thank you.' Peering around the hallway she says, 'This is just as I remember it, only smaller.'

I smile. 'I think the memory plays tricks with scale.'

She nods and walks through to the living room. I follow close behind, ready to referee if Antonia decides to misbehave.

'Hello, Antonia,' Gill says. She doesn't hold out her hand, which I think is a wise move. It would be too awful if Antonia refused to shake hands.

Antonia gives a brief nod. 'Gillian. You're looking well.'

Silence falls, so I usher them into the dining room.

'A beautiful spread,' Gill says, pulling out a chair.

'She only made the salad herself,' Antonia says. 'Everything else is out of a packet.'

'Take no notice,' I mutter, offering Gill the salad bowl.

'I wouldn't have wanted you to go to any trouble,' Gill says. 'Normally I only have a sandwich for lunch.' She smiles at Antonia. 'Made with supermarket bread. Though I do try to follow a healthy diet – not too much fat or carbohydrate.'

'Our mother used to eat dripping,' Antonia says. 'Bacon rinds and even the parson's nose. Didn't do her much harm, since she lived to a ripe old age.'

'I daresay she smoked forty a day, as well,' Gill jokes, but Antonia doesn't crack a smile.

I grip my knife. 'Tell us what it was like to move to Wales, Gill.'

Gill proceeds to describe the small village in South Wales where she lived with her parents. She takes out her tablet ('Very fancy,' Antonia remarks) to show us a few snaps, and Antonia seems to settle down, admiring the lush scenery in the photographs, reminiscing about our own childhood holidays in Devon.

I clear the plates away and take up Gill's offer to help me wash up.

'Is Antonia as you remember her?' I ask, not able to look her in the eye.

'Much the same, only more bitter, I think.' She rests her hand on my arm. 'Don't worry. She doesn't bother me.'

Some of the tension in my shoulders eases, and I put on the kettle to make a pot of tea. Gill helps me sort out cups and saucers. Once the tea is made, I pick up the tray and follow Gill into the living room. Antonia has set out a plate of Penguin bars and pink wafer biscuits, more suitable for a child's birthday party.

I pour the tea and hand a cup to Gill.

Antonia shakes the mantel clock and holds it to her ear.

'Has it stopped?' I ask.

'If I didn't know better, I'd think Antonia was giving me a hint,' Gill says.

Antonia glares at her and puts the clock back on the mantelpiece, which is covered with all manner of knick-knacks. She bends and picks up the plate of biscuits, holding it out to Gill. 'One won't hurt you, Gillian.'

They stare at each other but Gill is the first to crack. 'I needn't admit it in confession.'

'I'm sure God only has your best interests at heart.'

Gill opens her mouth but immediately shuts it and smiles, taking a pink wafer from the plate.

'Why don't you tell us about your husband?' Antonia asks. 'I must say, I was rather surprised to hear that you'd married, but I suppose people can change.'

'I'm sorry, I don't quite follow...?'

Antonia's smile is vicious. 'I never thought men were really your line. Apart from Philip, of course.'

Gill puts down the biscuit. 'I think it's probably best to draw a veil over the past.'

'Do you? I don't think Diana quite sees it that way.'

'Stop it, Antonia,' I say, 'you're embarrassing yourself.'

Antonia continues to stare questioningly at Gill, her chin thrust forward.

'My husband and I were very happy together,' Gill says. 'The past is of no consequence. I'm sure Diana understands that. I would like to think you do, too.' She doesn't look at me.

Gill finishes her tea quickly and stands. 'I'm afraid I must go. My friend and I are going into town a little later.'

'Of course.' I accompany her to the front door, trying hard to behave as if I'm not upset by Antonia's little outburst.

Gill steps outside and turns to face me. 'Perhaps it was too much to hope that Antonia—'

'Quite. I'm so sorry. Goodbye, Gill.'

I shut the door and lean against it for a few moments, my eyes closed. The thought of speaking to Antonia makes me feel ill, so I run upstairs and lock myself in my bedroom. Until I've calmed down, I must stay away from her, or there's no telling what I might do.

22

ANTONIA

Ridiculous, am I? Well, perhaps I am. Sisters, such devoted sisters... She bites into a Penguin. Diana always had a tendency to sulk. Their mother used to say how much she preferred Antonia's short-lived outbursts to Diana's epic sulks. 'I'd rather have fireworks than rumbling volcanoes,' she used to say, which only made Diana even more cross.

When Diana refuses to come down for dinner, Antonia doesn't worry unduly. Best to let her get on with it. She hopes that by the time Diana emerges from her room, her anger will have worn itself out. That's what usually happens.

Silly of Diana to get in such a tizz over her telling Gill a few home truths. Or is there more to it than that? Might Diana have found out the one thing she's always kept from her? That doesn't make any sense, but it's always been there in the back of her mind, she's always wondered what Diana would say if she told her. They've never talked about Antonia's long stay in Devon with those people, those vague "friends of the family". A short period of convalescence was how Mother and Father described it. Antonia's a bit peaky. She needs the sea air. Diana has never mentioned the subject and Antonia has always assumed Diana was too preoccupied with her own affairs to wonder what her sister was up to.

If it hadn't been for the baby, she might have tried to find someone else after Philip left. Her parents told her that having the baby adopted was the best thing for her, so that no man need ever know she was second-hand goods. As far as they were concerned, they had only her best interests at heart. But once she'd given up her baby, she couldn't contemplate the idea of getting involved with anyone else. Another baby, born within wedlock, would have done nothing to ease the gnawing ache caused by the loss of the first.

It's nine o'clock when Diana flings open the living room door. Her hair is dishevelled and she reeks of smoke. She used to be a heavy smoker, but gave it up years ago.

'Good heavens, dear,' Antonia says, flapping her hand, 'what have you been doing up there? I hope you haven't set fire to anything.'

'Do shut up.'

'But what is it? You look quite fearsome.'

'There have been times when I've come close to doing you some mischief; times when I've wished myself anywhere else – yes, even prison – than being stuck here with you.'

'Why are you saying such cruel things?' Antonia clutches her cardigan.

'Because I need to. I promised Mother I would always look after you, but I'm not sure I can stand living with you for the rest of my life. I'm sorry, but that's how I feel.'

'What are you saying?'

'I think I would like to live on my own. You can stay here, of course; I'll make my own arrangements.'

186

'Diana, you can't!' Antonia springs up from her chair and claws at Diana's arm. 'Please don't do this. I couldn't bear it.'

'We'll talk about it in the morning.' Diana shakes off Antonia's hand and turns to leave.

'But...' *You've had nothing to eat since lunch*, she wants to say – as if food matters at a time like this! At least Diana isn't planning to kick her out – not that she could, could she? – but Antonia doesn't want to spend the rest of her life alone. It's not what Mother would have wanted.

23

DIANA

I felt triumphant after making my announcement, but the next morning I'm ashamed of myself. I've been self-centred. Antonia loved Philip, and Gill's behaviour had been dreadful. I thought Antonia was wrong to harbour a grudge, but deep down I believed Gill and I could rekindle a relationship that ended forty years earlier. I'm really no better than Antonia, and I trudge downstairs feeling chastened.

'I'm sorry,' I tell Antonia. 'I was too hard on you, I know that. I was embarrassed, that's all, after I'd put so much effort into making everything nice for when Gill came round.'

'I've never liked her, you know that. And before you say anything, it's got nothing to do with – well, how you *are*.' As she speaks, I can smell her minty breath.

'You've good reason to dislike her, I know that,' I concede. 'Perhaps I didn't appreciate the strength of your feelings.'

'She liked people to be enthralled by her. You were, of course, so you wouldn't have noticed how she behaved with everyone else.'

'Which was how, exactly?'

'Oh, as if we didn't count. She liked playing games, toying with people's emotions, like she did with Philip.'

It all seems so ridiculous, Philip viewed as a trophy, a

possession, a symbol of adolescent triumph rather than a person. Perhaps that's really how it was, back then. Everyone had been hurt, except perhaps Philip.

'She told me Philip was only with me because he couldn't have her.'

'If Philip had really cared for you—'

I'm disconcerted by the tears that spring to her eyes. 'I loved him. I knew, after seeing him with Gill, that I could never trust him again, but it didn't make me stop loving him.'

'You told Gill's parents about us to make her go away, didn't you?'

'I had to! I knew the sort of person she was.'

I hang my head. Perhaps we should have talked all this through years ago, and perhaps the fact that we can talk about it now proves that we have reached a turning point in our relationship, enabling us to be more honest with each other. 'I was besotted.' I shut my eyes and rub my forehead.

'We've both made mistakes.'

The clock ticks in the background, reminding me of all the time that has passed and how little of it remains.

'Let's not talk about it anymore,' says Antonia. 'Would you like a cup of tea?'

I nod. She bustles to the kitchen. That, it seems, is that.

The sound of rattling teacups alerts me that Antonia is coming back, so I open the door for her.

'Thank you, dear.'

She fills the cups and hands one to me. 'Seeing Gillian brought everything back.'

'There was no call to be rude to her, though. She's not the same person she was then.'

Antonia regards me with her innocent cornflower blue eyes. 'Do you really think that? My own opinion is very different, you see. I believe that people don't really change much. If they alter their behaviour, it's because they learn what is acceptable and what isn't. But deep down they stay the same.'

'She was my best friend, as well as all the rest of it.'

'I don't doubt you were fond of her. If I were you, though, I'd be a little bit wary now.'

'Don't talk soft,' I mutter. 'It's not as if I have any illusions that we can be to each other what we were in the old days.'

'You won't be sad when she leaves, then? Will it be a relief to get your old comfortable life back again?'

I frown and stare at my cup. I'm never quite sure how to take Antonia when she's in one of her perceptive moods. It's rather like listening to a preternaturally wise child, not quite normal. Perhaps what I mean is that whenever she says something clever, I feel I've entirely misjudged her, which in turn makes me doubt my own powers of discernment and makes me wonder, too, if she sees far more than I give her credit for. This possibility makes goosebumps rise on my arms.

'I know she's only visiting. I'll be sorry when she leaves, but my heart won't break,' I say, rubbing my arms and wishing I believed it.

'That's all right then, isn't it? I would hate to see her hurt you again.'

I open my mouth to protest, but Antonia gets in first. 'She would have left anyway, eventually,' she says. 'She had quite an eye for the boys, she was a terrible flirt. You were just...'

Practice. Antonia doesn't finish the sentence, but I can read her mind. She blushes and I grip my saucer, wondering how much truth there is in what Antonia says. If it's true, that I was merely hors d'oeuvres before the main course, I've no idea what to feel. I never fell in love with that same intensity again, hence the memory of Gillian has attained far greater importance in my mind than it should have done. Is what Antonia says true, I wonder, and if it is must I go to my grave believing that I've spent all these years treasuring a memory more insubstantial than the steam rising from my cup?

I wake with a start, thinking I hear my sister cry out. 'Antonia? Was that you?'

Getting no answer, I jump out of bed. I grab my dressing gown, then search under the bed for my slippers. 'I'm coming,' I shout, sitting on the bed to steady myself while I force my feet into the slippers. I peer at my clock: it's just gone six.

Antonia's room is next to mine. I find her on the floor in the foetal position.

'Oh, my dear!' I crouch to see if she's conscious. 'You silly goose!' I say, wishing my hands would stop shaking. There have been many times when I hoped some harm would befall Antonia, but I get no enjoyment from seeing her on the floor, frail and frightened.

'Can you get up? I can't manage you on my own – I'll have to phone for help.'

Antonia manages to nod. 'I'll try.'

I help her into a sitting position, and manage to haul her dead weight onto the bed.

'What happened, dear?' I ask, examining Antonia's

head and finding a bump the size of a hen's egg.

'Must have fallen out of bed, and hit my head on the bedside table,' Antonia mumbles. 'A couple of aspirins will soon put me right.'

'It's more than aspirins you need. We should get you to hospital and have that bump checked out. I'll phone the vicar, he's bound to help.'

'Don't pester him.'

'Pester, indeed! He might as well be of some use.'

The vicar answers promptly in spite of the early hour, and when I explain what happened he agrees to bring his car round and take Antonia to A&E.

'The least he could do,' I report back to Antonia, grateful nevertheless that he offered his services without any hesitation.

'Aspirin,' Antonia says, gently feeling the bump.

'All right, I think there are some in the bathroom.'

A pink nylon frill disguises the washbasin's pedestal. I rummage around in the tiny, cobwebby cupboard beneath it. What a lot of rubbish Antonia keeps in here! Rusty razors. Dry, crumbly old soaps that refuse to lather. Tubes of foul-smelling pink ointment. A dirty black comb with a grey, fluffy deposit along the base of the teeth.

The aspirin, at least, is a relatively recent purchase.

Mr Fielding, as good as his word, arrives shortly after I've provided a glass of water for Antonia and got dressed.

'I can't go to hospital in my nightie!' Antonia protests.

'Nonsense; it's perfectly respectable. It's always overwarm in those places.'

'I don't care – I want proper clothes on.'

Reluctantly I help Antonia change into a dress.

'That's better.'

Once Antonia is what she calls "respectable", I call Mr Fielding into the room. He waves me aside and scoops up Antonia in his arms.

Antonia giggles. 'I feel like Tess of the d'Urbervilles,' she says.

'Sorry, I haven't read it,' he says.

'She's talking nonsense,' I say.

'Oh, you *must* remember, Diana – that scene in the film, when Peter Firth picks up lovely Nastassja Kinski and her friends to help them over an enormous puddle.'

Mr Fielding laughs. 'It must indeed have been quite the puddle.'

Antonia sighs and leans her head against Mr Fielding's shoulder.

'Don't get too cosy there,' I say. 'You're a great lump for anyone to have to carry.'

'Ignore her,' Antonia whispers loudly to the vicar.

He gives an embarrassed laugh and bends low to get Antonia into the front passenger seat of his Renault Megane. I scramble into the back, irritated by my sister now that the shock has worn off. She's far too old to be flirting with vicars. Why do men always fall for that simpering little girl act? At least Antonia is too old to turn his head.

During the half hour drive to hospital we listen to his customary classical music.

Mr Fielding sighs. 'Schubert – my favourite.'

'We weren't a classical family, I'm afraid,' I comment. 'Though our mother was partial to a bit of Gilbert and Sullivan.'

'*Was* she? I don't remember that,' Antonia says.

'You've had a bang on the head, it's probably affected your memory.'

Mr Fielding parks the car and helps Antonia out.

Antonia giggles. 'Such a lot of bother over a silly little fall.'

'You can't be too careful,' Mr Fielding says, 'especially with a head injury.'

I roll my eyes. Trust Antonia to cause such a fuss.

'They see to the children first,' I remark as we take our seats in the waiting room. 'We'll be here for hours.' I smile at a little girl sitting opposite, lolling across her mother's lap.

The girl keeps one eye scrunched shut and her mother tells her to stop rubbing it. 'But it *hurts*,' the child whines.

'It's only a bit of sand,' the mother tells me, but five minutes later mother and daughter are called in to see the triage nurse.

Mr Fielding wanders off in search of a drinks machine, but not before I've had a good old moan about the quality of tea from such machines. I could kick myself afterwards and can't understand why I have to go on and on about things. I make sure to sound very grateful when the vicar returns with a couple of beige plastic cups too hot to hold comfortably.

Finally a nurse calls Antonia and takes her to a room, pretty bare but for a couple of chairs and a computer. Antonia sits down and I stand behind her.

The nurse takes Antonia's details and assesses the seriousness of her injury. 'It's a nasty bump, isn't it?' She has a chunky pen on a cord around her neck and it keeps knocking against the table as she types in Antonia's details.

'Next of kin?' Her fingers hover over the keys and I open my mouth to speak, but the nurse has patently lost interest and is concerned only about her computer, which has locked up. 'Never mind – d'you want to go back to the waiting room? You'll be called when it's your turn.'

'How long will that be?' I ask.

The nurse frowns and shakes her head. 'Impossible to say. I'll do what I can.'

The waiting room is filling up.

'Let's just go home,' Antonia says, fretful now the excitement has worn off.

I put an arm around her. The only available seat is a rickety plastic chair. A man with crutches stands next to it, using the public phone.

'I could go and get sandwiches,' Mr Fielding offers.

'At this time of the morning?' I snap.

'Antonia Littlehales?'

Antonia looks up. 'Me?' Everyone is looking at her. Resentful, probably, that it isn't their turn.

Antonia walks into a cubicle and I follow her.

'It's nothing,' Antonia tells the doctor, but he wants to keep her in for observation.

'I don't want to,' she tells me.

'Now, Antonia...'

'I like to be in my own bed,' Antonia tells the doctor. 'I don't like hospitals. People always come out more ill than they went in, and that's if they come out at all. I want my own things around me.'

'It's only for one day,' I say.

'Just to get a few X-rays and make sure there's no lasting damage,' the doctor adds.

Antonia allows herself to be cajoled into a wheelchair and up to a ward. All the patients have the curtains pulled around their beds.

I stare distastefully at a darned hole in the top bed sheet and a small red stain (blood? Can it really be blood?) on the pillow.

'Do you have to go?' Antonia whines.

'It's only for today. We'll be back tomorrow to collect you. Don't worry, the time will pass in a jiffy.'

24

DIANA

Mr Fielding drives me home.

'You've been very kind,' I say.

'Give me a ring once you know when she's being discharged, won't you?'

'Of course. It's very good of you.'

'My pleasure.'

I remember what Mother used to say, whenever Antonia or I hurt ourselves: *I'd take your pain and bear it myself, if I could.* Her cool hands would seem to do exactly that as they soothed a clammy forehead. I can't give Antonia a mother's comfort, nor am I generous enough to wish I could bear Antonia's pain.

Mr Fielding comes into the house with me. 'You'll be all right on your own, will you?'

'Of course I will.'

It isn't so long ago that I really did consider, albeit half-heartedly, the prospect of moving out. I know I would never have done such a thing, but still, the thought was there, and it isn't because I would miss Antonia that I have given up the idea.

'Will you stay for a cup of tea?' I ask.

'Thank you. I could do with a decent drink.'

I put the kettle on. Tea is always acceptable, no matter what time it is.

'Only half a cup for me, please.' The vicar looks from his watch to my clock. 'I can't stay for long. I have so much to do today.'

'I'm sure Antonia didn't inconvenience you on purpose.'

'I'm sorry, I didn't mean to sound short. It's hardly Antonia's fault the NHS is under-staffed and under-funded.'

'Sit yourself down, then.'

We sit opposite each other, our knees almost touching. Mr Fielding keeps his knees pressed together. The phrase "like a virgin in a brothel" pops into my head. Now who can I remember saying that? Is it an old army saying, perhaps? Hardly something my father would have said. No matter.

Mr Fielding stirs sugar into his tea.

'You'll stir a hole in the bottom of that cup,' I say. 'Are you hungry? Can I get you a bite to eat? We've only cornflakes, I'm afraid. Not even Kelloggs. I don't normally bother. But if you want…'

'I wouldn't say no to a bit of cereal. No, no; don't get up. I'm sure I can find my way around your kitchen.'

I don't like to sit doing nothing while a guest does the work. Apart from anything else, there is always the worry that they might come across something embarrassing – an old pair of Mother's greying bloomers in the duster drawer, for instance. Every house has its secrets, and they are fragile secrets: all you have to do is die alone, or in suspicious circumstances, and all of your life becomes public property, picked over by some stranger in rubber gloves whose job is to do the dirty work of ferreting through other people's belongings. I shudder as I hear the clatter of crockery coming from the kitchen.

Mr Fielding returns with a bowl of cereal and makes short work of eating it. 'I'd better get along, if you don't mind,' he says when he's finished.

'Of course; I mustn't keep you from your work.'

The house feels strange without Antonia. It's neither worse nor better, just different. I experience a fleeting sense of freedom, then realise there is nothing I particularly want to do that I can't do when Antonia is present.

I mooch around the house, tidying up in Antonia's room, which I hardly ever enter. There are cotton wool balls under the bed, cotton buds and used tissues in the drawers. Such a mess! Antonia has always been careless. I put fresh sheets on the bed, give the room a squirt of air freshener, and close the door behind me.

In the freezer I find some bread rolls that I shove in the microwave to defrost, then I fill them with Quick Chips. Even by spinster meal standards it's a pretty poor effort, and the rolls haven't properly defrosted. I bin most of my lunch and rummage around in the larder until I find a bar of cooking chocolate.

I fill the rest of the day with odd jobs and housework, and in the evening I defrost a ready meal before settling down to watch some telly. It's odd having no one to talk to. Does that mean I miss Antonia, or have I just grown accustomed to her presence?

Although I'm not upset, a tear slips down my cheek, taking me by surprise. I wipe it away and shake my head. We are both too old to fight or to carry resentments to our death bed. Perhaps, in the end, we *are* as bad as each other.

I fall asleep in the armchair, waking in the early hours. I lack the energy to move from the chair to go upstairs to bed and when I next wake, with a crick in my neck, it's seven o'clock and time to start another day. I get to work.

The hospital calls to tell me I can fetch Antonia after two. I hope she won't be too cross when she sees how much stuff I've chucked out while she's been in hospital. Some of the cans were years past their sell-by date. Antonia always says the manufacturers stick any old date on them, just for something to put. But nothing keeps forever, and it isn't just food that goes mouldy and rancid. I've also thrown out the ice-encrusted ready meals in foil trays, defrosted the freezer, and intend to replace the packaged meals with wholesome home-cooked food. This isn't the first time I've made such a resolution, and I wonder how long it will be before we slip into the old ways again.

I think about the prospect of having Antonia back home. I'm sure she will milk her accident for all it's worth, lounging around on the sofa like Madame de Pompadour, flirting with Mr Fielding when he calls in. Antonia's romantic silliness might have enraptured a certain type of man, but why bother now? *No one's going to love you now, Antonia; no knight in shining armour, no Prince Charming, not even a lonely old widower or a timid vicar. You're past it – past your sell-by date.*

I tut when the doorbell rings. Now who can *that* be? Expecting to see the vicar, I open the door to Naomi.

'This is a nice surprise,' I say. 'Won't you come in?'

'Thanks. I heard about Antonia from the vicar. Is she all right now?'

'She's fine. She's coming out of hospital this afternoon, but the doctor says she needs to take it easy for a while. She'll be up and about as soon as she thinks she's missing something.' I squint as I regard Naomi. 'You look different. Have you done something to your hair?'

'It doesn't make me look too young, does it? One fears mutton dressed as lamb syndrome.'

'It suits you. Really, it looks lovely.' The decent haircut, with some expert layering, has taken years off her. I hope it will give her the courage to update her wardrobe. She has a good figure. A smart Boden dress would be so much more flattering than those cheap pencil skirts and tired-looking shirts she always wears.

'Come into the sitting room, dear,' I say. 'I'm afraid it's rather a mess – I started having a big clear-out while Antonia's in hospital, but as you can see, I've barely scratched the surface.'

Naomi flicks through a pile of old women's magazines dating back to the sixties. 'You could probably sell these on eBay.' She looks up, self-consciously brushing her hair away from her face. 'It's an auction site on the Internet.'

I smile. 'Yes, I know what it is. I'm not sure I can be bothered. Perhaps you could take them for the next church jumble sale.'

She stares at an advert for G Plan furniture in one of the magazines before setting it aside. 'Can I help you tidy?'

'There's really no point keeping all this junk – we've no one to leave even our good things to, let alone the rubbish.' I sit in an armchair and run my fingers over the embroidered covers. What are they for, exactly? To prevent wear and tear of the chair's fabric, I suppose. I whip them off and throw them onto the pile of things for the church jumble sale.

I can just imagine what Antonia will say: "You can't

get rid of them! Mother embroidered those!" And then I'll make some brusque comment such as: "Well, we can't take them with us", and another argument will ensue.

'What about the cabinet?' Naomi says, opening the oak dresser's front doors. 'There's a ton of stuff in here.'

'You tell me what's in there while I make a cup of tea. Would you like one?'

'Thanks, yes.'

When I return with the tray, I find Naomi crouched beside the dresser with a pile of old papers.

'What have you got there?' I set the tray on the table and go over to have a look.

'Letters, I think.'

'Let me see.' I reach for my reading glasses and settle them on my face.

Naomi hands the pile to me.

I stare at the neat handwriting and recognise it as Philip's. Antonia used to show me some of his letters. My hands tremble as one sentence in particular catches my eye. 'I can't believe it,' I whisper.

'What is it?' Naomi asks. 'Have you found something interesting? Can I see?'

'Nothing. Nothing of any importance. Put them back – I think I'll leave the dresser for another day.'

'If you're sure.' She drinks her tea.

I was glad of her company, but now I'm eager for her to leave. I need to reread the letters, to come to terms with the information they contain, before I see Antonia again. 'Thank you for offering to help, though. It's something I really must get around to one of these days, but I should probably speak to Antonia before getting rid of anything that belonged to our parents.'

'Of course. I only called round to make sure Antonia's all right.'

After Naomi has left, I find odd jobs to do, because – much as I need to confirm what I've read – I need to prepare myself. Once my tasks are done, I grab the letters and sit on the sofa. My heart pounding, I reread the letter that gave me such a shake-up.

Hotel Weber, Munich
27th March, 1975

Darling Antonia,
Please don't fret yourself. It could be a false alarm, couldn't it? But if it's confirmed, you know I'll stand by you. We'll get married as soon as possible. And you're not to worry about G – it was just a bit of flirting, nothing serious. You do believe me, don't you? Once my folks know there's a baby involved, they'll have to come round. They only dislike you because they've got the wrong idea about you. In time they'll learn to love you as much as I do. We're here until Tuesday, so only four more days. I'll see you very soon.

All my love,
Philip

A baby! But Antonia has never been pregnant. I would know if she had been. Antonia has never... My heart skips a beat as I remember that time when Mother sent Antonia to stay with friends of hers in Devon. I thought nothing of it at the time, even though Antonia was absent for the whole of the school summer holidays. I was working

203

in Miss Dodson's wool shop by then and merely envious that Antonia was gadding about at the seaside. I remember when she returned she looked no better – not that I'd been aware she was ill in the first place. She was thinner, certainly. Unhappy. I pestered Mother to tell me what was wrong with her, but she snapped my head off. Perhaps I didn't really care that much; I had my own friends, my own concerns.

Perhaps, though, Antonia hadn't been ill at all. Our parents were certainly the type to shunt her out of the way so they wouldn't have to confront the disgrace of having an unmarried mother for a daughter.

But what happened to the baby, if there was one? I scatter the letters on the sofa and hurry upstairs to Antonia's room. If she had a child, surely there would be some evidence, somewhere? I rummage through drawers, peer under the bed and in the wardrobe that stinks of mothballs. I find lots of dust and a few dead flies, but nothing to suggest Antonia ever gave birth.

Finally I turn my attention to the cupboard in the corner of her room. I tug on the handle, but it's stuck. There's no lock, so I pull harder, and stumble backwards as the door finally gives.

I blink rapidly a few times, bemused by the sight that greets me. Dozens of pairs of unblinking glass eyes stare back at me. The cupboard is stuffed with dolls: collectors' dolls, quite lifelike, very detailed, like the ones in Challoner's shop. Dolls with rosebud mouths, pink cheeks, glossy ringlets tied with ribbons. Some still have the price tags on. Dolls are supposed to be cute, but to me they are sinister. Their fixed smiles make them look cold and heartless.

'What in the...?' The words die in my throat and I shut the cupboard door with trembling hands, as though what are shut up in there are real children, suffocated by Antonia's love.

25

DIANA

I ring the vicar and ask if he can give me a lift to collect Antonia from hospital. I'm glad of his company, his small talk, the soothing music in the car. Antonia is groggy, her mouth pinched, she doesn't want to talk. She snaps at the vicar when he offers to help her upstairs, but he's not offended. 'She's not herself yet,' he says. 'A good rest is what she needs.'

'She rested in hospital.'

'Not the same, though. Noisy places, hospitals.'

I don't want him to linger, but after he's gone I feel oppressed by the silence, my thoughts, Antonia's nearness, the thought of her in that room with those dolls.

Relief floods me when the doorbell rings. Surprised to find Naomi on the doorstep again, I invite her in and lead her into the living room.

'Is this one of those arthritic chairs?' she asks as she sits down.

'It's the normal sort. We couldn't afford a proper one.'

I know the type Naomi means; I see them advertised on TV in the afternoons. Very cheap adverts, but intended to be reassuring to the elderly.

'Thora Hird. *She* must have made a packet. Don't suppose she knew what to do with it, at her age.'

'I wouldn't have any trouble,' I say.

Naomi fiddles with the brooch pinned to the collar of her blouse. 'I'm sorry to bother you. I always seem to be pouring out my troubles to you, don't I?' she says with a tight laugh.

The woman's lonely, that much is obvious. If she weren't clearly so bedevilled by her worries she's the sort of person I should like as a friend. Why *is* she so nervous and uptight all the time?

'I received a letter, you see, and it's shaken me up terribly.'

The last thing I want to hear about is letters. I have no idea how to broach the subject of Antonia's long stay in Devon. Or even if I should mention it at all. It might be better to let sleeping dogs lie.

Naomi takes the offending letter from her handbag and passes it to me. The words have been constructed from letters clipped out of magazines and newspapers. My first reaction is to laugh. 'It's like something out of Agatha Christie,' I say.

The writer has typed the address on the envelope, so there are no clues there.

The message is short. Perhaps the writer got fed up with sticking each letter down. *I know what you did. From a well wisher.*

'Well wisher my foot!' I say with a snort. 'I wonder what it means?'

'I know I should have put it straight in the bin, but what if they send more?' Her hands are trembling, her gaze fixed on the paper.

I tear it up. 'There. People who write these things don't deserve to have any time wasted on them.'

'I know what this letter means,' she whispers.

'Don't talk rot. It's so vague it could mean absolutely anything. It's just some twisted person who wants to shake you up. Probably chose you at random because you live alone. Even so, if you get another one, you should report it to the police.'

'Yes, I should. Perhaps there won't be any more.' Her fingers tug the brooch. She's in danger of ripping the thin material of her blouse.

'It's a cowardly thing to do. Whoever did it must be a bitter, spiteful individual.'

Naomi abandons her brooch and clasps her hands together in her lap.

'Would you like a cup of tea? Or something a bit stronger?'

'Yes, I would like a cup of tea. Perhaps a small nip of sherry, just to settle my nerves. I don't normally drink...' She takes a deep breath. 'That's the worst of living alone. When something like this happens, you do feel very vulnerable.'

I slip out to the kitchen and make tea, adding an extra spoonful of sugar to Naomi's cup as well as the splash of sherry. She looks as if she could do with it.

When I return to the living room bearing the tray, I find Naomi standing at the window, palms pressed against the glass.

'Where's Antonia?' she asks. 'Is she still in hospital?'

'In bed. She's still feeling a little fragile.'

'Oh?' Naomi turns, her gaze sliding between me and the tray. 'No broken bones, though?'

'Just a nasty bump on the head.'

Naomi's shoulders sag. She slumps onto a chair and

lays a hand on her forehead. 'I do apologise. I don't know what's got into me. Do you ever feel that no matter what you do, the past will never let you go?'

I sip my tea. 'Sometimes we have to make the effort to let it go.'

'But what if other people won't let you? If they insist on constantly reminding you? Oh, God, if only they hadn't found that body!'

'But it's not Brian, is it? You said the police are certain about that.'

'They are, yes, but… an anonymous tip-off and now a poison pen letter. Someone's determined to stir up trouble for me.'

'But why would they?'

'Antonia,' she whispers. 'You might have told her, and she… she's never liked me.'

'You think *she* wrote the letter and phoned the police?'

'Why not? She's hardly a saint, is she?'

'She's my sister,' I say. It's my job to defend Antonia, even though I admit to myself it's possible she could have phoned the police in a moment of madness. But she couldn't have sent the letter. It bears a first class stamp, so it must have been posted yesterday, when Antonia was in hospital.

'Oh, God, I'm sorry. Of course she's your sister, your own flesh and blood. What must you think of me?'

'Please, Naomi, don't give it another thought. You're clearly very upset.'

'Yes, I am.' Naomi picks up her tea cup and takes a sip, her hand still trembling.

Can it be that Naomi has got herself into such a stew

simply at the thought of people in the village gossiping about her? I know how people talk, and Naomi produced a great deal of fodder for the rumour mill; but how many people even remember Brian? And of those who do, how many of them are likely to think badly of Naomi simply for being married to a rogue? If anything, people will sympathise with her.

Although Naomi and I have lived in the same village all our lives, I've spoken more to her in the last couple of weeks than in the previous sixty years. However, despite the fact that we were never on intimate terms, working in the shop I heard the gossip about Naomi's husband, the insinuations that Brian was having an affair. Customers whispered about seeing Naomi with a black eye. In passing I mentioned this to Vera Dodson, who still owned the shop at that time. 'I'm not interested in gossip,' she said, cutting me off. But later, over a cup of tea, she apologised for snapping and told me that Naomi had enough on her plate, though she refused to elaborate.

Naomi sets down her cup. She stares at her hands as she pulls on cotton gloves the weather doesn't warrant. I can't help thinking of Frances Cornford's poem, "To a Fat Lady Seen from the Train". She isn't fat, but nobody loves her.

'I apologise for intruding upon your time and for behaving so appallingly. And I'm sorry about Antonia. I hope she feels better soon.'

Confused by Naomi's sudden change in mood, I nod, and stand to show her to the front door.

'Goodbye, Naomi,' I call after her, but she keeps on walking.

I, too, wish the body in the quarry had never been found. I'm not generally superstitious, but I can't help feeling that all the unpleasant things that have been happening lately stem directly from the disturbance to those old bones that must have lain there for years, troubling no one.

26

NAOMI

Naomi sits in her rocking chair, the wooden rockers creaking back and forth. She could kick herself for going off at the deep end with Diana. In her overwrought state, she sees enemies everywhere. With everything preying on her mind, it's hard to behave normally. She can hardly remember what "normal" is, what it feels like. The texture of her life has always been bumpy, like a sort of rough tweed. Now, though, she feels as if it has a quality more like barbed wire. Everything feels like an effort, something sinister always lurking just out of sight, waiting to ambush her.

Slowly but deliberately she unpicks the row of stitches she has made to the hem of a skirt. Her tears fall unchecked, her mouth gaping. The deputy librarian has "strongly advised" her to take some sick leave. She daren't, she's sure it's the council's way of trying to edge her out, make her feel she's no use anymore at the one thing that has always been her fixed point, the one thing she knew she could do, where she understood her role, where she never made mistakes. Oh, the odd minor mistake, but nothing vital, nothing that mattered.

I know what you did... But what does the anonymous writer know?

She took time off work when Brian blacked her eye. He wasn't a violent man as a rule. He had a temper, he could shout and swear for England, but physical intimidation wasn't his way. It was her own fault, for goading him, going on about Nigel after he found all the mementoes she thought she'd hidden so carefully. He cried afterwards, said he'd rather have punched the wall and broken his hand than harmed her. She believed him. It was the only time he ever hurt her physically.

How stupid she had been, to imagine that Brian would slot neatly into her life. To imagine that was what she wanted. She'd wanted a child, before it was too late, but that hadn't happened, either. All for nothing. All for the sake of being able to tell Nigel and Melanie she was married, they weren't to pity her anymore, she had someone of her own.

He chose *me*, she thinks; he *chose* me. She liked knowing that she could appeal to such a man: her, with her cardigans and her easy-iron skirts and her short, neat fingernails. He never had a regular job, but you couldn't really call him work-shy. Routines bored him. Staying strictly within the law bored him. She disapproved of him, but she found it exciting, too, after having spent her whole life being so careful, so proud of her cherished respectability. Where had it got her, that's what she'd like to know? A good citizen, a churchgoer, very correct, polite, but oh, it was such a tame life, wasn't it, so humdrum?

They married in a register office and it didn't feel like a proper wedding. She'd married Nigel in a register office, too, but they'd been young, full of hope, defying their parents who said they should wait. 'They were right. We should have waited,' Nigel told her, sadly, on the day she packed up her few belongings. 'It's only a trial separation,' Naomi reminded him. He couldn't look her in the eye. It was over. She'd never again sit on their squashy sofa reading a book while Nigel leaned back, a gentle smile on his face, listening to Brahms or Chopin or Schubert.

Naomi rethreads her needle and wishes Brian could have suffered as much as she has. She's tried to be a good Christian, but it hasn't always been easy. She reaches for a tissue to wipe away her tears. Some people, she tells herself, simply aren't meant to marry.

27

DIANA

The first thing Antonia does when she feels strong enough to venture downstairs is to head for the kitchen. I hope she won't be too cross when she sees how much stuff I've chucked out.

'What *have* you been up to, Diana?' she says, opening cupboard doors.

'They were old. Years past their best before dates, some of them.'

'Cans don't go off,' she snaps. 'They put any old date on them, just for something to put.'

I suppress a smile. 'Nothing keeps forever.'

'And you ate the cooking chocolate. Can't I leave you on your own for a minute without you getting up to mischief?'

I know she's not really cross. Hospital frightened her, brought her face to face with her own mortality. I saw the fear in her eyes when she was discharged, her lower lip trembling as she told me the woman in the bed next to hers had died that morning, suddenly, having been admitted after a dizzy spell, or so she said. 'Laughing and joking, she was,' Antonia reported. 'Said she didn't know what the doctors were making all the fuss about, and if it was anything serious she would have been in one of those high dependency wards with machines and monitors and such.'

'I'm sorry,' I say to her now. 'It seemed like a good opportunity to do a spring clean.' I can't tell her that I hardly knew what to do with myself without her around. If I was like that after one day, what would I be like after a week, a month, a lifetime?

I've never known how to comfort Antonia. She sobs in front of the larder, a tin of fruit clutched against her bosom.

'Come and sit down.' I steer her into the living room. I attempt to prise the tin from her, but she won't let go.

She looks old, I think. *That's what hospitals do to people*.

'How would I manage if you went off to live on your own? Who'd look after me then?'

I feel like an unfaithful husband who's been debating whether or not to leave his sainted wife for a young floozy.

'Put that can down.' I try again, but she grips it even more tightly.

'Perhaps you *should* go. If you want to go, you should get on with it. Get it over with. Better to rip out a bad tooth than put up with the toothache.'

'We've been through all that. I'm not going.'

'Promise?' Her eyes are glassy with tears.

I try hard not to sigh. 'Promise.'

I set the table for lunch. Antonia has been out of hospital for two days and, although it's Sunday, she didn't feel like going to church. I'm rather surprised that Mr Fielding hasn't bothered to check up on her, now that she's a regular attender. No doubt he's had a bellyful of us and our troubles.

I've yet to broach the topic of the letters, or the dolls. I can't help feeling we should discuss these things, but have no idea how to introduce them without upsetting her. It's all water under the bridge, perhaps; but the existence of the dolls suggests otherwise. I have to assume they are some sort of child substitute, but how worried I ought to be perhaps depends on what happened to her baby. If there was a baby.

Antonia sits at the table while I lay out the cutlery, place mats, and bring in plates of ham and bread and a bowl of mixed salad.

I sit opposite Antonia. 'There, now. We really ought to eat in the garden while the weather's so good.' Our garden furniture isn't up to much. Just two white plastic chairs and a tiny fold-out table that wobbles.

Antonia helps herself to a slice of ham and a few bits of lettuce, then pushes the plate away.

'Not hungry?' I ask.

Antonia shakes her head. 'I rarely am, these days.'

I grab a slice of bread and tear it into small pieces. No one, it seems, will be eating any lunch today.

'You were always the *good* one,' I say. 'Mother often told me she wished I were more like you.' In view of what I suspect Antonia to have done, this is rather ironic. But a favourite child is always a favourite, however badly he or she behaves.

'And where did it get me, ever?' She wipes her hands on a napkin. 'If only...'

If only, if only, if only... How long will we continue to torture ourselves with those words? I stand and scrape the ham off Antonia's plate back onto the serving platter. 'I might as well clear everything away. Such a waste.'

'Oh, what does a bit of waste food matter? You never could see things in proportion.'

'What do you mean?' I stand still, cradling the bowl of salad.

'It's ridiculous, how you carry on. I bet you laughed, didn't you, when you found out what Gill had done to me, how she took Philip away from me? He was *mine*, I tell you! You and your wicked ways! And you wonder why I told Gillian's parents what I did!'

I run into the kitchen. Antonia follows me.

'That's right – have a crying fit, pretend *I'm* the one who's being beastly!'

'I'm not crying!' I spin around, the salad bowl flying from my hand and landing with a crash.

Antonia raises her hand as if to hit me.

I cover my face.

Antonia's hand pauses in mid-air, then drops back down to her side. 'I'm sorry,' she whispers. She plods back to the living room, leaving me to clear up the mess on the floor.

I shudder as I pick up the broken china and scattered salad items, collecting them in the dustpan. I'll have to vacuum to get rid of all the small shards. I sit back on my heels. We are getting nowhere. Antonia claims she can't manage without me, yet at the same time it seems she can hardly bear to be in the same house with me. I sniff and try to calm myself. We could both live for another twenty years or more. We have to find some way of getting along.

I haul myself to my feet, deposit the rubbish from the dustpan into the bin, and get out the vacuum cleaner. I'm aware that I'm crying, but the noise is lost in the high-pitched whine of the Electrolux.

Antonia's had a shock, I remind myself; she's still not feeling one hundred per cent. And I don't have too many regrets about the past, all told. Sometimes I wish I'd gone to university, but I might not have been any better off. I had the brains for higher study, but not the confidence. My father taught history in a private school for boys and he made it plain that he didn't have much time for educated women. He believed, as I think some men still do, that women will get married and have children and give up their careers.

It was he who encouraged me to work in Vera Dodson's wool shop. She managed it herself until a serious illness meant she had to give up work. Her assistant decided she didn't want to work with anyone but Miss Dodson and took early retirement. Miss Dodson cared about the shop, but she was realistic enough to realise it was losing money. Knitting has become quite trendy again, but when Vera fell ill it was considered an old woman's hobby, and old ladies tended not to spend the kind of money that would have kept the shop afloat.

I've never told anyone about the arrangement Vera and I came to so that the business could stay open. Not even Antonia knows that Vera gave the shop to me on condition that it reverts to her niece after my death. I have an income for as long as I want it, but I can never sell the shop. The flat above the shop, however, is mine; another small secret I've kept from Antonia. Vera gave the flat to me on condition that I did it up. All my savings vanished into that flat, but what does it matter? I rent it out, and when I finally retire I will sell it and use some of the money to take one of those grand holidays I've always promised myself, but never managed to get around to.

I switch off the vacuum cleaner and check on Antonia. I find her sitting serenely in the living room, as if the earlier scene hadn't occurred. I decide to leave her be and shut the door. The presence of the dolls upstairs, and Antonia's little peculiarities – the emotional outbursts, the mood swings – make me wonder if she's on the verge of another breakdown.

I wish I could be the kind of person able to listen to her sympathetically. I remember how Vera came round to the shop one day to collect the books and found me in tears.

She told me to sit down while she made me a cup of tea and supplied me with a large handkerchief. After I'd cried myself out, she asked me what was wrong.

'I think I'm doomed to be alone forever,' I told her. 'I meet people, but never anyone I could love.'

Miss Dodson shook her head. 'You wish to marry? You think you would be happy then?'

'No, not really. Not marriage.' I blew my nose and drank my tea, certain Miss Dodson wouldn't understand. She was too old, too much of a spinster to understand the particular pangs of my heart.

Now I wonder if Miss Dodson understood more than I gave her credit for. She was always a very self-sufficient person, content with her life. If she never married, it was because she didn't want to. I should go and visit her, I want to talk to her; to ask her how much she really understood, and to apologise for assuming she was too old to understand how I felt.

On Monday morning, Antonia tells me she doesn't want to come to town with me. I should be grateful, yet it disturbs me that Antonia no longer wants to follow our usual routine.

'Are you sure?'

'Not today. Feeling a bit peaky. But you go.'

I can't be bothered to take the bus into town, but once I've done my few bits of shopping at the Spar and called in to see Stella at the shop, I feel in need of a pick-me-up and wander along to the village café.

As I enter, I see Naomi sitting alone at a corner table with a drink and a biscuit. I think of her as being in that grey, ill-defined place between acquaintanceship and friendship.

I walk over to her. 'Hello, Naomi. I've not seen you in here before.'

She gives an apologetic smile. 'Sometimes it's hard to know what to do with myself on my days off. I get sick of staring at my own four walls.'

'I'll just get a cup of tea, then I'll sit with you, if I may?'

She nods.

'Shall I get you a refill?'

'Please. I'll pay, of course.'

At the counter, a surly girl with lank black hair and a spotty face fills an aluminium pot with teabags and water, then mumbles the amount due.

Carrying the tray carefully, I edge between the seats and sit at Naomi's table. 'Shall I pour?'

I'm aware of a couple of women at a nearby table staring at us. I smile at them; by far the best way of getting rid of that sort of attention. It doesn't work with the young, though; only with people of a certain age who've been brought up with some manners. Even if they forget them sometimes.

'What are they staring at?' I mutter to Naomi.

'Me, probably. They've been staring like that since I got here.' She dunks a biscuit in her tea. 'So, what have you been up to?'

'Very little.'

'And how is Antonia?'

'Driving me potty, if I'm honest. Snapping at me half the time, and sulking the rest.'

'She's become very dependent on you, hasn't she? Part of her probably begrudges that. I expect she goads you to see how much you're prepared to put up with.'

Naomi can be a perceptive woman. I put this down in part to the fact that she's educated, though perhaps this says more about the value I place on education than on her actual capabilities.

'I suppose, if I'm honest, I need her as much as she needs me.'

Naomi nods. 'You need friends, at our age. It's different, I think, when you have a family. Children, I mean.'

'Yes, quite.'

'Perhaps she needs more interests. Get her to come to the library.'

'She's not a big reader.' Other than the odd Georgette Heyer, I can't recall seeing her read anything but magazines since she was in her teens. She claims books make her head ache.

'A pity. Well, she has her knitting, I suppose...'

*

222

When I get home, I find Antonia in the garden, secateurs in one hand and a trug in the other.

I tiptoe through the long grass and stand beside her. 'Lovely roses,' I remark, pointing to a thorny bush. I bend down and carefully cup a fleshy rose. The smell always reminds me of stale water.

Antonia clips off a perfect flower. 'I know I shouldn't take it,' she admits, 'but it's so pretty. And it'd die whether it's on a bush or in a vase.'

'Fancy a bite of something?'

'All right.'

She sits at the dining room table while I prepare tea and a snack. She twirls the rose between thumb and forefinger and a couple of petals fall off.

'Here we are, then – oh, dear – your lovely flower!'

'It doesn't matter. Roses are shockers for dropping,' she says, clearing away the limp petals and chucking them into the grate.

'Are you all right?' I ask.

'Tired, that's all. I might go and lie down for a bit.'

'You haven't had your tea. I got you a snack, too.'

'Not now, thank you.'

I settle down to reread *Where Angels Fear to Tread*, but my mind wanders. I recall the first time I read *Maurice*, which Gill lent me. We didn't speak about the subject matter of the book, but when I handed it back after reading it, her smile suggested complicity.

'Did you like it?' she asked.

'I think it's beautiful.'

'He's rather good, Forster, isn't he?'

As I gaze at the cover of *Where Angels Fear to Tread*, which depicts a scene from the movie, I remember the first time Gill and I kissed. We'd been sitting under the shade of the trees on Minster Hill on a blistering July day. She wore jeans with a white cheesecloth blouse, her bra visible beneath the thin material. We lay beside each other and Gill took my hand. For a while we stayed like that, but after a minute or two she shuffled closer to me, till our shoulders touched.

'Diana,' she whispered.

I turned my head, so that I was face to face with her. As if we both had the same idea in mind, we leant forward until our lips touched. That first tentative kiss was as sweet as new grass. When we moved apart, Gill stroked my shoulder and kissed my throat, her hair tickling my chin. Afraid to break the spell, I kept my hands by my sides, perfectly still.

I shake my head and apply myself to the book, but images of Gill keep reappearing, coming between me and the pages. I remember the poems Gill used to write to me. It was only years later I discovered that the poems hadn't been her compositions at all; she must have copied them from obscure anthologies of long-forgotten minor poets. People don't write letters anymore, it's all emails and texts, but nothing beats the thrill of receiving a handwritten love letter.

I hear Antonia walking around upstairs. Have I truly forgiven her? I can only decide the matter by facing the most painful memory of them all.

Gill and I were lying on my bed, reading poetry to each other. Gill recited Juliet's first words to Romeo: 'If I profane with my unworthiest hand, This holy shrine, the gentle fine is this: My lips, two blushing pilgrims, ready stand, To smooth that rough touch with a tender kiss.'

Moved both by the sentiment and by Gill's lovely speaking voice, I rolled onto my side and touched her cheek. Without speaking, she untucked my blouse and undid the buttons before removing her own. Arms around each other, we kissed. We were locked in this embrace when Antonia burst into the room.

Antonia screamed. Mother came pounding upstairs to find Gill and I hurriedly dressing. Our faces must have announced our guilt.

'Get out!' Mother shouted at Gill. Then she glared at me and made me stay in my room for the rest of the day.

She wanted to draw a discreet veil over the incident, but Antonia insisted that Gill's parents should be told. When Mother showed no marked enthusiasm, Antonia took it upon herself to tell them.

I saw Gill only once after that, her parents allowing us the masochistic pleasure of saying goodbye to each other. I held out my arms, wanting to hug her, but she took a step back, giving me a cool smile.

'Mum says to pretend it never happened,' she said. 'I think that's the best way.'

At the time, I thought she was putting on a brave face, cowed by her parents into giving me up. Now, I suspect her coolness was entirely genuine. I gave her my gold chain to wear, to remember me by. It had belonged to my grandmother. I can't help but regret my sentimental gesture as I wonder what she did with the necklace. I'm almost minded to ask for it back, but that seems petty, and she will probably deny all knowledge of it.

28

NAOMI

Naomi glances at her watch. It's the first meeting of the Silversurfers today. The library has a full programme of activities for children, but Naomi's suggestion that they provide more for older people has been taken up with enthusiasm. Volunteers – a retired accountant and a younger man, recently made redundant and using his golden handshake to start his own business – will provide the computer expertise. She will supervise, and hand out tea and biscuits after the session.

She's made more of an effort than usual with her appearance, and she knows this is silly. The retired accountant is an attractive man, and a widower, and he reminds her of Nigel.

'Foolish woman,' she mutters, but her foolishness is forgotten when Jim-the-retired-accountant strides over to her before the session begins and engages her in conversation. They don't talk about anything significant, but it's nice to speak to a man who isn't a vicar or a police officer; a man who wants neither to introduce her to God nor catch her out. From the corner of her eye she can see two young volunteers whispering and giggling. She wishes she didn't immediately assume she is the source of their amusement. What does it matter? They are silly young women, the sort who coo over babies but seem unable to grasp the complexities of the Dewey system.

'Can't wait to get started,' Jim says.

'I don't know what skill levels they'll have. I hope you're patient.'

'It'll be fine. In my experience, older people are more computer-literate than we give them credit for. And I'm speaking as an older person myself.'

She wants to prolong the conversation, but it wouldn't do to make it obvious. She'll pretend she must get on. The silly women won't be able to accuse her of being needy if she's the one who ends her chat with Jim.

'Mustn't keep you from your work,' he says, before she has the chance to make her excuses.

'It's quite all right,' she finds herself saying. 'I don't have anything pressing to do.'

'Still, I'd better make sure everything is set up for the session.'

'Yes, of course.' She glares at the two young women, who are staring at her. It's a pity they have to rely on volunteers. Impossible to treat them like paid members of staff; instead one must pretend to be endlessly grateful to them for the few miserable hours they put in each week.

Ten people have signed up for the first Silversurfer session. She's assumed that most of them will want to learn how to Skype their grandchildren and order shopping online, but she knows it's wrong to make assumptions. Many of those attending could be younger than she is, which is a sobering thought.

Although she dressed with care today, she still looks dowdy. Why shouldn't she wear pretty clothes? In the staff room she finds a Boden catalogue, presumably belonging to one of the volunteers. She flicks through it, admiring the bright colours and pretty patterns. Unable to help herself, she rips out a page showing a beautiful wrap dress, turquoise with pink dots. It would look lovely with a little pink cardigan. She can't believe she'd have the nerve to wear such a dress, but she wants it anyway. She folds the page twice and slips it into her shopping bag. The dress costs nearly one hundred pounds, but after all, why not? What else does she spend her money on? Why shouldn't she?

A head peers around the door. 'Mrs Wilkinson? Just to let you know the surfers are all here.'

'Thank you.'

She isn't expected to participate, but she's curious to know the type of people who've come along today. It's her library, after all; not officially, of course, but she runs it, she keeps everything ticking along.

She waits half an hour before she shows her face. That will give everyone plenty of time to settle, once the initial introductions are made. It's a two-hour session, but very informal, and there's no timetable. Jim and Liam will be guided by the needs of the attendees.

'Hello, everyone,' she says, trying not to keep her eyes on Jim for too long. 'Everything all right?'

Everyone smiles at her. There are only two women, one of whom is vaguely familiar, but she can't put a name to her. Probably someone once seated next to her in the hair salon.

'Smashing,' Liam says. 'Everyone is doing really well.'

Naomi smirks as she notices one of the women rolling her eyes. 'I'll let you get on. Tea and biscuits at the end, so that's something to look forward to.' She's pleased that this earns a titter from one of the male participants, and a beaming smile from Jim.

She carries on with her regular duties, keeping an eye on the time. Tea and biscuits will be taken in the staff room, since drinks aren't allowed anywhere near the computers. They'll have to make do with Bourbons; they haven't the budget for fancy assortments. Still, a free biscuit is a free biscuit.

Jim and Liam lead the way once the session is over. They are accompanied by six of the attendees; the other four had prior engagements.

The woman Naomi thought she recognised is among those who wish to partake.

'I'm sorry there's no choice of biscuits,' Naomi says. She should have bought some out of her own money. Next time, she will.

'Everyone likes Bourbons,' Jim says, handing the tin around.

'You're wondering why you recognise me, aren't you?' the vaguely-familiar woman says.

'I expect our wire baskets have crossed in the supermarket.'

'You were married to Brian, weren't you?'

Naomi's stomach somersaults. Of course: that's why she recognises her. This woman with badly-dyed red hair was one of Brian's floozies. 'I was.'

'You're better off without him,' the woman says, taking a Bourbon from the tin. 'Sorry, but I speak as I find,' she adds, acknowledging the raised eyebrows. She steers Naomi towards the far corner of the room. 'I'm sorry if I embarrassed you,' she says.

'He was my husband. For all his faults.'

'Let sleeping dogs lie, eh?'

'What do you mean? You said you speak as you find.'

'Always thought it was funny, him being married to someone like you.'

'He wasn't very polished, it's true.'

'Polished! My God!'

'None of us is perfect,' Naomi says, edging away from the woman, who narrows her eyes and says, 'I wonder if you know what he was really like? Not good at taking no for an answer, our Brian.'

'Please don't say any more. I don't want to know!'

The woman grips her elbow. 'When I heard about that body being found, I hoped it was him. I won't be sorry if he's dead, not one little bit.'

'Please – leave me alone.'

The woman lets go. 'Poor cow,' she says. 'Be thankful you're shot of him, that's all I can say.'

Naomi pushes past Jim and the startled attendees. She must get some fresh air! That dreadful, common woman, her nasty insinuations.

She runs outside to the back of the building where there is a wooden bench. Whimpers as she sits down heavily, hugging herself. 'I hate you, Brian. I hate you, I hate you, I hate you.' No one will come to look for her; they'll assume she has one of her migraines. It's just as well, she thinks, because if someone showed concern for her now – one of her colleagues, Jim, that tart with the red hair – she would tell them everything. She shakes her head at the thought of Jim's startled expression and takes gulps of air as she tries to compose herself. Dull, dependable Naomi; nervy, can't take a joke, lives for her job.

That's who she is. She stands and makes sure her blouse is tucked in neatly before re-entering the library.

She finds the staff room empty apart from Jim and Liam. She's grateful that, despite their concerned smiles, neither of them ask her if she's all right.

'Everyone gone?' she says.

'Yes,' Jim says. 'They all enjoyed it. Wendy asked me to pass on her regards and to apologise if she upset you.'

'There was no need,' she says stiffly. 'I'm glad it was successful.'

'Till next time, then,' Jim says, placing the lid on the biscuit tin.

'Yes. Goodbye.' She walks smartly from the room. 'Haven't you anything to do?' she snaps at one of the volunteers.

The woman gazes at her blankly. 'I...'

'It creates a poor impression if staff are standing around idle, even if they're only volunteers.'

She will likely tell her friend what a bitch Naomi is. Naomi doesn't care. She can't stand pity, and that's what she read in Wendy's eyes, and in Jim's, and it makes her hate them.

29

DIANA

I'm on my way to the post office when I catch sight of Gill coming out of Challoner's. I slow down, not wanting to draw attention to myself, but Gill waves to me from across the road, so I feel justified in crossing over to talk to her.

'I'm trying to find something to take back for Ian, but I can't decide what he'd like. Do you know if there are any pottery shops around here? Ian is buying me the most beautiful oil painting from a gallery in Devon as a wedding gift; I'd like to get him a really nice piece of studio ceramics.'

'It must be a very exciting time,' I say. My voice sounds hollow as an Easter egg. Gill speaks of her forthcoming marriage as though it's an exciting adventure, like a midnight feast in a boarding school dormitory; and to her, no doubt, it is. For me, though, it's the end. I know I'll never see her again. All these years I've not seen her, but there was always the possibility that I *might*, and she's taking that away from me.

She sighs in what strikes me as a rather self-satisfied way.

'It *is* exciting, but it is a big step. Ian and I are both quite set in our ways, we shall both have to make compromises.'

I grasp hopefully at the suggestion of doubt in her voice. 'You sound like you're getting cold feet.'

'Not really. I think it's just that the enormity of what we're doing hasn't quite sunk in. It sort of sneaks up on me sometimes when I think about it. Anyway, I mustn't keep you from your errands.'

'Oh, I'm only taking this parcel to the post office. A dress Antonia ordered, but it doesn't fit.'

'Time for a coffee, then?'

Even now, I find it impossible to say no to Gill. Where she goes, I want to follow.

In the café, the tired décor strikes a gloomy note after the warmth and sunshine outside. We each grab a tray and queue, then sit at a table near a window. For a while we don't speak, as we deal with the business of setting out drinks and plates. Gill then takes both trays back to the counter.

I watch her walk back. She isn't looking at me, or at anyone in particular, and I resent the constant smile on her face, her serenity, the elegance of her beautifully-cut bob, the sophisticated pale pink silk blouse and tailored cream linen trousers. I feel slightly grubby in baggy trousers with an elasticated waistband and a checked shirt with a hole in one of the cuffs. Her snowy hair is far less ageing than my iron-grey crop.

I can't bring myself to ask her about Ian. I picture him as a thin, tall man, wearing pressed jeans and a Guernsey sweater. For all I know he's fat and red-faced, with bow legs, but even if he is, I wouldn't feel any better.

My biscuit sits untouched on my plate. Gill has eaten hers. 'Want mine?'

She slides my plate towards her. She eats my biscuit

then daintily wipes crumbs from the corners of her mouth.

'How is Antonia?' she asks. As if she cares!

'All right, I think.'

'I still think it's a pity she never married. It's what she wanted, isn't it? Why didn't she find someone else, if she wanted marriage and children so much?'

'She got it into her head that Philip was the love of her life.'

'How very silly of her.'

Anyone watching us would never believe all that we once were to each other. Just two women of uncertain years gossiping over coffee. What could be more banal? I almost start to wonder if I imagined the past.

'I can't help thinking it a shame,' I say, choosing my words carefully, as if each one were a hand grenade, 'that I'll possibly never see you again when we've only just renewed our acquaintance after so many years.'

'We can still send postcards and emails,' she says. Is she cold-hearted or simply thick-skinned?

'It's hardly the same as being able to chat over coffee, face to face.'

She frowns. 'Well, no.'

'I could come and visit you, perhaps. Once you've settled in.'

She gives a noncommittal smile, but I know she won't invite me to stay. I will never see her again – *never*. This gives me a boldness I've lacked up till now – I have nothing to lose, because soon I will have lost her forever. 'Did you ever think about me after you left Morevale?'

'Of course I did. You were my best friend, after all.' Her expression is guarded, her polite smile not reaching her eyes. If she fears I'm going to bring up the past in all its messy glory, she has only herself to blame for being so infuriatingly discreet.

'But – the rest – all we meant to each other, once... did you think about that at all?'

She touches the silver stud in her ear, her eyes darting from left to right. 'I'm not quite sure what you mean.'

'We *were* more than friends.'

I've gone too far. Her eyes have that steely look, and I know she's going to deny everything.

'You and me, Gill. Remember, how we lay side by side on top of Minster Hill?'

She raises her eyebrows. 'I remember a picnic, and you complaining that midges kept biting you, and you got upset because a bottle of ginger beer leaked and soaked your cardi.'

'But – don't you remember the rest?'

She looks genuinely perplexed. '*What* rest?'

'You kissed me.'

I don't recall the midges or the damp cardigan, only the sweet pressure of her lips on mine and thinking it the happiest moment of my life and wanting to freeze it, for us to stay like that forever, the moment fixed in time.

She doesn't reply, and the pause in conversation extends until I become self-conscious about breaking it. In an attempt to mask my nervousness, I take small sips of my drink, while Gill gazes around the café with an abstracted smile on her face.

Gill shakes her head slowly. 'I think you must have mixed me up with someone else.'

How can she be so unkind, so cold? 'You don't remember Antonia finding us together in my bedroom, and her telling your parents, and them saying we couldn't see each other again?'

'We left Morevale because Dad got a better job, in Wales.'

'But—'

She pats my hand. 'Don't apologise. Sometimes what we think happened is only what we *wanted* to happen.'

'No.' I shake my head violently. 'No, I won't have it!'

Gill glances at the people sitting at the table opposite. 'Don't upset yourself,' she tells me in a repressive tone.

'I'm sorry if I'm embarrassing you, but I must clear the air.'

She sighs and leans back in her seat, grabbing the strap of her handbag.

'No – please don't go!'

'I think I must if you're going to be hysterical.'

I lay my hands flat on the cold table, feeling dizzy, the world shifting beneath my feet. 'Please.' My voice comes out as a whisper.

'We were friends. I was very fond of you, but – well, I must be brutal, it seems – leaving Morevale was no great wrench for me.'

'All these years – I've loved you.'

Gill clicks her tongue. 'This is hardly an appropriate conversation.' With quick, irritated movements, she slides out of her seat and hurries to the door, the heels of her cream-coloured court shoes ringing on the floor tiles.

I follow her, as I'm sure she knew I would. 'Gill!'

She speeds up, but I catch her easily and we fall into step near the church.

Repugnance distorts her features. 'Please leave me alone,' she says.

'I can't – not until I've said my piece.'

She snorts.

'Let's sit down.' I lead her over to a wooden bench outside the church. I sit and wait for her to do the same. Once she's seated, I take a deep breath. 'Remember when you lent me your copy of *Maurice*?'

'*Did* I?' She sits with her legs pressed together, clutching the handbag that sits on her lap.

'Yes, you did. Oh, I know you'd never acknowledge our relationship and exactly what we meant to each other, but that book told me you understood.'

'Understood what, precisely?'

'That you and I – that we loved – that we were lovers.'

She gazes at me, her expression shocked, her eyes wide. 'Lovers?'

For the first time, I believe I really have misremembered the past, that I only dreamed what happened between us. Her shock seems so entirely genuine.

We look out over the graveyard, the proximity of memorials to the dead a sobering reminder that all lives are short. Many of my ancestors were lucky to make their fiftieth birthday. Even a person who lives long enough to get a telegram from the Queen has lived but a brief moment. One hundred years. That's nothing.

'What are you thinking?' Gill asks.

'That the greatest human tragedy is our ability to comprehend the fact that one day we will die.'

'How morbid.'

'Why don't you remember, Gill?'

'Because there's nothing *to* remember. You were my friend, nothing more. When we went to Wales, I made new friends. I married.'

'Yes, I know—'

'I'm not homophobic, and it's true that I have read and enjoyed *Maurice*, but I've only ever been attracted to men.'

I shake my head, unable to comprehend what she's saying. 'All I wanted from you was an acknowledgement; just for you to say it all happened as I say it did.'

Her expression softens. 'But it didn't. I can see how upset you are, and that pains me, but I can't give you what you want.'

Stubbornly, I feel if I pester her for long enough, eventually she'll give in. I yearn to take her hand in mine and reminisce about our shared past, but she's colder than the stone angels standing guard over the old graves.

'Let it go,' she says softly. 'I told you a lie when I said I removed my wedding ring because of a dog bite. I took it off and reverted to my maiden name because that part of my life was over.'

'Why would you lie about it?'

'Because...' She sighs. 'I didn't want you to know that my marriage wasn't entirely happy. You would have asked questions, wanted to know too much. I prefer not to talk about it, that's all.'

'Did you throw it away?'

She laughs. 'I'm not *that* callous. No, it's in a jewellery box.'

'I wish we understood each other.'

She shrugs. 'What do you expect me to say? The past you remember is not the one I lived.'

I bite my lip. I feel sure, now, that she knows as well as I do, but refuses to accept the truth. 'We went to the cinema once, and we had our only row, because you flirted with a boy.'

Gill gives a short, irritated sigh. 'I remember going to the pictures with you, and we argued... well, I don't remember exactly why, but it was over something stupid and trivial, nothing to do with any boy.'

'I have photos, of you and me together.'

'Of course you do. What do *they* prove?'

'Can't you just...' I raise my hands, helpless in the face of her denials. I feel as if someone has taken a photo of us and ripped it down the middle. Does she still have pictures of me? Has she mentioned me to Ian? She's made it clear enough she has no use for the past, and I feel the pointlessness of my need to hold on to it.

'Humour you? No, I won't do that. If you're going to keep repeating the same things, I might as well go.' She stands and gazes down at me. 'Goodbye, Diana.'

I watch her march smartly down the gravel path without so much as a glance back. She did a good job of making me doubt my memories, but something has in any case changed. My memories are tainted. I can never think of our times together with the same happy glow and must draw a curtain over the past, which she has spoilt forever.

Is this, then, "closure"?

I return home to find Antonia eating a slice of fruit cake. She's scattered crumbs all over the carpet.

'What a mess,' I mutter, handing to her the magazine she asked me to get.

'I'll see to it. Don't fuss.'

'No, *I'll* do it.' I get out the carpet sweeper and clear up the crumbs.

Antonia glares at me when the sweeper knocks against her ankle. 'I said I'd do it.'

I thrust the sweeper back into the pantry, unsure if I'm more annoyed that she ate the cake or that she made a mess. Most of all I'm annoyed with myself for making a fuss over nothing.

'I'm going to clear out the rest of Mother's things.' After she died, I left her bedroom more or less as it was. I rarely enter the room except occasionally to dust. I've never needed the room for any other purpose, and it seemed easier simply to shut the door and ignore it. But it really won't do.

'I like to see her things in her room,' Antonia says. 'It's a comfort.'

'Don't be childish.'

Nevertheless, I experience a frisson of naughtiness as I rummage through Mother's personal items. She was a modest, private person and no one was allowed to touch anything of hers while she was alive. I collect the detritus together, throw the junk into a bin liner and put the good stuff to one side (silver hairbrush and mirror, silk scarves, a set of pearl buttons still on the card: a meagre assortment of treasure).

'What have you got there, Diana?' Antonia asks when I bring the bin liner downstairs.

'Mother's bits and pieces. Her catarrh inhaler and Friar's Balsam. All the rubbish out of her drawers. Just look at it, and all these ancient boiled sweets and... and all this hair. Disgusting!'

Later, Antonia brings in a tray of refreshments. She lifts the woolly cosy from the teapot and gives the tea a stir. She's brought out a plate of chocolate Hobnobs, though the plate is chipped and lacks a doily. Not that it matters, but it's evidence of how far our standards have slipped.

She removes her pinny and folds it on the arm of the chair before settling herself like a hen getting comfy on its nest. 'What brought this tidying fit on, then?' she asks. 'You've waited ten years to get rid of Mother's things, so why now?'

'I'm like you, Antonia; I have difficulty in letting things go.'

'Like Gillian, you mean?'

'Like Philip,' I retort.

She glares at me, tight-lipped.

I decide to tell her about Naomi's poison pen letter and see how she reacts.

'People who send those things want the attention,' Antonia says. 'If everyone just threw them away and never discussed them, she'd get bored and stop.'

'She?' I say.

'The name says it all,' she says. 'Poison pen, I mean. Poison is supposed to be the woman's weapon, isn't it? Historically, I mean.'

'Lucrezia Borgia and all those Victorian matrons cheerfully bumping off their husbands.'

'I don't think they were particularly cheerful, else they wouldn't have wanted to murder their husbands.'

'But who could have sent her such a thing?'

'Some prank played by a teenager, I expect. Some of them, well, they're into all this heavy metal music and Satanism, aren't they?'

'I think you're a little behind the times, dear.'

'Oh, I don't know, then. Why should I?'

'You don't like Naomi, do you?'

'I don't like a lot of people. Do you think *I* sent it, is that what you're getting at? I didn't.'

'No, of course you didn't. You were tucked up in hospital.'

'And that's the only reason you believe it wasn't me? That's nice, I must say.'

'Antonia...'

'Don't "Antonia" me!' She grabs her knitting, the needles clashing as she works another row.

'Be careful, Antonia – your wool's caught on the chair leg.'

'What?' In her fury, she yanks the wool and the stitches tumble from the needle. 'Oh, *blast* it.'

'Can't you put it back on the needle?'

'It's not as simple as that!'

'Let me help.'

'Leave it be. You'll only make matters worse. You're too soft; always were,' she says.

'Soft? You're forever telling me how unkind I am.'

'Anyway, I didn't send that poison pen letter. Forty-odd years ago I might have done such a thing, but not now. Why would I? She hasn't had much of a life.'

Antonia the magnanimous. 'And the anonymous tip-off to the police? I suppose that wasn't you, either.'

She pokes her knitting needles into the mangled ball of wool. 'Think what you like,' she mutters.

'I see.'

'Yes, I expect you do.' She looks me in the eye. 'What do you intend to do about it?'

'Nothing, of course. I don't approve of eavesdropping.'

'I'm not going to say I'm sorry. I did it for you.'

'I know.'

'You won't tell Naomi?'

'Since the body wasn't Brian's, I don't see much point.'

'I'm sorry it wasn't Brian,' Antonia says. 'He was a horrible man.'

'How do you know? You were living in Ipswich, weren't you?'

'I saw him sometimes when I came home to visit. He leered.'

Poor Naomi, who'd put up with five years of leering. "Not as such" she'd said when I asked her if she killed him. Perhaps she'd wished him dead; murdered him in her heart. After all, what else could she have meant?

30

NAOMI

Naomi remains convinced that Antonia is responsible for the poison pen letter. Antonia might not be much of a reader, but she likes the telly, and might well have seen the Joan Hickson dramatisation of Agatha Christie's *The Moving Finger*. How dare anyone point the finger at her? She is not the only person who has sinned, and at least she has the decency to regret what happened to Brian.

She remembers being in the hair salon and overhearing Antonia telling her stylist her theories about Brian's disappearance. 'I'll bet you anything he's left her for another woman, but she's too proud to say so. He's not my cup of tea at all, of course, but at least he had a bit of life in him.'

The stylist nodded sagely as she brushed dye onto Antonia's hair. There must have been plenty of decent stylists in Ipswich, but she always visited the village salon whenever she paid one of her brief visits home. Showing off, Naomi always thought; boasting about her responsible job, her marvellous girls, the prestigious school at which she taught. It was a bit rich. Antonia taught sewing and cooking to a bunch of spoiled young madams, not a proper academic subject.

'Everyone knows about Brian's little indiscretions, don't they?' Antonia continued, not even trying to keep her voice down. She must have seen Naomi was there, must have noticed the woman cutting Naomi's hair glancing nervously at her client in the mirror as she snipped.

Antonia's stylist cast a nervous glance around the room and caught Naomi's eye. 'Best not jump to conclusions,' she said.

'People will, though,' Antonia said. 'You've missed a bit, dear,' she added, pointing to her head with a red-taloned finger.

Once her own hair was done, Naomi walked past Antonia's chair. Antonia didn't even blink, let alone give any indication of embarrassment. She must have known her voice was loud enough to carry throughout the salon. She simply didn't care.

Naomi, better than anyone, knows Antonia has nothing to feel superior about. One day she was sitting at the kitchen table, studying, when Antonia's mother came round to see hers. All in a tizzy, Mrs Littlehales stood in the kitchen and spewed out a garbled story about Antonia being in some sort of trouble.

Naomi bent over her books, but her attention was all on Mrs Littlehales.

'Calm down and tell me what's wrong,' Naomi's mother said, leading her over to a chair in front of the range.

Mrs Littlehales took a gulp of air and began again. 'Antonia's in trouble and we don't know what to do.'

Naomi's mother shushed the woman and glanced towards Naomi, who immediately began to scribble in her notebook as if oblivious to their conversation.

The women spoke in hushed tones, but Naomi's hearing was sharp enough to catch the gist of what they said.

'Philip's a good boy, surely he'll do the right thing?' Naomi's mother said.

Mrs Littlehales shook her head. 'His parents won't have it that the baby is his. You can imagine how Edward took *that*.'

'Oh, men take these things very much to heart. All they can think about is how their daughter's reputation has been sullied. They don't consider the practicalities.'

'But that's just *it*!' Mrs Littlehales said. 'What should we do? She can't possibly have a baby, not if she can't get married.'

Naomi's mother cleared her throat. 'Naomi, dear,' she said, 'why don't you go and study in your room?'

Naomi left without demur. She'd already heard enough, and when she later learnt that Antonia had gone for a lengthy visit to family friends in Devon, she drew her own conclusions. Antonia wouldn't have been the first girl to be packed off by her parents to have a baby in secret and for it then to be quietly adopted.

When Antonia returned from Devon, Naomi tried to speak to her and ask how her holiday had gone, hoping Antonia's superiority might have been worn away by her experiences, but Antonia gave her a look so cold it could have frozen water.

'What's it to *you*?' Antonia asked.

Her face hot, Naomi said, 'You were away a long time. Your mother said you were ill.'

'I'm quite well now, thank you,' Antonia snapped. 'And in future I'll thank you to keep your nose out of my business.' She turned on her heel and flounced off.

Naomi stared after her, mouth hanging open. The cheek of the girl! Still giving herself airs and graces. She ran up to Antonia and grabbed her arm. 'I know,' she said. 'I know why you were away for so long. I heard our mothers talking. The baby—'

The colour drained from Antonia's face. 'How dare you? Take your hands off me!'

'I only want to help.'

'I don't need anyone's help, least of all yours. And I'll thank you to keep your disgusting lies to yourself in future.'

Naomi's eyes narrow as she remembers that scene and her anger at being spoken down to by a girl who'd been so wicked.

At five o'clock Naomi makes her way home from work. Nearing her house, she sees her neighbour trimming a shrub in her garden. Walking on, Naomi nods in greeting, but Mrs Fisk rushes over to her. 'Heard you've had one of them nasty poison pen letters. Such a terrible thing. Have you told the police? You should, you know.'

'I threw it away,' she says, wondering how Mrs Fisk knows about it. No point asking; part and parcel of living in a village.

'I can't say as I blame you. Not that I know exactly what it said, of course, but who'd want to show that type of thing to anyone else? Best to forget all about it, dear.'

'I suppose so, yes.'

Mrs Fisk shakes her head, her expression mournful. 'This used to be a nice area when I was a girl.'

'People these days have no respect.'

'And no morals,' Mrs Fisk adds. 'Anyway, I must crack on. Nice to see you.'

Typical. The woman doesn't speak to her from one year's end to the next, but people like her can sniff out gossip and dirt. She wanted to know what was in the letter and why she was singled out. Naomi's damned if she'll tell anyone. Unlike Antonia, she can keep other people's secrets as well as her own.

After she'd received such a terse response to her enquiry after Antonia's health, Naomi confided in her mother that she'd heard her talking to Mrs Littlehales, so she might as well tell her the rest, mightn't she?

'Oh, Naomi – you shouldn't have eavesdropped.'

'I couldn't help it. I wasn't *trying* to listen.'

'No. Well. You must never tell a soul, d'you hear me? The poor girl has been through enough.'

Naomi pretended to feel sympathy for Antonia, otherwise her mother would have refused to tell her anything more. 'At least she can still go to university,' she said. 'She can put it all behind her then, can't she?'

Thinking back, Naomi remembered Antonia coming to school wearing a baggy jumper, even on days when it was warm enough for short sleeves. And always missing PE lessons with one excuse after another.

'I suppose it's been adopted, has it?' Naomi said.

'I haven't spoken to Mrs Littlehales since that day when she came to see me. Embarrassed, I expect. Can't say I blame her.'

'I wonder if she had a boy or a girl?'

'Oh, Naomi – what does it matter? She'll carry that with her for the rest of her life. It's not something you can just forget.'

'No, I suppose not.'

'Naomi, whatever you do, promise me... At least...'

'It'll never happen to me,' Naomi said. 'I'm not as stupid as her.'

Age has gone some way towards mellowing her antipathy towards Antonia, although the call to the police and the poisonous letter have made her think that Antonia hasn't really changed at all. Antonia has never shown any humility, no empathy with other people. If only Naomi had had a child of her own. If Nigel hadn't divorced her. If—

Oh, the past; the stupid past that makes no sense. She opens a tin of new potatoes and a tin of tuna. Heats the potatoes in a saucepan. Takes a slice of bread from the packet and spreads it with butter. Sits at the table. Pours herself a small glass of whisky. Forces herself to eat, tries not to cry.

The house is always cold, always empty; always somewhere she doesn't want to be, and the only place where she feels safe.

31

ANTONIA

Antonia understands why people might think she sent that horrid letter to Naomi, but it's true what she told Diana, it's not a thing she would ever lower herself to do, not these days. She hates Naomi for knowing about the baby, blames everyone for poking their noses in, for involving themselves in something that was between her and Philip, but she knows that's unfair. She lost him with no help from anyone else. She pleaded with him to marry her, begged him. He was horrified, physically backing away from her, afraid of her messy fertility, blaming her.

'It doesn't have to spoil our lives,' she told him, aware of what a sight she was, her eyes red and puffy.

'But it will,' he said. 'We're not stupid people. It would be tragic if we couldn't go to university. I want to make something of myself.'

'Can't you make something of yourself with me? Can't we, together...' She tailed off. He was shaking his head. As far as he was concerned, there was nothing to discuss.

Vividly she remembers sitting down with Philip and his parents in their plush living room, the soft cushions, the deep-pile carpet, the family photos in silver frames ranged around the room. A room that smelled of money and privilege. Philip's mother in a floaty silk and chiffon dress, fur-trimmed mules on her feet. Philip's father standing with one hand resting on the black baby grand piano polished to a glassy shine.

'We want what's best for both of you,' Philip's dad told her. 'You're only sixteen. You could ruin the whole of your lives.'

His mother nodded. She was holding a tall thin glass of gin and tonic. Antonia could see the smeared imprint of her chalky pink lipstick on the glass.

'We'll pay for the very best care,' Mr Belmont said.

Antonia felt the tears spilling down her cheeks. She was being given no choice. Philip was no use at all. He sat next to his mother, staring at the carpet.

'We're not *angry*,' Mrs Belmont said, 'just disappointed. You're both bright enough to have had more sense.'

Antonia's father drove her all the way to Devon. On the journey, he didn't speak one single word to her. When she got out of the car, he stared blankly ahead. He didn't get the suitcases out of the boot for her.

She was told never to speak of it to anyone, even Diana. Antonia knew she would always be her father's favourite, but he struggled to look her in the eye after that, even when she graduated and he told her he was proud of her.

She was proud of herself, too, and again when she landed a job at a private girls' school, but she wasn't a natural teacher. Her subjects weren't considered to be of much importance even by the other teachers. Even physical education was taken more seriously. Domestic science, later rebranded as home economics. "Training for housewives" as one physics teacher dismissed it. Antonia swallowed, smiled, said everyone should know basic cookery and how to sew on a button, but in her heart she knew she'd made a mistake. Miserable and browbeaten she persisted, never allowing herself to confide in her parents or in Diana how foolish she felt, how she allowed herself to be manipulated by her pupils. Worse, the girls saw how other teachers treated her, how they made fun of her, belittled her.

She shared a small house with another teacher, who taught Latin. She was a sensible woman who told Antonia that children were no better than a pack of wolves, and like wild animals they could smell fear. 'And you stink of it,' she told Antonia, who wept. Her friend plied her with cheap wine, told her to buck up, that teaching was kill or be killed. She gave her advice on class management and for a while things got a little better. She managed to get through some days without once retreating to the staff toilets to weep, but she still felt that tightness in her chest every Monday morning, a sense of dread, a wish to pretend to be ill so she could have one more day of peace.

In hindsight she is sure the girls were working up to something, that something being to push Antonia over the edge. 'Why don't they like me?' she asked her friend. 'I never shout at them, I don't mock them when their work is poor.'

'That's not the way it works, as you well know.'

She did. Some of the most respected, most admired teachers were those who pushed the girls to their limits, who reduced the more sensitive ones to tears.

She's never tried to make excuses for what happened, but she had only just recovered from a particularly nasty bout of flu and hadn't eaten properly in days, weeks even. She should have talked to someone, but pastoral care wasn't really a thing at that school, for teachers or pupils.

It was so stupid, too, the silly words on the whiteboard that had caused her to flip. *Miss L is a sour-faced old virgin, hands up if you agree!* Typical girlish adolescent nonsense. She should have rubbed it out, said nothing, raised an eyebrow, given them a withering glance. She got as far as picking up the cloth, but when she saw her hands shaking she spun around, picked up a marker pen and threw it wildly, aiming at all of them, all those stupid ignorant girls who hated her. Well, she hated them, too. 'You're all vile!' she screamed. 'Vile, hateful, ignorant little bitches!' Then she stormed out of the classroom, feeling much better. She left the building, walked across the playground onto the field. Then she didn't know what to do with herself. She wanted to sit in a pub, smoke and get drunk. She couldn't just walk out, could she? But it was all over anyway, wasn't it? She'd lost control. She could never face any of those girls again.

No one came to look for her. What had happened to her class? Were they still sitting there, cowed from her outburst, or had they shrugged, walked out, laughing at their victory?

Antonia walked back into the building and knocked on the door of the headmistress's room. She must have heard by now what had happened.

'Come!'

Antonia opened the door, saw from the headmistress's face that she did know all about it. Antonia felt her eyes fill with tears as the headmistress told her that the marker pen had hit a girl on the head, just a glancing blow, but there would be repercussions. They couldn't allow that sort of thing in the school.

'I understand,' Antonia murmured.

She would be granted sick leave until the end of term, which was very generous, as the headmistress pointed out.

'And after that...' There was no point finishing the sentence. The headmistress was shaking her head in a sad, disappointed way.

The end of the road; the end of her teaching career; the end of everything.

'I do appreciate the difficulties you've had,' said the headmistress. 'And I know some of the girls can be troublesome. But.'

Yes; but.

Antonia's friend said she'd miss her, but it was probably for the best. She had already found someone to replace Antonia in the house they shared.

'You'll keep in touch, won't you?'

'Course I will.'

She hadn't, of course. Out of sight, out of mind.

She'd sobbed during most of the long train journey home. She couldn't bring herself to tell Diana exactly what had happened. At some point Diana must have realised that she'd lost her job, but nothing was said. Even now, she's aware of term dates, of the waxing and waning of the school year. The particular rhythm of the academic year is in her bones. She wishes it were otherwise, but it has defined her life.

She was forty years old when she bought her first doll. It wasn't even for her; she'd bought it ready to give to one of her younger colleagues, who'd just returned to the school after her maternity leave. They were throwing a little party for her in the staff room after lessons ended, but, for reasons she can't now recall, Antonia was unable to go, and the next day the two women had a minor argument. After that it never seemed to be the right time to give the doll to her, so she kept it.

It wasn't even a very nice doll, but making clothes for it gave her something to do in the evenings, and gradually she grew fond of it, gave it a name, invested it with a personality. She never meant to buy any more, but every time she sees dolls on shop shelves she feels as if they are waiting for her to rescue them. They don't want to be given to rough children who will cut off all their hair and lose their clothes. She ought to know how thoughtless children can be, after what happened to Diana's old doll.

Collecting them is no stranger than collecting stamps or snuffboxes. She would like to have them all out on display, but she knows Diana wouldn't understand. Diana would think Antonia sees them as baby substitutes, that she thinks she's their mother. That would, of course, be mad. Antonia isn't mad. She knows the dolls aren't real people. But they're so realistic, some of them, with pearly pink fingernails, eyes that open and close, perfect little teeth. They like being clean and tidy, so she regularly dusts their patent leather shoes, gives their hair a tender brush, uses a damp cloth to wipe their faces. It's not mad, it simply shows how well she looks after them. Their faces show their contentment, their approval.

She couldn't explain to Diana how much joy they give her, and it's such a harmless thing. It's not as if she's a secret drinker. The dolls bring her comfort. They depend on her. When she's asleep, she can feel their gentle breath, sense their gratitude and affection. They aren't people but they're real, to her they're real, and they ask for nothing except to exist.

32

DIANA

Almost as soon as I get in, the phone rings. 'Hello?'

'Diana? It's Gill.'

I take a sharp breath and sit down.

'Sorry if it's a shock, but I felt I owed it to you to let you know that I've left Morevale. I thought you might not answer if I rang your mobile and you saw my number.'

'I see.' I'm irritated that she felt the need to phone, yet at the same time glad to know for certain that she's gone and will never come back.

'I expect you hate me now, don't you?' she says.

I could never hate her, but my feelings for her are too complicated to express in simple terms.

'Diana? Are you still there?'

'Yes, I'm here.'

'Since we're unlikely ever to see each other again, and I can't see the look on your face, I want to apologise. I'm too much of a coward to admit to certain things, even to myself. And... I couldn't possibly tell Ian, you see. I can't take that risk.'

I should feel relieved that I didn't imagine it, but I'm overwhelmed by a sense of betrayal. Why couldn't she tell me any of this to my face? I don't understand her.

'Why did you come back?' I ask. 'You must have

257

known that I would – that I might – that...' I can't put it into words. She knows what I mean, surely?

'I know. And I wanted to talk about old times – properly, I mean. But when I saw you in the flesh, so to speak, I couldn't cope with it.'

'So why didn't you leave after that? Why did you stick around?'

'I wanted – I thought – I don't know.' She sighs heavily. 'I'm not the person I was then. What happened between us shouldn't have. It wasn't—'

'You're ashamed.'

'No! It's not that, really it isn't... I'm not who you thought I was.'

That much I have managed to work out for myself. 'You never loved me, did you?'

'It wasn't like that for me.'

A phase; an experiment; exactly as Antonia implied.

'I'm so sorry,' she says.

I hang up, replacing the receiver gently, without saying goodbye. The done thing would be to have wished her good luck in her new life, but the words would have choked me. I *don't* want to wish her luck. If that makes me sound childish, so be it.

Much later that same day, when I'm getting ready for bed, the phone rings again. I'm sure it's Gill, but I steel myself not to answer. The next morning I dial 1471. It *was* Gill, and this leaves me feeling both spitefully gratified (she needn't think I'll still come running whenever she wants) and also bereft (she's gone forever; she won't phone again).

'Are you all right?' Antonia asks.

I open my mouth to say something bright, but instead I burst into tears. I tell her about Gill's phone call.

258

She pats my shoulder. 'Thank God she's finally gone!'

I sniff and dab my nose. 'Is that supposed to be supportive?'

'What else can I say? Why don't we book ourselves a nice holiday?'

'How will that help?'

'We never have holidays. I think we should treat ourselves. I've always wanted to go to Venice. Shall we get some brochures when we're in town next?'

She has at least managed to put me off my stroke, enabling me to think of something other than Gill.

Antonia wanders off happily, as if this holiday is a done deal. I slouch in my chair, listening to her singing in the kitchen, the "Just one Cornetto" song. Tears slide unchecked down my cheeks. I have nothing against Venice, but I don't want to go on holiday with Antonia. These romantic places she favours are for lovers, not faded spinster sisters. I can't bear the prospect of sitting in a gondola with Antonia giggling and flirting grotesquely with the gondolier while I trail my fingers in the water wishing it were Gill who was seated next to me, her white hair glinting in the sun, her hand resting lightly on top of mine.

It's getting on for four o'clock in the afternoon. I offer to make a pot of tea and load a plate with sweet treats: chocolate digestives, marshmallows, and her favourite garibaldis.

'What's this in aid of?' she asks when I bring the tray through. 'Normally I'm lucky if I see a rich tea finger when you make the tea.'

I set the tray on the coffee table and pour. 'I want to talk to you, and I don't want you getting upset.'

'Oh, I see. So you're trying to soften me up with biscuits, is that it?'

'If you like.'

'Let's get it over with, then.'

'Antonia...'

She glares at me. 'Well?'

'When you were in hospital, I tidied out the dresser.'

'Really? I hadn't noticed.'

'No, I didn't get very far.' My mouth is dry and I take a few sips of tea, aware that she might well fly off the handle the moment I mention that I've read her letters.

She selects a marshmallow, pinching it between thumb and forefinger before popping it in her mouth.

'I found some letters,' I say, bracing myself for fireworks.

'What letters?'

'Letters to you, from Philip.'

Her eyes blaze. 'How dare you!'

I hold up my hand. 'Antonia, please. I didn't realise what they were. If I had, I would have put them back immediately.' I'm not sure if this is true, but it feels true. Wanting to know the truth is not the same thing as prying, is it?

She rubs her arms, a hurt expression on her face. 'It was a big joke to you, wasn't it, my friendship with Philip?'

'No, it wasn't, but I could have been a bit more sensitive.'

She snorts.

I decide to plunge right in, to what matters. 'Did you have a baby?'

For a few moments, the room is eerily still, both of us motionless, our eyes locked.

'You know,' Antonia whispers.

'Not until then I didn't. Oh, Antonia, is it true?'

Her eyelids flicker. I have the sense that she is torn between flying into a rage and slumping in her seat, defeated.

I hold my breath, letting it out only when the hint of a smile touches her lips. 'I never would have told you.'

'I know. But I wish you had. What you must have gone through!' For the first time in many years, I'm entirely on my sister's side. I've always considered her childish and irritating, but right now I feel she's rather admirable to have kept such a big secret for all these years, never once hinting at it. 'You went to stay with some people in Devon, didn't you? Is that where you had it?'

'It was all arranged by Philip's father. A nursing home of some sort. No one around me that I knew, just strangers.' She spoons sugar into her tea. 'I expect it cost a lot, but Mr Belmont could afford it. I wonder if they ever spared me a thought at all while...'

While she was giving birth to their grandchild. 'Antonia, you poor thing.'

Her eyes open wide. 'I thought, if you knew, it would be one more thing to throw at me and make me feel guilty about.'

'Good heavens—' I pause as a wave of shame rolls over me. 'Tell me what happened – if you feel able.'

She shrugs. 'I'm sure you've worked it all out for yourself by now.'

I nod. 'I want to hear it in your own words.'

She sighs and leans back in her chair, fingers playing with a curl of her thin red hair. 'I told Mother and Father, and they spoke to Philip's parents. At first, it seemed everyone was agreed that we'd get married as soon as possible, but then his parents changed their minds, said we were too young, we would ruin our lives.'

'But what about Philip? Wasn't he allowed an opinion?'

'Oh, I think he was quite glad for his parents to get it all out of sight, clear up the mess for him. Even though it was a mess he helped to make, I know they blamed me.'

I wince to hear the bitterness in her voice.

'He was their only son, you see, and he was to have a career and get on in the world, become a solicitor like his dad. They didn't want him saddled with a wife and child. Not with *me*.'

'Brutes,' I mutter.

'I can see their point, now.'

'Can you?'

She gives me a sad grin. 'I loved him, but he didn't feel the same way about me.'

'So that was that?'

'He moved away with his family and I never saw him again. They rented out their house, didn't even stop long enough to sell it, don't you remember?'

I take a few moments to digest this. How alone she must have felt, how helpless.

Antonia takes a biscuit from the plate, but she doesn't eat it. As she speaks, she picks at the biscuit, chipping off crumbs. 'It was my baby. He or she would be middle-aged now. How odd is that?'

She gives a shuddery laugh and a tear slides down her cheek. I have an urge to reach out and squeeze her hand, but we've never been physically demonstrative with each other.

'I was only a foolish teenager, after all.' She takes a deep breath. 'I used to spend hours walking back and forth across the beach at Dawlish, whatever the weather, wishing the wind would blow away my thoughts. Or, better, blow *me* away.'

'And after...?'

She rummages in her skirt pocket for a hanky and blows her nose. 'They said they had adoptive parents all lined up and waiting. Waiting to snatch my baby from me.'

I stare at the floor, tears stinging my eyes. What can I possibly say that won't sound trite?

Antonia clears her throat. 'Everyone said I'd get over it, that I should pretend it never happened, but how could I?' Sniffing, she scrubs her eyes with the hanky. 'So now you know it all.'

We both stare at the teapot. 'Shall I make a new pot?' I ask.

'Not for me.'

'I think I'd like another.' I take the tray into the kitchen, needing to be alone for a few moments. Although I suspected everything she told me, hearing the truth from her own mouth has knocked me for six.

When I return to the living room, Antonia is standing by the mantelpiece, staring at the picture of us as young women, outside the gift shop.

'I'm sorry, Antonia.'

She turns her head and gazes at me, her expression softening. 'Me too. It was unkind of me to tell tales to Gill's parents.'

'Water under the bridge.'

I put down my cup and walk slowly towards her. Together we stare at the photograph.

'I know you loved her,' she says, 'and hurting you didn't make me feel any better. Well,' she adds after a pause, 'only for a few moments. I didn't dislike her without good reason, you know.'

'I know.' I place my hand on her shoulder. 'Reading between the lines, it sounds as if this fiancé of hers is worth a bob or two.'

Antonia gazes at me, her eyes narrowing. 'You were too good for her.'

For some reason, this strikes my funny bone, and I laugh as if she's made a good joke.

'Why are you laughing?'

'I'm sorry, dear. I'm not laughing at you. I think I'm just—' There is a sudden catch in my throat and I find myself weeping. Antonia pats my shoulders and I lean against her. 'Oh, what was the *point*?' I take a few deep breaths to stem the tears and lurch towards the armchair. Sitting down heavily, I wipe my damp face, though more tears come anyway.

'Best to let it all out,' Antonia says.

Once my crying jag passes, I feel empty, as if I haven't eaten all day. My head aches. The tears offered only a temporary release. I'm left with a grey-tinted aftermath, the acceptance that Gill was shallow, that our relationship meant nothing to her. Possibly it wasn't a relationship at all, and my memories have made more of it than there was, weaving a story out of fragments.

'What are you thinking about?' Antonia asks.

'Only what a fool I've been. I knew deep down that I didn't mean anything to Gill. I pretended she felt as strongly about me, but I've always known that wasn't true.'

'Shall we look at photos?' Antonia suggests.

'Are you sure?'

'Yes, I'd like to.' She goes to get the albums from the dresser.

I'm not sure this is a good idea. We've established that our past contains many painful episodes. A trip down memory lane seems designed to make the old wounds sting even more.

Antonia returns with a leather-bound album, the photos attached to the thick pages with corner mounts, some of which have lost their glue and fallen off.

I sit next to her. Antonia turns the pages. The pictures are captioned in faded ink, in Mother's hand.

There are pictures of Antonia and me from childhood – more of me than of her, which I believe is normal, the novelty of having a child wearing off with the birth of the second.

Later pictures were mostly taken for specific occasions – twenty-first birthdays, weddings, the christening of Sheila's son, an occasion I don't particularly remember, though the picture exists to say I was there.

We come to a picture of Antonia, aged sixteen, with Philip. I hear her sharp intake of breath and place my hand over hers. 'Antonia...'

'It's all right. He was a handsome boy, wasn't he?'

He looks awkward, his arms and legs too long for his body. His ears stick out and he wears a daft expression on his face. My sister, though, is beautiful, like the young Elizabeth Bowes-Lyon. Antonia's hair is a cloud of soft waves, her big romantic eyes cornflower blue, her face a perfect heart shape. She looks delicate and fragile next to gawky Philip.

Antonia sighs and turns the page. The next picture of her was taken when she turned twenty-one. She was still beautiful, but I see such sadness in her eyes I wonder how I've never noticed it before during the hundreds of times I must have looked at these photos.

'It'll be all right,' I say.

33

NAOMI

Things came to a head one sunny day in March. Spring seemed to have come early and Brian suggested they take a picnic to Minster Hill. At the last minute, Naomi complained of a migraine, and suggested they choose another day for their excursion.

'It'll likely be raining again tomorrow,' Brian said, filling a stone bottle from a jug of homemade lemon cordial and twisting in the cork stopper. He said the drink would keep cooler in that than in a lighter plastic bottle. 'We should make hay while the sun shines,' he added with a wink. He told her to take a couple of paracetamol and stop making a fuss about nothing.

Brian buckled the straps on the picnic hamper and stood at the front door, waiting for her. 'Come on, then, if you're coming.' Whistling tunelessly, he led the way. The open ridge top ran eight miles across the land and was popular with walkers who enjoyed the stunning views. Brian preferred the more secluded areas lower down the hill. While the ridge itself was open and often windy, the lower slopes were covered with a range of woodland and scrub. The stony soil supported gorse, bramble and bracken interspersed with silver birch, mountain ash, hawthorn, sycamore and pines. The trees were stunted at the higher levels, but in the valley floor they grew thick and lush.

'Did we have to come this far?' Naomi asked, sweating from the exertion of trudging through so much dense vegetation.

'We want a bit of privacy, don't we?'

Naomi made no reply.

'We'll stop here, I reckon. Over there's one of the old quarries.' He pointed to his right, where Naomi saw a battered "Danger" sign warning people to keep out. Naomi had no interest in quarries, but Brian's grandfather had worked as a quarryman. On the wall in the kitchen he'd hung an old photograph showing eight workers with the wheelbarrows they used for carrying away the stone. He claimed the man at the front, his face almost obscured by a flat cap, was his granddad.

Brian laid a large plaid blanket on the ground and unbuckled the hamper. 'Sit yourself down, then.'

She felt pine needles spiking her through the woollen blanket.

Brian grinned and held out a Tupperware box containing her egg and cress sandwiches. 'Have summat to eat, then. Put some meat on them bones.'

Naomi shook her head, nauseated by the sulphurous smell of the sweaty sandwiches.

He shrugged. 'Suit yourself.' Unable to hide her distaste, Naomi watched Brian make short work of sandwiches, pork pie, and a Scotch egg.

Her migraine had reached the point where the headache was no more than a nagging pain, but nausea threatened to overcome her. If she could just manage to ignore the food, to stop thinking about how her stomach would churn if she so much as nibbled a sandwich... She took deep breaths, telling herself Brian would soon get bored and they could go home.

Naomi knelt and tried to keep perfectly still as she watched a grey squirrel scamper between the trees.

'What're you staring at?' Brian asked.

'A squirrel.'

'Vermin.' He balled up one of the sandwiches and aimed it at the squirrel.

Naomi sighed. 'Why must you be so coarse?' she asked.

'Coarse? Me? I know how different I am from your precious Nigel. You never stop reminding me, do you?'

'I try my best.'

'You do nothing but nag. You're ashamed of me, aren't you?'

'Only when I see people staring at me, whispering, pitying me. You could at least be discreet, for God's sake.'

'You'd know all about that, wouldn't you? I've never kept any secrets from you.'

'I've kept none from you.'

'Stop writing to him, then. I know he sends your letters back. Doesn't even bother to open them, does he? That's how much he thinks of you.'

'Brian... don't you think we should end this farce of a marriage? We're better off without each other, you know that.'

'Divorce? Been no divorces in my family. You got what you wanted, didn't you? That ring on your finger?'

'It's not enough.'

'Maybe it's enough for me.'

She knew she never nagged him, though there was

plenty about Brian with which she could find fault. He came and went as he pleased, he took money from her purse without asking, he invited his pals from the pub round to the house at all hours. The din they made, laughing and shouting, when she had to get up early for work the next morning. He would never change, because she'd made it too easy for him not to.

He took the bottle of lemon cordial from the hamper and removed the stopper. 'Ladies first,' he said, offering it to Naomi.

She shook her head. 'I'd like to go home.'

'I wouldn't.'

She began to get up, but he caught hold of the hem of her skirt and pulled her down. 'You'll leave when I say we're ready to leave,' he said.

Dancing flashes of light told her the headache she knew was coming would soon thump into the side of her head with the force of a wrecking ball. 'I'm not well! I need to lie down.'

She doubled over and retched, but she'd eaten so little that nothing came out. She groaned.

'Christ Almighty,' Brian muttered, pulling the picnic basket towards him.

'I can't help it, I'm ill.'

'Always summat with you, isn't there? "I can't help it, I can't help it",' he mocked. 'You're no sort of wife to me.'

'Not this again, please,' she groaned. 'Not now.'

'I've been patient, haven't I? Put up with more than most men would.'

He edged towards her and placed a meaty hand on her knee.

She inched away, but this time he wasn't going to give

up so easily. He squeezed her knee, pushing the thin cotton of her dress up her thigh.

'Not *now*, Brian. I'm not well.'

'I've had enough of your excuses, missus. I've waited long enough.'

He lunged at her, his wet lips smothering hers, his hands pawing her breasts. Roughly he pushed up her dress and lay on top of her.

She pummelled his back with her fists. 'Leave me alone! I'll scream!'

'No one'll hear you,' he panted. 'I mean to have what's rightly mine, so you might as well stop struggling.'

Sickened by the feel of Brian's warm breath upon her neck and the groans of pleasure he made, she reached out her arm, seeking the stone bottle. Once it was in her grip, she lifted it and cracked it down onto his head.

A split-second glance passed between them. Naomi has replayed that moment in her mind so many times. She wonders if perhaps she thought the blow would be only a glancing one. The bottle was a solid weight, but could she wield it with sufficient heft to... but what was the point of doing less? To hurt him, to knock him out: that would have achieved nothing. Which must mean that when she brought down the bottle on Brian's head, she knew what she was doing. What she intended. What she wanted.

He fell to one side. At first Naomi felt only relief as she put her clothes straight with shaking hands. She scooted backwards, away from Brian, keeping the bottle in her hand, ready for when he regained consciousness. That's what she thought, isn't it? It couldn't be that easy to kill someone, could it?

But minutes passed and he remained still.

Naomi felt a tightness in her chest as if she were struggling to breathe. As if the air around her were being sucked away.

'Brian?' Naomi slapped his cheek.

Shivering, she sat back on her heels.

Blood oozed from his head.

The enormity of what she'd done made the hairs prickle on the back of her neck. She half suspected Brian of mucking around, waiting for her to come close enough so that he could grab her, laugh at having fooled her. "Gave you a good scare, didn't I?" She could just imagine him saying that. He liked practical jokes, did Brian.

More minutes passed. Had she really killed him? She was such a small woman, no match for a brute like him, and yet he did look dead.

She pulled his body further into the thicket of trees, breathing heavily from the effort, and from fear. No one would believe that his death was an accident. Naomi hauled his body towards the "Danger" sign and peered down the cliff face, the rocks scarred by nineteenth-century quarrying, but covered thickly with trees. A pool had formed at the base of the quarry. She crouched and tried to gauge how far he would fall if she shoved him down.

Using every bit of her strength, she pushed the body over the cliff and watched him tumble down, landing in a thicket of trees. She rolled large rocks down after him, until she could no longer see him.

Once she'd caught her breath, she returned to the picnic site, heart hammering, her hands and dress filthy, the scent of the pines sickening her almost more than the odour of hard-boiled eggs had done. She packed away the picnic, then cleaned herself as best she could before returning home.

Looking back, she's amazed she could have behaved so calmly. What thoughts ran through her head as she trudged back to the house? She can't remember. She must have been in shock.

She washed her hands then went straight to bed to sleep off the migraine.

When she woke, some four hours later, she felt much better. Then she remembered what she'd done. Still a little woozy from the migraine, she toasted two slices of bread and spread them thickly with butter and Marmite. Then she poured herself a glass of wine and thought about what she needed to do. First of all, she must get her story straight.

Brian suggested the picnic. It was out of character, but it was a nice day. When I felt unwell he got annoyed, so he stormed off in a huff, leaving me to take the picnic basket home while he went in search of his pub cronies.

But he never arrived at the pub. Did it matter? Everyone knew of Brian's propensity for suddenly disappearing, sometimes for days at a time. He'd go off in search of cash in hand work, the sort of work Naomi didn't want to know about.

'Everything will be all right now,' she murmured. If not, what was the point of him being dead?

Naomi removed her wedding ring and placed it on the table. *You can't get rid of him that easily...*

As time went by and Brian remained absent, she expected questions from people she knew, but no one asked, so she said nothing. People must have assumed he'd left her and didn't want to make her feel worse by referring to it.

Every day she expected the police to knock on the front door; would have almost welcomed it. She had made up her mind to take the blame, if Brian's body was found. She would claim she hadn't meant to hit him that hard, but she had used more force than she should have. More than was necessary. She would accept the punishment for that, whatever it might be. And the more time that elapsed, the more she tried to convince herself that her actions had been justified, that he'd deserved to die, and eventually she could go for days without thinking of him at all, until they found the body in the quarry.

34

DIANA

After tea, I decide to serve custard with the rhubarb crumble, but I can't be bothered to make it from scratch so I snip open a carton of the ready-made stuff and bung it in the microwave.

'It's such a time-saver,' Antonia says, a note of wonder in her voice. 'It still makes me giggle to see how quickly it cooks things.'

Once the microwave has pinged, I remove and squeeze the carton. The bright yellow custard emerges with a farting noise and flops out into the bowls.

The rest of the evening passes in the usual blur of bland television programmes until it's time for the news. At that moment, the phone rings.

'Don't answer it,' Antonia says. 'It can't be important. Anyone worth speaking to would phone at a decent hour.' Our parents drummed it into us that it's bad form to call anyone after nine in the evening.

It seems unlikely that salesmen would phone at this hour, so I pick up the phone.

'Hello, is that Antonia Littlehales?' a woman's voice says.

'To whom am I speaking?' I reply.

'This *is* the right number, isn't it?'

'I'd like to know who you are before I divulge that information.'

'Sure. My name's Florence. You don't know me.'

I'm about to slam down the phone, when she continues, 'You did, however, know my father, Philip Belmont.'

Speechless, I glance at Antonia, whose gaze is fixed on the television.

'Are you still there?'

'Yes; yes, I'm still here.'

'The thing is, I'm compiling my family tree, and I came across some letters addressed to my dad from an Antonia Littlehales of the White House, Morevale. If I may, I'd love to come and talk to you.'

'Why?' I realise I must sound rude, but don't much care.

'My dad never talked a great deal about himself, about his childhood or anything. I'd like you to tell me a bit more about him.'

'Can't you ask your mother?'

'She doesn't like speaking about the past.' She gives a nervous giggle. 'She says people only start asking you about the past if they think you're going to die soon.'

I raise my eyebrows. 'I doubt I could tell you anything useful.' I realise this Florence person has assumed I'm Antonia, but I've no intention of correcting her.

'I'm just trying to get a better picture of my parents' backgrounds – what they were like when they were young.'

I pause. Antonia looks up and mouths, 'Who is it?'

When I shake my head, she shrugs and returns her attention to the telly.

'Could I come and see you?' Florence asks. 'I promise I wouldn't take up too much of your time.'

I want to say no. What would be a reasonable excuse? Or should I just be downright rude, put her off that way? She knows where we live. What if she comes anyway?

'I'm sorry, it's really not convenient at the moment,' I say. 'It's also rather late.'

'God, I'm sorry! I never thought. I was so excited about finding the letters that I—'

'Have you read them?' I interrupt.

'Glanced at them, that's all.'

If she reads them, she will find out. She will know. 'Don't you think you ought to discuss them with your mother first?'

'To be truthful, I suspect they're love letters. I'd rather not worry my mother with them.'

But it's fine to worry us? The cheek of the woman. I have to get rid of her. I must protect Antonia. I don't want her to know Philip has a daughter, a wife – widow, I suppose. It clicks with me, finally, that Philip is dead. I would like to ask her about him, but I can't possibly do that while Antonia is in the room.

'Could you call back tomorrow morning?' I say. 'I'll give you my mobile number.'

'I suppose it was a bit rude of me to call out of the blue and expect an immediate invitation to tea.'

Yes, it was. The young are so thoughtless. Though she might not be as young as all that, depending on when Philip married.

'Who was that?' Antonia inevitably asks when I put the phone down.

I try to recall what I said. I made a reference to "your mother", so I can't pretend it was Naomi. 'It was Stella,' I say, inspiration striking in the nick of time. Antonia knows

277

my shop manager, of course, but not well. Nor is Antonia particularly interested in what goes on at the shop.

'Nothing wrong, I hope?' Antonia says, but I can sense her interest has passed.

'A minor domestic emergency. Nothing that can't wait till tomorrow.'

I grab the telly remote and turn the volume up a notch. Rather aptly, it's one of those programmes in which celebrities delve into their family tree, getting pointlessly emotional because their great-grandmother ended her days in the workhouse.

The next morning I'm on tenterhooks waiting for Florence to call, hoping I can manage it without Antonia knowing. Trying to explain to Florence why I let her believe I was Antonia will be awkward. At some point I might have to tell Antonia about this, depending on how our conversation goes, but not yet; not yet.

My phone vibrates. I can't take the call, not with Antonia in the room. Did she hear it vibrate? 'I think I'll go and check on the washing,' I say, hoping my expression does not betray me.

'It won't be dry yet.'

'Still; fresh air. I won't be long.' Is she suspicious? She gives me an odd look as I hurry from the room. I can't dwell on that now. One thing at a time, Diana.

'Yes?'

'Antonia? I was just about to leave a voicemail.'

'Yes, I'm sorry.'

'No worries. Are you sure I couldn't pop round to see you? I'm only in Shropshire for a couple of days – looking up parish records, that sort of thing.'

'It must be fascinating,' I say, wanting her to hurry up, to reach a point where I can quiz her properly.

'Yes... Look, I need to come clean, I did have a squint at some of those letters – *your* letters, I should say. I realise there are some things in the past – in everyone's past – that we'd rather other people didn't know. Personal things.'

Here it comes, I think. 'As you say, those things are in the past. It takes a lot to upset me.' I wince. I'm speaking on Antonia's behalf, about letters she would definitely not wish anyone to see. 'Tell me, Florence, when did your father die?' I've been frank with her, or so she thinks, so I hope she will reciprocate.

'I suppose you haven't seen him since—'

'No. Not for decades.'

'Well, he married quite late. He was nearly forty, my mother was a lot younger. He worked as a solicitor – conveyancing, very dull. My mother was his secretary. I think they were happy together.'

'And you...'

'I was born not long after they married. A bit of a shotgun job, by all accounts, although I'm sure they would have married anyway. I mean, they always seemed devoted to each other.'

'You are their only child?'

'Yes. I'm studying history at uni. I'm particularly interested in oral history.'

I'm having to adjust my ideas about Florence.

'I'm sorry to hear your father is dead.'

She sighs. 'Poor Dad. He was always so stressed out by his job. He took on far too much work, but couldn't bear to turn any down. I don't know why. People are always buying and selling houses, aren't they?'

'Is it long since...?'

'Two years. My mum fell apart a bit, so I delayed going to uni for a year to look after her till she got back on her feet. She was quite old-fashioned, gave up work when I was born and never went back. She does a bit of voluntary work now, I think she quite enjoys it.'

'It must be difficult, when your world has revolved around someone.'

'Yes. Look, about these letters—'

'Did Philip ever talk about... the past?'

'I knew he'd had other girlfriends, if that's what you mean. It would be a bit weird if he hadn't, wouldn't it? And there are the photos, of course. Not many, but... You were very beautiful.'

'Thank you.' Antonia would be delighted to hear that. But I'm not Antonia. What I'm doing is wrong. Even so, I don't correct the error. It's too late for that; I must know about the letters.

'The thing is,' Florence continues, 'I feel like you should have the letters back. They're very personal, very... they're quite upsetting. I mean, it's not like they're just bog standard love letters, is it?'

Isn't it? What on earth are they, then?

'Florence, I need to correct an error. An assumption I did nothing to correct, to my shame. I'm actually Diana. My sister is Antonia. She's not a strong person and I didn't want you speaking to her. I'm sorry.'

The line goes silent and I assume she's disgusted with me and has hung up. 'Florence?'

'Yes, I'm still here. I think I can sort of understand that. I'm sorry, too. I haven't been very sensitive, have I?'

'Antonia has been living with me for the past five

years. Before that she was a teacher, but she had some kind of breakdown.'

'I see. So you don't know about the letters?'

'I've seen a letter from Philip in which it's clear Antonia suspected she was pregnant.'

'Have you spoken to your sister about it?'

'Yes. She told me everything.' Everything? Unlikely. But I need to know the contents of the letters Florence has. I must make her believe Antonia and I have no secrets from each other.

'I wish my dad was still alive,' Florence says. 'It's so difficult when you only know one side of the story.'

'I'm not sure he could shed much more light. Antonia got pregnant and was forced to give the child up for adoption. A sad thing, but I daresay it happened quite a lot before people stopped caring about babies being born outside of wedlock.'

'But... But she didn't,' Florence says.

'Didn't what?'

'She didn't have a baby. To be honest with you, the letters are a bit mad. She was clearly very troubled when she wrote them.'

'I'm sorry, I don't understand.'

'I spoke to my mum about it. She told me – well, I mean, it wasn't something she and my dad had talked about much, but they had discussed it – and she said that, according to Dad, Antonia had some sort of phantom pregnancy. I mean, she was utterly *convinced* she was pregnant, but she wasn't. She... caused a certain amount of trouble, I gather, for Philip and his parents. They tried to be kind, but in the end they got fed up. It seems Antonia's parents – sorry, your parents, too – bundled her off to stay with family friends till she could pull herself together.'

'But... I don't remember any of this. I would have done, surely. I was living in the same house, for God's sake.'

'Yes, well; families are good at keeping secrets, aren't they? Especially from one another.'

Antonia and I weren't close as children or teenagers. We had our own set of friends, and for the most part we ignored each other. Even so, if Antonia behaved as strangely as Florence is suggesting, I would have noticed *something*.

'Will you tell Antonia that you've spoken to me?' Florence says.

'I don't know. How can I?' But what if Florence's mother lied to her daughter? I can't know any more unless I see Antonia's letters, but it would be an act of gross betrayal if I read them without letting Antonia know.

'I'm really sorry,' Florence says. 'My mum said it was a bad idea to rake up the past, but with my studies and everything, family history is something I'm really interested in, and – I got a bit carried away.'

'Yes...'

'Look, I'll leave it with you. I'll be around if Antonia wants to speak to me, and maybe you or she could get back to me and let me know what you want to do about the letters.'

'Burn them,' I say without thinking. 'Please.'

'You were out there a long time,' Antonia says. 'Was the washing dry?'

'No, not quite.'

'You were on the phone. Stella again, was it?'

I take a deep breath. 'No, it wasn't Stella.'

'Who was it, then?'

'It was a girl called Florence. Florence Belmont.'

'Belmont?'

'Sit down, Antonia.'

She does so.

'Florence Belmont is Philip's daughter.' I ignore her sharp intake of breath and carry on. 'She sounds like a pleasant young woman. Studying history at university. She's researching her family tree or somesuch, wants to speak to people who remember...'

'Philip,' she whispers.

'Yes. I told her there was nothing we could tell her. I didn't want her pestering you, you do see that, don't you?'

'Of course. Thank you, Diana. But I would like to meet her.'

'Would you? Do you think that would be wise?'

'I would like to see what a daughter of his looks like.'

'She might upset you.' I don't for the life of me know why I've decided to tell Antonia about Florence, except that it feels wrong to keep it from her. I feel disloyal for speaking to Florence.

'We could show her the photos,' Antonia says. 'It's not her fault, is it, what happened in the past?'

'No, but...'

Antonia gives me a cheerful smile, tells me to call Florence and ask her to pop round. When I call her, she sounds delighted. I warn her not to contradict anything Antonia says, however nonsensical it sounds. 'I understand,' Florence says. 'The last thing I want to do is upset anyone.'

Already Antonia is rooting around in the dresser to find all the relevant photo albums. What is she thinking, what is she hoping? A nice little trip down memory lane? Perhaps that's all it will be.

The next morning I tidy up a bit, and both of us make an effort to dress a little more smartly than usual. Antonia's roots need touching up, but otherwise she looks nice in a calf-length pink skirt and floral cotton blouse. Only her blue fluffy slippers spoil the outfit.

'Will she want feeding, do you think?' she says.

'Shouldn't think so. We can give her tea and biscuits. I doubt she'd expect anything more than that.'

Florence raps on the front door at a quarter to eleven. Antonia and I stare at each other.

'Let her in, then,' Antonia says, glancing at herself in the mirror above the mantelpiece.

Opening the front door, I find Florence to be a slender young woman with naturally blonde hair and freckles, wearing a leather jacket over skinny jeans and a black Led Zeppelin T-shirt.

She smiles and holds out her hand. 'Miss Littlehales?'

'Diana.' I shake her hand and usher her in. 'Can I take your jacket?'

After a moment's hesitation she removes it and hands it to me. Her arms are covered with golden freckles. She must get her colouring from her mother; Philip's family were all dark-haired with olive skin.

I take her into the living room, as nervous as I've ever been, worried how Antonia will react when she comes face to face with Philip's daughter.

'Antonia, this is Florence.'

Antonia nods and smiles. 'I would have liked a daughter,' she says. 'A dear little girl to cosset.'

'My sister is a sentimentalist,' I say, not unkindly. 'Shall I make some tea?'

'I'm fine, thanks,' Florence says, a little too hurriedly. 'I don't want to take up too much of your time.'

'Would you like to see some photos of us when we were younger?' Antonia says. 'There are a few of Philip that might interest you.'

'I'd love to.'

We sit on the sofa, Antonia in the middle, turning the pages of the album. She stops when she reaches the photos taken when we were in our teens. 'Can you tell which one is which?'

Unerringly Florence picks us out. I wish she'd hesitated a little before guessing that I am the least pretty sister, my hair in a fussy style that doesn't suit me, a roll of fat visible over the belt of my best dress.

'You look unhappy,' Florence says to me. 'In the picture, I mean.'

The photo was taken long before I met Gill, but I see that she's right. 'I never liked having my picture taken, especially with Antonia.'

'I never knew that,' Antonia says.

'People always said what a pretty girl you were. They never noticed me, and goodness knows I was big enough.'

I feel we're all deliberately avoiding the subject of Antonia's relationship with Philip and decide to get it over with. 'Antonia was only sixteen the last time she saw Philip.'

Florence looks from Antonia to me. 'I'm so sorry. I don't want to bring up any bad memories.'

'Not bad ones,' Antonia says. 'I loved Philip and I believe he loved me back, but he was spineless. Spineless...'

Florence blushes. 'He was a gentle man, certainly.'

'Spineless!'

'Miss Belmont, perhaps...' I gesture with my head towards the door. She follows me to the kitchen. 'I do apologise,' I say once we're alone.

'No need.' But her small, tight smile suggests she's upset. 'I'm really sorry what happened to your sister. I don't think my dad treated her badly, do you?'

'I really don't know. I don't suppose we ever shall.'

My gaze wanders to the door. I hope Antonia isn't listening, but I can just imagine her crouching there, ear pressed against the keyhole.

'I think I'd better go,' she says. 'I think... I don't think this is very good for your sister, is it?'

I hand her jacket to her. She removes a bundle of papers from an inner pocket and presses them into my hands. 'I know what you said, about burning them, but I can't bring myself to do it.'

Once I've shown her out, I return to the living room, but Antonia isn't there. I go upstairs and find her lying on her bed. The curtains are shut and she looks to be asleep, so I leave her be. Of course it was a mistake to invite Florence round. I suppose I've salved my conscience about keeping Florence's phone calls from Antonia, but now I'm stuck with the letters, so I haven't escaped at all. They're my responsibility. Their destruction, too, will be my responsibility. I still haven't decided whether or not to read them first. Either way it will be the wrong decision.

I clear away the photo albums. A picture falls out: Antonia and Philip. She's staring straight ahead, squinting; the sun must have been in her eyes. Arms behind his back, Philip stands a little apart from her. He smiles for the camera: a warm, generous smile. I wonder who took the picture.

35

NAOMI

On Sunday, Mr Fielding gives a nice little sermon on the theme of forgiveness and compassion, but the atmosphere in church remains as chilly as the marble font. Strange, Naomi thinks, that she's never noticed how little joy there is in her religion. She's sure most of the other worshippers give lip service to the idea of forgiving their enemies, but in practice it's a different story.

As parishioners shuffle from their pews after the service, she catches someone saying to his neighbour, 'They lack guts, these religious types.'

Forgiveness as a weakness. Turn the other cheek and someone will slap it. She's said the same thing herself.

She is one of the last to leave. Mr Fielding offers to carry her bag for her. She thanks him, but when they're near her front gate, she can't help crying out, 'Watch my bag – it's dragging in the dirt.' Immediately she bites her lip. Why must she criticise when only gratitude is due? 'I'm sorry.'

He frowns. 'Are you all right, Mrs Wilkinson?'

'Yes, fine.'

She unlocks the back door and the vicar follows her into the kitchen, where he puts down her bag.

'Sit down, Mrs Wilkinson.'

'I really ought to get on.'

His eyes twinkle. 'With what?'

'Tidying. Cleaning. The usual.' She damps down a spurt of irritation. Men have no idea how long it takes to clean a house thoroughly.

'You can spare a few minutes, can't you?'

Reluctantly, she sits opposite him. He's a pleasant enough, inoffensive man, but she finds it hard to relax in his company. On the way home, she toyed with the idea of confessing to him about Brian, but she doesn't know him well enough to gauge how he's likely to react. Would he have to tell? He's not a Catholic, for all that he acts like one.

'Lately I've been wondering how much of a difference I really make,' he says.

'It's a calling, isn't it? I can't imagine you'd take to being a computer programmer or anything along those lines.'

He crosses his legs, revealing navy blue socks at half-mast and surprisingly hairy legs. 'I suppose so. Perhaps it's merely – envy? That I've never been the kind of man I wanted to be. I've known some charismatic vicars, but I fear I am not one of them.'

It's almost amusing; she entertained a half-hearted intention of confessing to him, and yet it's he who's decided to open his heart to her. 'That sort of thing shouldn't matter. In my experience, charismatic people are often rather shallow, relying on charm rather than wisdom.'

His foot bounces up and down. 'I'm not sure I agree, but you're right that substance is more important than outward show.'

'Sounds to me like you're having a crisis.'

'Of confidence, not of faith,' he says quickly, though she never made any such suggestion. This in itself makes her wonder if it's certainty that he lacks. If God exists, wouldn't he give his mortal representatives the talents to engage and attract people? Mr Fielding is not by any stretch of the imagination a stimulating person. He's rather like those timid curates in the novels of Barbara Pym. They're easier to handle than the oily Obadiah Slopes of this world, but they hardly inspire admiration.

'People want miracles and quick fixes,' she says. 'The Anglican Church never offered those things, nor should it.'

He smiles. 'You've always struck me as a woman with very firm convictions.'

'I am, for all the good it does me. I have moral standards and I can't approve of things I find repugnant.'

The church may try as hard as it likes to modernise itself, but she will never accept services for pets, or electric guitars instead of the organ. No one mentions sin anymore, but it exists, and Mr Fielding has no business turning a blind eye. No one can tell her that she should be forgiven her sins.

'What did you think of today's sermon? The theme, I mean.'

'I don't forgive my own faults. How much harder it is to forgive those of other people.'

He gives her a smile she interprets as patronising. No doubt he thinks she's too dull to have committed any really big sin. Inoffensive Mrs Wilkinson, set in her ways, judgemental, as interesting as a bowl of porridge.

'You know nothing about me,' she snaps, knowing her comment to be unfair. What, after all, does she really know about *him*? He may have hidden depths.

'You've never volunteered very much,' he says.

'I'm not the type of person who enjoys talking about herself.'

'I'm well aware of *that*, Mrs Wilkinson.' He steeples his fingers and rests his chin on them. 'What concerns me is that you can come across as a little unapproachable, so that people aren't always keen to try and get closer to you.'

'These days everyone seems to want to know everything about everybody else.'

He frowns, perhaps thinking she's not understood him. 'We all need friends,' he says.

'Have *you* so many?'

She gasps, feeling she's overstepped the mark by some distance. 'I apologise. I shouldn't have said that.'

'Please don't worry. I'd be a pretty poor vicar if I were so easily offended.' But his face is flushed, and it's clear she's hit a nerve.

'I'm a difficult woman,' she says quietly. 'I know that. I say the wrong things. I put people's backs up.'

'Why is that, do you think?'

'It's just the way I am. I'd better press on now.'

He scratches his ear. If he intended to say something in particular to her, to make a point, it seems he's failed. They are no nearer to knowing each other. He'll never be allowed to see into her heart. If he thought he'd win her trust, her affection, by revealing his weaknesses to her, he's mistaken. That way lies disillusion. She still remembers with pain the shock she felt when visiting the house of a woman she'd got friendly with: an unmarried woman in her thirties, a committed Christian. On her way to the loo, Naomi peeked into her friend's bedroom. There on the dressing table, in full, brazen view, was a packet of contraceptives. She could never feel the same way about her after that and the friendship soon lapsed.

What if she entered the vicar's bedroom and found dirty underpants on the floor, or discovered that he uses a pink floral bedspread? She could no longer take him seriously.

'Just one thing before I go.' He takes a slim book, more of a pamphlet really, from his inside pocket and holds it out to her.

'What's this?' she says, distrustful.

'I hope you won't think me interfering, but I wondered – as I know you're a big reader – if you might enjoy this.'

She takes the book and reads the title: *Practical Christianity – When Charity Begins at Home*. 'What on earth—?'

'It's about how, as Christians, we need to love ourselves as much as others.'

She raises an eyebrow. 'A self-help book. Surely these things are of no real benefit?' Except, she wants to add, to the self-obsessed and weak.

'As Christians, we have a duty to accept our flaws as part of our basic humanity.'

She suppresses a snort. 'Thank you for the thought,' she says, flicking through it. There's an awful lot of psychobabble and tree-hugging nonsense, but one paragraph in particular catches her attention: *To err is human; to dwell on our faults is mere self-indulgence. Does God love us in spite of our faults, or because of them?* In spite of, surely, she thinks, but hasn't she been guilty of mental flagellation, of wallowing in her imperfections and hating herself for things she can't change?

She pushes the book aside. 'Thank you,' she says, unable to look Mr Fielding in the eye. He leaves soon afterwards. For an hour or more she sits staring out of the window, trying to see herself through others' eyes. When her lip trembles and tears threaten to fall, her first instinct is to reach for the whisky bottle. Instead, though, she remains seated and allows the tears to flow, and sobs till her throat aches.

Once she's cried herself out she feels silly, but also cleansed; almost – but not quite – as if she's been absolved by a God who bears little resemblance to the God of hellfire and brimstone she thought she could trust.

She wipes her eyes. To forgive herself would, she feels, be pointless unless she can also learn to be more tolerant of the failings of others. Is that the sticking point, after all? What right has she to look down her nose at those teenage girls pushing baby buggies? She only does so because she's envious. Her own life is empty; no one loves her. She shuts her eyes and tries to pray, but the words won't come. She imagines God saying, "You're on your own now, kid. Come back and see me again when you've worked out what it is you want from me". She moves to the living room window and opens it. In front of the house opposite, Mrs Fisk is working in her garden. Naomi waves to her. A startled expression on her face, Mrs Fisk stares at her for a few moments before slowly lifting her hand and waving back.

36

DIANA

The dark clouds in the sky suggest it will rain later, so I stuff my mac into my bag and set off, certain I'm on a fool's errand. I stand outside Naomi's house for a few moments, rehearsing what to say; but that never works; conversations always go in unexpected directions. Best to play it by ear.

The front door has seen better days; blue paint has chipped off in many places. Naomi is clearly no gardener – weeds run riot in front of the house.

She immediately answers my tentative knock.

'Diana. Come in.' I've never called on her before, never stepped inside her house, yet she expresses no surprise that I should do so now, out of the blue, at eight in the evening.

She leads me into the kitchen. A strong smell of bleach hits my nostrils. Cold grey tiles cover the floor and there are no little feminine touches. For once I appreciate Antonia's frills and ornaments.

Naomi invites me to sit at the small table. There's no tablecloth, and the wood is covered with rings from mugs.

She stands with her back to the dark Welsh dresser, her arms folded. She's wearing a shapeless brown cardigan over a pale blue blouse, brown skirt, and purple carpet slippers.

'So what brings you here?' She doesn't seem surprised to see me, but she's oddly defensive. What does she fear? Me? *Is* it fear or simply belligerence?

I stare at the table, not sure how to begin. 'I wish you'd sit down.' I dislike having her looming over me.

She scrapes back a chair and sits, placing her hands on the table.

'I don't know why I'm here, really... For advice, I suppose, as daft as that sounds.'

'Advice about what?' She looks a little more relaxed now.

'I've learned something about the past – about Antonia – and I'm not quite sure... You knew her better, you were – are – the same age, in the same class at school. All that.'

'Antonia and I disliked each other. You know that.'

'Yes, I know. Tell me, do you know why Antonia went away so suddenly and for so long, that summer before you both went into the sixth form?'

'Yes, I do. I've never told a soul. I heard my mother speaking to yours. I'm sorry, but at the time I thought it served her right. To have to deal with *that*.'

I tell her, as succinctly as I can, about my conversations with Florence. The baby that wasn't. 'Don't you remember Antonia behaving oddly?'

'She always was a bit— No, not really. I was just annoyed with her. I didn't approve of what Gill did, but I didn't stop her, either. At that age, you don't pause to wonder what other people are going through. It's all about your own pain, your own little bubble.' She sighs. 'How *do* we make amends for all the people we've hurt, the mistakes we've made?'

She gazes around the kitchen, which is bleak enough to make anyone miserable, and I wonder if she lives like this as some sort of penance.

'I think I'd like a drink,' she says. 'A proper drink.'

I follow her into the living room, where she keeps a drinks cabinet. Everything in the room is a muddy brown: carpets, curtains, cushions. One wall is lined with bookcases. 'You certainly have a lot of books.'

I browse the collection, which consists mostly of nineteenth century novels. There's a whole set of Dickens and all of Jane Austen's books. There is a lot of contemporary fiction, too. I notice she has all EM Forster's novels and, bizarrely, the *Rough Guide to Florence*. 'Are you planning a holiday?' I ask, gesturing towards the latter.

'I don't know how that got there. I can't remember the last time I had a holiday. I've never even been abroad.'

'I see you admire Forster.'

'Yes. *Howards End* in particular.'

'An unusual choice.'

'Which is your favourite?'

'*Maurice*.'

Naomi and I lock eyes. 'I always knew about you and Gill,' she says.

'I suppose... What does it matter now? What did it ever matter?'

'She made a lot of trouble for a lot of people. She liked to stir things up, to make things happen.'

There are no pictures on the walls, but on one of the bookcases stands a framed photograph of Naomi in her graduation hat and gown.

'Join me, for God's sake,' she says, pouring two generous measures of whisky. 'I very nearly bared my soul to the vicar yesterday. I'm glad I didn't. He wouldn't have understood.'

'Because he's a man, or because he's a vicar?'

'Because he's not me.' She takes a long slug of whisky. 'It doesn't matter, anyway. It wouldn't have changed anything. Same with you and Antonia. However much you talk about things, it doesn't alter the past.'

'But what she believes—'

'Is what she needs to believe. Burn the letters, Diana.'

Somewhat shamefacedly, I take the bundle of letters from my bag. They seem to have become the booby prize in a ludicrous game of pass the parcel. But if I hold on to them, Antonia might find them. Worse, I might read them, and I could never unsee their contents.

'Leave them with me, then,' Naomi says. 'I've no wish to know what they say.'

'Thank you. Did you get any more of those poison pen letters, by the way?'

She hesitates, then, 'No.'

'How odd.'

'Yes, isn't it?'

She seems unconcerned.

I pick up the photo of Naomi. 'You were a good-looking woman.'

'Was I? My husband is the only person who's ever told me so. My first husband.'

'I never knew him.'

'No. I'll walk with you when you go, I need to get some bread from the Spar.'

'Life goes on.'

'Yes. Life goes on.'

*

We walk in silence until we near the cemetery. Naomi slows down and gazes through the locked iron gates. 'One day I will be buried in here,' she says. 'Next to my parents.' She shivers.

I jump when I hear voices coming from inside the gates.

'Just teenagers,' Naomi says.

'They climb over the gates?' They're a good twelve feet high.

'No, they climb over where the wall's lower.'

'But what do they do in there?' I ask.

Naomi laughs softly. 'What do you think?'

'Oh! Surely not?'

'What harm can it do? The dead have no feelings.'

'But isn't it sacrilegious or something?'

'Probably.' After a pause she continues, 'I've been reading the Bible a lot of late. The New Testament. I've had enough of the God of vengeance.'

'I wonder what Mr Fielding would think if he knew youths were going in there and getting up to all sorts.'

'I don't know. *I* certainly shan't tell him.'

We walk on and I try to engage her in conversation, but her monosyllabic responses to my chatter suggest her mind is elsewhere.

'Do you believe in ghosts?' she asks, apropos of nothing.

I pause before answering. 'I'm not sure. It's funny, isn't it, that I have no trouble in saying I don't believe in God, but I find it much harder to state categorically that I don't believe in ghosts.'

'Perhaps because the feeling of being haunted is something most of us sense from time to time.'

A sudden chilly breeze makes me shiver. In silence Naomi and I stare at each other. There are so many things we could tell each other, but perhaps silence is the better way.

'Goodbye,' she says. Abrupt as always.

I watch her walk away, her head bent, and wish I'd tried to prolong the conversation. But I don't call her back, and feel only relief when she disappears from view.

37

DIANA

I stop in my tracks when the local news comes on the radio and it's announced that the body found in the quarry has finally been identified.

'They took their time,' Antonia says.

'Shh!'

'...Mr Collins,' the velvet-voiced female newsreader says, 'was an experienced hill climber who was reported missing more than fifteen years ago. At the time he was believed to be walking in the Lake District, having taken time off work following the sudden death of his young son.'

'What a thing!' Antonia says. 'The poor man.'

'And his poor family, looking for him in quite the wrong place.'

But I don't spend any more time thinking about Mr Collins. I never knew him, therefore I can't mourn him. I'm thus a little perplexed when I learn that Mr Fielding has decided to hold a memorial service for him.

'It's ridiculous,' Antonia snorted when she saw the announcement in the parish newsletter. 'He has no connection with the area apart from dying here. And his family live in Scotland, apparently. They're hardly likely to want to traipse all the way down here for a church service, are they? Shall we go?'

'What for? We never knew him.'

'Oh, I know, but since it's been organised, it would be awful if no one turned up.'

She wanted me to know that she thought it a mad idea, but she can't bear to miss out on what might be a pleasantly ghoulish occasion. Or will it? I assume there will be others who will turn up, like Antonia, out of a macabre desire to see how this event will pass off.

I believe the coroner eventually ruled an open verdict, which I assume means that it's impossible after all this time to ascertain precisely how Mr Collins died, which is hardly surprising.

I put off making a decision until the last moment, but on the day of the service I realise that Antonia isn't going to settle, so we might as well put in an appearance.

'It's always funerals, isn't it, at our age?' she says. 'Never a nice wedding or a christening.'

I decide smart but casual is suitable for the occasion, and change my loose trousers for a neat black pair, which I team with a grey silk blouse. I half-expect Antonia to emerge wearing solid black and a hat with a veil, so am pleasantly surprised when she comes downstairs wearing a navy-blue suit with matching sandals.

We leave the house and walk in the direction of the church. Antonia asks if we can stop at the paper shop to buy sweets. She picks up a family-size bag of mints and squints at the price. I tell her to treat herself.

Outside, Antonia laboriously unwraps a shiny, stripy mint. She glances around, presumably looking for a litter bin. Seeing none, she screws up the sticky wrapper and stuffs it in her pocket.

'You've started to shuffle, Antonia. Like an old woman.

And you're only sixty, that's no age at all.'

The sigh she gives is one I've heard too many times. It expresses her disappointment and unhappiness. I hate it, but bite back the urge to tell her to shut up.

'I hate getting old,' Antonia mutters. 'I honestly never expected it. The aches and pains, feeling like an old crock. Thinking over all the things I've never done...'

'I know, dear. It's the same for me.'

I link arms with her and we walk up the hill towards St George's. The graveyard is filled with broken headstones dating back to the eighteenth century, perhaps earlier. Most of them are too weather-beaten to read. Anyone who dies now is interred in the cemetery near the library, but I like to see the old graves. They remind me that life has gone on in our village for centuries, the continuous cycle of birth and death, and that anything that seems important now will be worn away by the years until it no longer exists.

We crunch along the gravel path that leads to the church. Gargoyles leer down at me, their eyes rolling back in their heads and their long tongues lolling out from bestial mouths. I shiver and wonder what the point of gargoyles is, beyond their functional purpose. To amuse, to frighten, to induce awe? A joke, or a visualisation of a soul in hellish torment?

Several people stand outside, none of them making eye contact. There's an odd sense of embarrassment in the air. We all had to come, but really we have no idea why we're here.

A man drops his half-smoked cigarette and screws it out with the heel of his shoe. It takes me a few moments to recognise him as our butcher. I'm used to seeing him in a blood-stained white apron.

He nods in greeting. 'Miss Littlehales.'

'Good morning, Mr Burton.'

He jerks his shoulder. 'There's already quite a crowd in there. Dunno why I've come, to be honest with you. It was the wife's idea. Churches give me the creeps. Just look at those gargoyles up there.'

'Grotesques,' Mr Fielding says, pacing towards us. 'Strictly speaking, gargoyles are waterspouts. Grotesques are simply sculptures, with no practical use. From the French, *gargouille*, meaning throat, as in gargle.'

Mr Burton stares at him with eyebrows raised.

'Fancy,' Antonia says. 'I never knew that, did you, Diana?'

I shake my head.

'If you'd like to come inside?' Mr Fielding says, his arms outstretched, ready to gather in his flock.

The interiors of churches make my skin prickle. That musty smell, every tiny whisper seeming to amplify and echo, and the long stained-glass windows showing saints with pious eyes rolling upwards to heaven as if in disgust. I can't look at them, and keep my eyes firmly on the floor, like a penitent sinner. The holy figures seem to point their fingers at me, accusing me of not belonging. Antonia, on the other hand, looks quite at home.

I notice Naomi sitting in the front row and I steer Antonia towards her, the hard clack of our heels ringing out on the stone floor. I bend and whisper to Naomi, 'All right if we sit next to you?'

She nods. 'Please do.' Her skin is without colour, her lips pinched. She looks as if she's going to be sick at any moment. In her black-gloved hands she clutches a hymnal – her own, rather than one of the set belonging to the church. I'm pleased to note that she's wearing a pretty dress, dark grey with a discreet print, that can only be a Boden.

A gentle susurrus of voices fills the church like rustling leaves on an autumn day. Not all the pews are full, but it's a decent turnout for a man none of us knew. Perhaps, like me, people are wondering what Mr Fielding will find to say about this stranger.

The vicar takes his place and clears his throat. He welcomes us and leads us in prayer before launching into his sermon.

'David Collins was one of those men people describe as the salt of the earth. A man of simple tastes, he devoted his life to his work as an engineer, and to his family...' And so on and so forth. The exemplary worker, the family man, the charitable works. Antonia passes me a mint.

I breathe a sigh of relief once the farcical service is over.

'It wasn't too awful, was it?' Naomi says.

I shrug. 'Could have been worse. Would you like to come back to ours for some lunch?'

'Oh – well – all right, why not?'

I've no idea how Antonia will react to this impromptu invitation. I gaze around, wondering where she has gone, when I notice her bending over a pram, admiring a baby.

'Antonia? It's time to go. Naomi's coming back with us for a bite to eat.'

She beams at the baby's parents before walking back to my side.

'Did you see that baby?' Antonia says. 'Such a dear little thing.'

'They all look the same to me.'

'I'd like to buy a toy for it.'

'Why? It's not yours.' I regret my words immediately. Antonia's face crumples. 'I'm sorry, dear. Thoughtless of me.'

'It doesn't matter,' she says.

Back at home, Antonia sets to work making sandwiches no one wants, while I chat to Naomi in the sitting room. Our talk is constrained, both of us too aware that Antonia is in the house, perhaps crouched with her ear to the door.

Eventually Antonia returns with the sandwiches. 'I wonder if they'll ever find Brian?' she says.

Horrified, I glance at Naomi. She blinks rapidly, then chuckles. 'You never cared about offending people, did you, Antonia?'

Antonia purses her lips. 'I've no idea what you mean.'

'Not much you haven't. It's all right, I know it was you who phoned the police. Obviously you were wrong, but I suppose I can't condemn you for your public spiritedness.'

'Well, he *did* disappear very suddenly, didn't he?'

'To everyone's relief, I daresay,' Naomi says.

'You know, don't you? You know where he is.'

'What does it matter? Unlike Mr David Collins he has no one who will mourn him; no one who could stand up and say what a fine man he was, what an excellent husband, what an asset to his community.'

'That's hardly the point, is it?'

'Maybe not. I don't know.' Naomi rubs her forehead. I glare at Antonia.

'I should be getting home,' Naomi says.

'But you've only just got here,' Antonia says.

'And she didn't come here for the third degree,' I snap.

'It's all right,' Naomi says. 'I know you've never liked me, although you must believe that what Gill did was nothing to do with me.'

'You could have stopped her,' Antonia says.

Farcical, sad, that two sixty-year-old women are still arguing over a trivial incident that occurred when they were teenagers. 'How could I? You know what she was like. And if I'd told you what she had in mind, you wouldn't have believed me. What *could* I have done?'

'Naomi's right,' I say. 'None of us behaved very well, back then. But it's a lifetime ago. What does any of it matter now?'

Philip is dead. Gill will soon be married. We need to let them go, those birds of passage who caused so much harm. Naomi, I think, is ready to let go. I'm less certain about Antonia.

'All I could think of during today's memorial service,' Antonia says, 'was Mother's farce of a funeral.'

Naomi gets to her feet. 'I'm going now.'

Antonia watches her leave with raised eyebrows. 'What a funny thing!' she says once the front door bangs shut.

'Naomi? I don't think so. No funnier than us.'

'She's close. You never really know what she thinks about anything – or anyone. I wouldn't be at all surprised if she *did* kill Brian.'

'Don't talk daft. People like her don't commit murder.'

'People like what? Educated people?'

I put my cup on the saucer with a crack. 'What possible reason could she have had for killing him?'

'No smoke without fire, that's what I say.'

I don't believe Naomi is the kind of woman whose temper would snap and lead her to attack Brian. For one thing, he was a stocky man, and she's always been a slip of a thing. Nevertheless, anything is possible, and I think it foolish to indulge in the kind of gossip Antonia enjoys.

38

NAOMI

She can smell autumn in the air. It's faint, but it's perceptible. Soon the shops will fill with Halloween novelties: pointy witch hats, buckets of trick or treat sweets, and pumpkins. She always keeps a few bags of sweets and chocolate in the house, just in case, but her curtains are always closed, there will be no glowing grinning pumpkin head in the window, and usually she is left alone. Then there will be Bonfire Night, the foggy tang of fireworks in the air the next morning, the spent cardboard tubes littering fields and gardens.

And then Christmas, a time of year she neither dreads nor welcomes. She enjoys the church services, attends midnight mass every year, feels a warm glow of community when the vicar invites everyone to shake hands with his or her neighbour. But always she goes home alone, returns to her cold, dark house where there will be no tree, no presents wrapped in shiny paper, no turkey to prepare. And then, back at work, everyone asking everyone else what kind of Christmas they had. How many kinds are there? 'Quiet, thanks,' Naomi will say. 'Quiet and peaceful.' She will help with the taking down of the tree in the library, packing away baubles and tinsel, everything back to normal.

But she's getting ahead of herself. There are days and days to get through before she has to deal with that. Sometimes she wishes Diana would call round, but why should she? Why should anyone?

She picks up the *Rough Guide to Florence*. How did it get there? It must be Nigel's; Brian never even had a passport. There are traces of them both scattered throughout the house. The little Wade Whimsie animals Brian used to buy for her, always careful not to buy duplicates of ones she already had. (She's tried to blot out all the times he was thoughtful, it makes it easier to accept what she did.) The records Nigel bought for her, early in their relationship, his disgust palpable when he discovered the only classical music in her collection was a compilation of "soothing popular melodies". Nigel never understood the need for consolation. She decides not to send him a Christmas card this year. He might not even notice its absence. He might assume she's dead. She realises she doesn't care. Finally, she doesn't care.

She might get a dog. They had a cat once, a half-wild thing that Brian rescued. It went for Naomi one day, drew blood. Cats don't care about anyone, but dogs are loyal. She'll get a rescue dog, one that needs her more than she needs it.

She thinks, as she hasn't thought for a while, of the Gypsy fortune teller. *You'll see him again, but you'll wish you hadn't. It's not going to end well.* You were wrong, she thinks. You got it wrong. You saw the wrong body.

39

DIANA

I'm looking through travel brochures with Antonia when the phone rings.

'Hello, Naomi.' Any distraction from the business of listening to Antonia wax lyrical over Venice is welcome, though of course Naomi is not the type who likes to spend ages yakking.

'I wonder if you'd do me a favour?' she asks.

'What is it?'

'I want to visit the place where that man's body was found, but I don't want to go on my own. Would you come with me?'

Before I can respond, she adds, 'I understand completely if you don't.'

'It's not that. I'm concerned that it might distress you.'

'It will, but I do feel it's something I need to do.'

Closure. It's a word constantly bandied around, but it's an elusive, slippery concept. Gill's final phone call should have provided me with closure, but I still feel as if I have unfinished business to deal with.

'All right, then,' I say. 'Do you want to go now?' I ask, hoping she'll say yes.

'Only if you're not busy.'

I cast a jaundiced glance on a photo of black gondolas, backlit by the setting sun. 'Nothing that can't wait.'

'Oh, what a shame!' Antonia says when I tell her I need to go out for a while.

'You carry on looking at the brochures,' I tell her.

'It's not the same on my own. I want this holiday to be something we share from start to finish.'

I turn my head to hide my wince from her. She wants this holiday so much, and for her sake I must grin and bear it and never let on how hateful I find it.

'Take a brolly,' she shouts after me. 'It looks like rain.'

There are a few grey clouds in the sky, but not enough to suggest a downpour is imminent. Nevertheless I stuff a brolly into my bag before going out.

I trudge up the hill. Naomi is there to greet me about halfway up. Thickly covered with vegetation, Minster Hill always makes me think of Tennyson's line about nature being red in tooth and claw. For all anyone knows, dozens of bodies could be buried up here, hidden under bushes and trees. It's a wild sort of place, and it seems to me to epitomise the Shropshire landscape that so inspired Mary Webb.

I'm glad I wore thick trousers, for once we're off the beaten track we have to force our way through tangles of branches and thorny stands of gorse. I'm sweating once we reach the place where David Collins' bones were found. As I look at the spot, it's easy to understand how his body lay undisturbed for so long. There's something eerie about the tall pines, the chilly air. Sunlight barely penetrates through the thick branches. Pine needles cover the ground. A scrap of crime scene tape flutters on one of the trees.

'Here we are,' I say, wondering exactly what Naomi hopes to find here.

'You'd hardly know, would you?' she says, staring down the sheer cliff face.

What did she expect? No one would be likely to erect a memorial or lay flowers here.

'But this isn't the right place,' she adds.

'It must be.' There is evidence of much trampling and digging.

'Not Mr Collins. Brian. That's why I'm here.'

'Brian? But—'

'I was so sure it was Brian they found. I know he's here, you see. I can't understand why... Did I imagine it? Dream it?'

'Dream what, Naomi?'

She tucks stray strands of hair behind her ears. 'That I killed Brian.'

She tells me her story. I don't know whether or not to believe her, but on balance I think I do.

Naomi points to a spot some way ahead of us. 'Over there,' she says, and we walk towards it, past a "Danger" sign erected to warn people to stay away from the potentially dangerous old quarry.

'Does this help?' I ask after she's stood for a few minutes in silent contemplation.

She shrugs, the material of her anorak rustling like a crow's wings. 'I don't know what I expected to feel. I can visualise so clearly the scene of the picnic – the pattern of the blanket we sat on, the weight of the bottle in my hand... But it feels like a dream. As if it never really happened.' She looks at me, her eyes teary. 'But I'm glad I came. I needed to come back.'

'We all try to bury our secrets,' I say, 'but nothing stays buried forever.'

'Some people manage it, I suppose.' She gives me a quizzical glance. 'What's *your* secret, Diana? You and Gill, I suppose.'

'Did you disapprove?'

'If you'd set up home together I probably would have done. I had a very firm moral compass, for all the good it did me. Perhaps the old Naomi would have thought you'd been punished enough, because Gill only ever made you miserable.'

'Not at the time she didn't.'

'I think she did. I think you always knew she'd let you down.'

'How could I?'

'I used to see you together. You always looked so worried, so desperate to keep her with you. And she ignored you, smiling at all the boys. Don't you remember?'

I snap a twig beneath my foot but say nothing.

'I always thought that my sexuality was my big secret,' I say eventually. 'I thought it ruined my life – the sense that I wasn't like most people. But I was wrong.'

'What, then?'

'Antonia,' I say. 'All my life I resented her, hated her, even. I promised Mother I would always look after her, but duty is the worst of reasons for doing something.'

'You feel Antonia ruined your life?'

'I did, but it's not true. You're right, Gill would never have stayed. She was never mine.'

'And now?'

'I can never leave Antonia. I'm stuck with her. And I'm sure she knows how I feel, but she can't say anything because she can't let me go, either.'

'What a pair we are! And what a waste.'

'Are you ready to go yet?'

She nods. 'I shan't return.'

We make our way back to the path and stop to remove brambles and burrs from our clothes.

'Will you come back to mine for a cup of tea?' she asks, in such a way I feel I can't refuse. I appreciate that she doesn't want to be alone just yet. Tea is merely an excuse. It always is.

There's something different about Naomi today. I sense she's less tightly-coiled. Even the way she sits is different. Usually she sits with her knees locked together, her shoulders high and tensed. She looks almost relaxed.

I bring the cups to the table and set one in front of her.

'Your tea's there,' I say after a while, as she's made no move to drink it.

'Thank you. What would we do without tea?' But still she doesn't take a sip. 'I'll always worry that the police will eventually catch up with me,' she says.

'You're hardly a fugitive from justice. The police have plenty of crimes to investigate without worrying about Brian.'

'But you do hear about what they call cold case crimes being solved, even after decades have passed.'

'It's over, Naomi. No one is going to come after you now.'

'I couldn't cope with prison,' she says, apparently not heeding any of my comments. 'But I am a criminal.'

'They couldn't prove a thing. Dwelling on it will do you no good.'

'I know, and yet I do, because I feel the moment I let it go someone will find out what I did.'

'That's not logical.'

'I know. I'm the same with fortune tellers,' she says. 'I'm sure everything they say is rubbish, but I always give a coin to them anyway, just in case.'

'In case of what – the Gypsy's curse?'

'Exactly. After all, it's no stranger than believing in the power of prayer. It's all superstition, really, isn't it?' She gives me a wry smile. 'I know you're not religious, so you don't understand how it's possible to believe in something that can't be seen.'

Finally she takes a sip of tea. She puts down her cup and gazes at me. Her eyes are dry, but her expression is pinched, the suggestion of relaxation gone.

'You look as if you've the cares of the world on your shoulders.'

'This house depresses me. It's so filled with memories.'

'Sell it, then. Buy a nice new house with no memories or ghosts.'

She shakes her head. 'I think they'd come with me.'

I check my watch. 'I ought to be getting back soon. I'm supposed to be looking through brochures with Antonia. All she can talk about is Venice.'

'You're going on holiday?'

'It would seem so. Antonia persuaded me, though I must admit my heart isn't in it.'

'I'm sure it's a fascinating place.'

'No doubt. But not with Antonia.'

'I wonder, would it help to have a third in your party? I'd pay my own way, of course.'

'Would you really? I'm not sure I can stand travelling just with Antonia.'

'I'd like to come.'

There will be no romance for me in Venice, but friendship needn't be a poor second. Naomi and I have shared so much, but more than that I have come to enjoy her company. I feel this is a pivotal moment in our relationship, an acceptance that we are friends, not just people who happen to know each other. I want to say something along these lines to her, but fear it will sound overly sentimental.

Her gestures of friendship give me reason to believe there is hope for both of us; that the rest of our lives needn't be a monotonous grey shuffle towards the final sunset.

I sense that we both have something we want to say. Naomi breaks the silence, scraping back her chair and walking over to the dresser. She opens a drawer stuffed with greetings cards. 'I ought to get rid of them, but I don't think I can just yet.' She glances up. 'Nigel knew what happened. About Brian, I mean. I can't think why I told him. I just couldn't believe that he felt nothing for me. I always hoped, you see, that he would realise what kind of person Melanie is. That he'd realise I... But it's no use. You can't go back, can you?'

'How did he react?'

'I'd tried to phone him, you see. But it was always Melanie who answered. She told me to leave them alone. She even threatened to get the police involved. So I wrote him a letter – a long letter, omitting nothing. I was so... so stupid. I typed the address on the envelope so Melanie wouldn't open it.'

'And?'

She shrugs. 'I was sent a letter from his solicitor. A "cease and desist" letter. It shook me up. For the first couple of years after our divorce he sent me a Christmas card. I thought that meant we were still friends. Then the cards stopped. I continued to send one to him, and every year they're sent back. Return to sender. I've kept all of them.'

The cards in the drawer. Not from Nigel to Naomi, but from Naomi to Nigel. Unread, unwanted.

'I suppose he must have told Melanie about the mad letter I sent. She must have read it, mustn't she?'

'The poison pen letter...'

'Melanie, of course. I doubt David Collins ever made the national news, but after I'd sent that terrible letter I expect they kept their eyes on the regional news stories.'

'But it *was* Antonia who made that anonymous call to the police.'

'Oh, yes. And I was quite glad, really. It brought things to a head. I suppose, when David Collins' name was revealed, Melanie must have thought I'd made everything up, that the letter I sent was the product of a deranged mind. Perhaps it was. I couldn't believe it, when I was informed it wasn't Brian's bones they'd found. Sometimes I wonder... But I *know* what happened, I was there.'

'It's all over now. Isn't it?'

'I suppose so. Yes. It should feel more final than this, shouldn't it?'

'Things rarely do. They're more likely to tail off.'

'It's very unsatisfactory.'

'A greater challenge, perhaps,' I say. 'Learning how to carry on in the absence of proper closure. I'm glad you felt you could confide in me. And I know I haven't always been very nice about Antonia, but she only made that call to the police because she was worried I might go to prison as an accessory after the fact.' Her phone call wouldn't have helped me, of course, but Antonia never did think things through.

'I know. I hold no grudge, I promise.'

I leave Naomi's house feeling as if I've had a few sherries. Even the spots of rain that fall, as Antonia predicted, aren't enough to dampen my mood.

I reach home and open the front door. 'Antonia!' I call, ready and willing to return to brochure duty. I receive no response. 'Antonia?' I say, more softly, as I enter the living room. It is empty. The brochures are scattered all over the floor. My stomach lurches. I assume Antonia got fed up with waiting for me and threw a tantrum. I tread warily up the stairs, not sure what to expect, not knowing if she's still in a foul mood or if her fury has worked itself out.

'Antonia?' I whisper, gently pushing open her bedroom door.

The curtains flutter in the breeze coming through her open window. The sill is wet with spots of rain.

I take a few steps into the room, until I can see the bed.

Antonia lies on top of the quilt, apparently fast asleep – legs splayed, mouth lolling open. Lying next to her, in the crook of her arm, is a doll. It's the doll that was originally mine and later given to Antonia by our mother. The doll is quite bald, the scalp covered with a layer of dark yellow dried glue. No clothes. When she was first given to me, she was wearing a gown of blue silk.

I lean in closer. The doll's open, lifeless eyes meet mine. Cornflower blue glass, horribly realistic. I reach out a hand and gently lower the doll's eyelids. Its black lashes brush the top of its cheeks.

I breathe a sigh of relief before leaving the room. Careful to make as little noise as possible, I shut the door behind me.

ACKNOWLEDGEMENTS

Massive thanks to Louise Walters for helping me to bring this book to life. Thanks also to the whole Louise Walters Books team and to all the amazing, supportive and talented LWB authors.

I would like to thank my friends who have kept me going through every difficult moment. Extra special thanks are due, as ever, to my always enthusiastic first reader, Chris Wyles.

Louise Walters Books is the home of intelligent, beautifully written works of fiction.
We are proud of our impressive list of authors and titles. We publish in most genres, but all our titles have one aspect in common: they are brilliantly written. Further information about all our books and authors can be found on our website:

louisewaltersbooks.co.uk

The Last Words of Madeleine Anderson

Helen Kitson

*"Writing is like a love affair, or should be.
You get to know your story, it intrigues you,
if you're lucky it enthrals you, and ultimately
it ends, leaving you wretched and abandoned."*

ONCE UPON A TIME Gabrielle Price wrote and published an extraordinary novel.

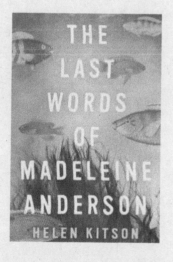

But twenty years on her literary star has dimmed, her "work of genius" is all but forgotten, and no further novels have materialized. She now lives an unremarkable life: middle-aged, living alone in the sleepy village she grew up in, and working as a housekeeper for the local vicar. Her lonely existence is dominated by memories of her best friend Madeleine, who died young, in tragic and mysterious circumstances.

Gabrielle's quiet world is turned upside down when she meets and befriends Simon – young, attractive, a would-be writer, and enthusiastic fan of the astonishing novel that Gabrielle published all those years ago. Charmed and flattered, she recklessly invites him into her home and her heart. But Simon is mysterious and manipulative, and it's not long before he forces Gabrielle to confront the demons in her past. Gabrielle's obsession begins to destroy her carefully cultivated life, and she comes to feel increasingly threatened by Simon's presence. Who is he? Why did he seek her out? And what does he really want?

The debut novel from acclaimed poet Helen Kitson is a joy to read: mysterious, reflective, and darkly humorous. Diana Cambridge describes it as "Barbara Pym noir".

Available in paperback, e-book, audio, and large print.

Don't Think a Single Thought

Diana Cambridge

"Hello? Hello? Emma, is that you?
Emma! It's only me... Hello? Are you there, Emma?"

1960s NEW YORK: Emma Bowden seems to have it all – a glamorous Manhattan apartment, a loving husband, a successful writing career. But while on vacation at the Hamptons, a child drowns in the sea, and suspicion falls on Emma. As her picture-perfect life spirals out of control, old wounds resurface, dark secrets are revealed, and that persistent voice in Emma's head that won't leave her alone threatens to destroy all that Emma has worked for...

Taut, mesmerising and atmospheric, *Don't Think a Single Thought* is a novel of dreams and nightmares, joy and despair, love and hate. It lays bare a marriage, and a woman, and examines the decisions – and mistakes – which shape all of our lives.

Diana Cambridge's debut novel is beautifully written, and tackles big themes in few words. Sophisticated and refreshingly short, this is the perfect holiday or handbag book.

Available in paperback, e-book, and audio.

The Naseby Horses

Dominic Brownlow

*"I only know Charlotte is not dead. I feel it within me,
her heartbeat the echo of my own. She is with me still.
She is near. I have to save her, for that is all in life
I have ever been required to do."*

SEVENTEEN-YEAR-OLD Simon's sister Charlotte is missing. The lonely Fenland village the family recently moved to from London is odd, silent, and mysterious. Simon is epileptic and his seizures are increasing in severity, but when he discovers the local curse of the Naseby Horses, he is convinced it has something to do with Charlotte's disappear-

ance. Despite resistance from the villagers, the police, and his own family, Simon is determined to uncover the truth behind the curse, and rescue his sister.

Under the oppressive Fenland skies and in the heat of a relentless June, Simon's bond with Charlotte is fierce, all-consuming, and unbreakable; but can he save his adored sister? And does she want to be saved?

Drawing on philosophy, science, and the natural world, *The Naseby Horses* is a moving exploration of the bond between a brother and his sister; of love; and of the meaning of life itself.

Literary, but gripping and readable, this was the first Louise Walters Books hardback.

Available in hardback, paperback, e-book, and audio.

In the Sweep of the Bay

Cath Barton

*"They forgot the happiness. Or rather, pushed it away.
But it was there, all their lives, waiting to surprise them."*

THIS WARM-HEARTED tale ex-
plores marriage, love, and
longing, set against the majes-
tic backdrop of Morecambe
Bay, the Lakeland Fells, and the
faded splendour of the Midland
Hotel.

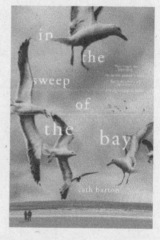

Ted Marshall meets Rene in
the dance halls of Morecambe
and they marry during the frail
optimism of the 1950s. They
adopt the roles expected of
man and wife at the time: he the breadwinner at the family ceramics firm, and she the loyal housewife. But as the
years go by, they find themselves wishing for more...

After Ted survives a heart attack, both see it as a new
beginning... but can a faded love like theirs ever be rekin-
dled?

A beautiful second novella from Cath Barton which, in
just one hundred and four pages, takes the reader by the

hand and leads them through a long marriage, and several lifetimes. Magical stuff!

Available in paperback, e-book, and audio.

Louise Walters Books extends its gratitude to our Supporters. Supporter subscriptions are invaluable to a small publisher like us.

Please visit louisewaltersbooks/lwb-supporters if you would like to receive a year's worth of books, invitations to launch parties, exclusive newsletters, early glimpses of forthcoming covers, and many other nice bookish things.

Heartfelt thanks to:

Claire Allen
Edie Anderson
Karen Ankers
Francesca Bailey-Karel
Tricia Beckett
JEJ Bray
Melanie Brennan
Tom & Sue Carmichael
Liz Carr
Penny Carter-Francis
Pippa Chappell
Eric Clarke
Karen Cocking
Louise Cook
Deborah Cooper
Tina deBellegarde
Giselle Delsol
James Downs
Jill Doyle

Kathryn Eastman
Rowena Fishwick
Harriet Freeman
Diane Gardner
Ian Hagues
Andrea Harman
Stephanie Heimer
Debra Hills
Henrike Hirsch
Claire Hitch
Amanda Huggins
Cath Humphris
Christine Ince
Julie Irwin
Merith Jones
Seamus Keaveny
Moon Kestrel
Ania Kierczyńska
Michael Lynes

Karen Mace
Marie-Anne Mancio
Karen May
Cheryl Mayo
Jennifer McNicol
MoMoBookDiary
Rosemary Morgan
Jackie Morrison
Louise Mumford
Trevor Newton
Aveline Perez de Vera
Mary Picken
Helen Poore
Helen Poyer
Clare Rhoden

Gillian Stern
John Taylor
Julie Teckman
Sarah Thomas
Sue Thomas
Mark Thornton
Penny Tofiluk
Mary Turner
Ian Walters
Steve Walters
Elizabeth Waugh
Alexis Wolfe
Finola Woodhouse
Louise Wykes